Praise for *Philip Davison's Work*

A Burnable Town

'Part le Carré, part Graham ... ...dialogue'

—*Independent*

'Each word in this bleakly humorous novel promises to explode and bring light to the shadows . . . Davison never fails to surprise, compel and intrigue with dry philosophy and grim wit.'

—*Times Literary Supplement*

'Davison writes well about betrayal and loss, and what matters most in this strain of fiction is the mood rather than chapter and verse. Maddening if you feel a bit left out; but possibly addictive.'

—*Literary Review*

The Long Suit

'Davison writes with the intelligence and intent of a James Lee Burke, flecked with the mordant wit of a Kinky Friedman.'

—*Arena*

'Sharp. Funny. Hip. Learned. Surprising. . . . If you haven't experienced Ireland's equivalent of Graham Greene with a dash of Le Carré and the readability of Len Deighton, then treat yourself to *The Long Suit*.'

—*Evening Herald*

'Philip Davison is a gem of a writer, and this is a glittering read, deceptively leisurely in pace, with killer flashes just when you least expect them.'

—*Irish Times*

'This is unlike any other crime novel you'll read this year; funny, poignant and gripping by turns, it will leave Davison's many fans eager for more.'

—*The Good Book Guide*

McKenzie's Friend

'Chilly, elegant and disconcertingly comic. Rather like a collaboration between two notable Green(e)s – Graham and Henry – and quite safely described as original.'

—*Literary Review*

'Davison shares Beckett's knack for making the down-at-heel appear surreal.'

—*Times Literary Supplement*

'A subtle undercurrent of humour: well written, weird'

—*Time Out*

Eureka Dunes

.

First published in 2017 by
Liberties Press
Terenure Place | Terenure | Dublin 6W | Ireland
+353 (0) 86 853 8793
@LibertiesPress
www.libertiespress.com

Distributed in the UK by
Turnaround Publisher Services
Unit 3 | Olympia Trading Estate | Coburg Road | London N22 6TZ
T: +44 (0) 20 8829 3000 | E: orders@turnaround-uk.com

Distributed in the United States by
Casemate IPM | 1950 Lawrence Road | Havertown | Pennsylvania 19083 | USA
T: (610) 853 9131 | E: casemate@casematepublishers.com

ISBN: 978 1 910742 64 8

2 4 6 8 10 9 7 5 3 1
A CIP record for this title is available from the British Library.
Cover design by Roudy Design
Printed in Ireland by Sprint Print

The publishers gratefully acknowledge
financial assistance from the Arts Council.

'A Quiet Spot' by Derek Mahon from *New Collected Poems* (2011) is reproduced
by kind permission of The Gallery Press.

Eureka Dunes

Philip Davison

LIB
ERT
IES

for Connie

It's time now to go back at last
beyond irony and slick depreciation,
past hedge and fencing to a clearer vision,
time to create a future from the past,
tune out the babbling radio waves
and listen to the leaves.

from 'A Quiet Spot', by Derek Mahon

Part 1

CHAPTER 1

Magnus, the Boy in the Desert

This is what Magnus remembers. It will only make sense when he speaks it out in his head. Then, it is his story.

Magnus shades his eyes and looks into their faces. They stand as they are, inviting his inspection. They follow his eyes with a steady, inscrutable gaze. The hairs on Magnus' arms stand up. He doesn't know why. He isn't afraid of them. He puts out his hand. They don't appear to be impressed. He is about to retract it when the oldest one reaches, and they shake. It is 1976. Magnus is fourteen years old.

Magnus can't determine whether the lightness of touch is in the shaking or in his own head. These men don't appear to want to speak to him. Mojave Indians, though Magnus does not know them as this. Two tall men and a boy teenager. One of the men is old. He has the deepest vertical creases that Magnus has seen on a human face. To his eyes all three are strong and effeminate, but not like girls. There are just two feathers, both in the old man's hair. They hang down, they don't stick up. Eagle feathers fixed into a thin braid, with what Magnus thinks would be bone glue. These men stare without grinning. They are beautiful, like his mother.

They speak to each other. Their talk is even, deep-throated and sleepy. They aren't shocked or angry. What are they saying?

At first, they appear to be not listening to each other. If they talk to him, Magnus will reply in a whisper.

The three take turns looking into the distance. They look in all directions in a lazy way, it seems to Magnus. If any one of them comes to some conclusion, it seems, they make a point of not sharing it. The old one recognises that the burning boy has come out here on a mission, sees he does not know how to put himself in the way of healing.

They give Magnus water from a big plastic jerry can. Carefully pour it into his mouth as though he were a kid goat. The heavy rain that has fallen is already in the ground, or has evaporated. They give him all he needs without him choking. His eyes take in what they can while he drinks. He observes that they take no real interest in the stranded car. He glances at their feet. Their muleskin boots, he thinks, are two sizes too small. The two younger men, he is sure, are wearing eye makeup.

'You run out of gas?' one says.

These words come as a shock. Magnus nods.

The other young man grunts disapprovingly. 'You break the top?' he asks, without looking again at the car or indicating with a gesture.

Magnus shakes his head. He does not feel responsible for the convertible roof being stuck a quarter of the way up, though it had failed with an electrical fizzle when he had thrown the switch.

The old man shakes his head and scowls. He touches his lips with the tips of the fingers of both his hands, shades his eyes, then taps the crown of his head.

Magnus indicates with a nod that he takes this to mean that a boy in his position will die of thirst after he had gone blind from the sun and mad from the heat. He is puzzled that they make no move to investigate the broken roof. Make no move to fix it. They just stand waiting for him to speak.

Finally, the old one moves forwards and speaks at the side of Magnus' head. Magnus' face is lightly whipped by the ends of his long grey hair. 'You come with us. We'll bring you to a gas station.' He points imprecisely.

The use of the phrase 'gas station' prompts Magnus to turn and flinch, with a little spurt of panic and excitement. He nods.

They don't ask his age. They make no move to lay a reassuring hand on his head or his shoulder. Nor do they seek an explanation. They aren't saying whether or not they are taking him to the gas station to get gas or dump him. The teenage one slings the jerry can in the back of the truck. One of the men opens the passenger door for Magnus to get in. The bench seat is high off the ground. There is a sweet human musk and the smell of stale tobacco: this is inviting.

The old man drives, the teenager sits in the middle, and Magnus by the passenger door. The other one is sitting splay-legged on the flatbed. Except for the last part, when they come off a trail onto the highway, the journey across the hardpan to the gas station is bone-shaky. The bumpiness is good, Magnus thinks.

A short distance on, they cross the slot canyon. Magnus doesn't see it coming. They bounce through shallow floodwater in an instant. The desert air still smells smoky damp, but that aroma will be gone even before they reach their destination, which is not far now. Already, there are dry sand particles coming out of the tyres and blowing down the road in their wake.

The three are mostly silent, but the old man does speak his name. Pete. Could he really be called Pete? The teenager doesn't give his own name, but points to the back and identifies the other one by the name. Judd. Magnus wants their secret names, but keeps his mouth shut.

'And you?' the old man asks with a sustained look to Magnus. He appears to be threatening not to look back to the dirt road until he has a response.

'Magnus,' comes the reply, in a whisper.

The old man repeats the name – speaks it at the windscreen. He isn't surprised by it, nor is he curious, though, Magnus supposes, he may have never met a Magnus in his whole long life. His name falls nicely out of this old mouth.

He wants to ask the name of their tribe but doesn't dare, lest they take offence.

'Where you from?' the old man asks.

Magnus doesn't answer. The old man doesn't press him.

The teenager has been studying Magnus' clothes and his shoes. He now adopts the same sustained look as his elder. 'Did you dream you'd be out here?' he asks.

CHAPTER 2

Stella, Magnus' Mother, in Hospital

'I've been shot,' Stella said, lowering her voice so that the other patients on the ward didn't hear.

It was ridiculous, of course, though it was a fantasy solution Magnus had been running in his imagination for years. It was 2008. His mother was old but his resentment hadn't slackened. He found that there was no solace in her cooperating with this particular fantasy. She was too resilient for a bullet. He might have known she would endure.

'Really?' he said, pitching his voice well above hers. 'And who shot you?'

She gave an impatient wave of her scrawny hand. 'I'll give you the details later.' This, Magnus assumed, was a demonstration of his mother's frustration with the recovery process that went with surviving a shooting. It was an extension of her long-standing denial of reality. The shooting explained how it was she had come to be in hospital. Somebody else was responsible for her condition. She had had no part in it. Her being old, organs failing, arteries collapsing: these things had nothing to do with it. She was opening and closing her mouth. He noticed the lipstick on her dentures.

'Have they operated?' he asked. There was a deviousness in his voice but there was no plan to back it. No prospect of her being brought down by force of reason.

'It's still in there,' she said.

'Is it?' he retorted and followed presently with the obvious next question: 'Why would anybody want to shoot you?'

There was another dismissive wave, this one weaker than the last.

'It's complicated,' he said helpfully, answering his own question.

The Guards had been in, she told him.

'To find out who shot you.'

'Yes.'

'To find out what happened?'

She had been shot. The Guards were going to get those responsible.

There was a surge in his deviousness. He might yet undermine her conviction. 'They'll want the bullet,' he said.

The point was deflected. The one who actually interviewed her, he was a handsome Guard, she told him. But he wouldn't say which barracks he was from.

'They're trained that way,' Magnus replied with a heavy heart. Some burner in him switched off, leaving only a pilot light. 'I couldn't get here any quicker,' he mumbled. 'There were delays at Heathrow. A bomb alert.' His mother wasn't interested. 'Where is he?' Magnus continued, looking over his shoulder. 'Where's this decent Guard now?' It was a futile line of enquiry, of course, but he couldn't resist.

Stella curled her lip. This facial expression Magnus recognised as being normally reserved for withering any reference to her marriage to Magnus' father, Edwin. The marriage was moribund, but Edwin seemed to think something more would come of it, even at this late stage. Wasn't that a gas?

The stout countrywoman in the adjacent bed spoke up. 'I've been praying for you,' she said, sitting up and leaning around Magnus to make eye-contact with her neighbour.

Stella was not impressed. 'Have you?' she retorted.

Confidence undiminished, the stout woman assured Magnus that she had, indeed, been praying.

'Thank you,' Magnus replied. Evidently, she had not yet learnt that bestowing God's blessing on his mother would certainly invite suspicion.

Turning again to his mother, Magnus wondered was she, imaginary bullet notwithstanding, finally on the way out. Something else might have got her. Some new strain of germ. He looked into the sullied luster of her watery eyes, but could not hold her gaze. He saw that her mouth was hanging open. Was she aware of the slackness of her jaw?

'What are you thanking her for,' she asked, the jaw suddenly springing into action.

Magnus couldn't hold back. 'You could just say thanks, you bitch.'

She seemed to give this serious consideration for a moment. Magnus realised that she took it he meant *Thank the bitch*. In any case the answer was no, she couldn't. She waved his good intentions away with a bird claw. 'Did you see she has a full-time beard?'

The beard obliterated all credibility, was her point.

Yes, Magnus did see the lady had a beard, but he wasn't about to acknowledge it.

Stella was truly annoyed at her son's put-on innocence. 'There's no use talking to you,' she said. The mouth closed. She set the jaw firmly, but couldn't hold it.

Under the circumstances, Magnus was forced to conclude that an opportunity had been lost over the beard. Actual or otherwise, it was life and death here. He should have sided with his ailing mother and tugged on the beard, instead of taking the high moral ground.

'I'm dying,' the frail Stella blurted. Evidently, there was still some desire to talk.

Magnus nodded gravely and kept his mouth firmly shut.

'I see you have a lot to say for yourself.'

'I hear you,' he said, 'but maybe you have it wrong. Maybe you're already on the mend.' This was a mistake. He knew it was a mistake.

'I'm dying,' she asserted in a bitter whinny. She was demanding he drink this acid. Her eyes widened in anticipation of the transfer regurgitation that would surely follow, but Magnus would not oblige. Instead, he nodded wearily. 'I'll talk to the doctor,' he said.

Stella scoffed. 'You don't know the half of it.' There was another bird-claw wave.

'I'll talk to the doctor in charge, then I'll talk to the Guards.' Magnus tried to give her some additional reassurance by supplementing his nodding with the raising of his eyebrows.

She waved him out with her knuckles.

Standing in the corridor, waiting for his father to appear, Magnus gets a flash from his childhood. Something in his subconscious sets the dumb-waiter in motion, which sends up a reminder that it was ever thus. This is a message of reassurance from the centre that provides for his well-being, his survival. His mother is riding a tall, black bicycle. Bouffant hair-do, pencil skirt, red lipstick. He sits astride a cushion clamped in the back-carrier. The back-carrier sways left and right. He holds on tightly to the tail of her short woollen jacket as they gather speed downhill. He is afraid of her rolling hips. To hold on here, he would have to press his palms hard in and spread his fingers to get any kind of grip. The movement of the hips together with the sway of the back-carrier would set up a dangerous momentum that would throw him off the bike. He knows his mother as a clothed woman's body with a beautiful face that beams in many directions. The suddenness of her attention, he believes, exposes a boy to harm. He might, for instance, be flung from a moving bicycle. She is making no attempt to dodge the potholes. Apparently, she is oblivious to his distress. She is his mother, so it must be all right.

'Let go, Magnus,' she calls over her shoulder, but he does not let go. He will not let out one fiber of her hounds-tooth jacket from his fists. He keeps his mouth firmly shut. She waves at men. They all wave back.

She doesn't say much. Stella is concentrating on her performance, to which there is no narration. Magnus feels that he, too, should concentrate. That's a way to please his mother. That's what makes people cool as well as glamorous.

He thinks she is pulling faces for the men as she rides past them in their stationary cars, but young Magnus can't see. He can't be sure.

'Who are you, anyway?' Stella asked when her son went back into the ward.

'It's Magnus, mother.' He shook his head at the absurdity of this third-party introduction.

She came back instantly – 'Magnus? You have me up in the pump room.' It was an accusatorial tone.

'What?'

'The pump room. The pump room.'

'What is the pump room? Where is it?'

She gave him a hard look: hard, that is, for somebody who was close to delirium. Her watery eyes seemed to lock in focus momentarily for this show of indignation. 'Och,' she shouted belatedly, and dismissed him with yet another wave of her hand. 'You have me destroyed.'

In happier days, Stella had declared she did not seek out love. If it was there, well and good. She had said she did not want to be remembered. Did not want to be an influence in the lives of those who remained. This, Magnus took as a robust declaration of her desire to live. To carry on in the hope that she might be lifted out of her present malaise and set down in a better place. It didn't have to be a familiar spot. Magnus could visit, if he liked. The whole thing could be improvised.

'Look at that hair,' she said loudly, indicating the young woman with dreadlocks who was visiting the patient opposite, and whom Stella had already described as 'a rip'. 'She needs a good comb-out.'

The DTs had not yet set in for Stella. She was lucid in the moment, as it were. Whatever her ailments, delirium had not yet rendered her entirely senseless. When the DTs set in, she would be prodding bottles floating in the air.

'Shut it,' Magnus said. 'Everybody can hear you.'

'What's wrong with you?' she wanted to know. 'I've done nothing on anybody.'

This, Magnus correctly took as an all-embracing denial. He walked to the window with religious forbearance, but really, he was smarting. It was a beautiful day. He looked out across the hospital car park. There were poppies and discarded plastic bottles along the curb, tall rusty weeds in the waist-high grass beyond, a clatter of aging, broken-down trees, construction cranes in the distance. A person could light a campfire or bury a dog in that meadow, he thought incongruously.

'I'm not staying here, I can tell you,' his mother called out.

To which Magnus replied: 'It's a nice day outside.' His eyes had focused on the smudge on the windowpane where someone had leant their forehead.

'I want a drink,' his mother wailed.

'You can't have one.'

'I'm thirsty,' she said, exhibiting some element of shock. 'I need a drink.'

'Ask the nurse.'

Yes, she wanted a whiskey, but she also wanted something to quench her thirst. 'You want water?'

'Seven-Up will do,' she replied.

There was a sign on the bedstead: 'No Solids, No Liquids'. They had her on Thick-and-Easy, the nutritious sludge they gave patients whose swallow was compromised.

Drug-induced or otherwise, self-delusion needed to be fed. If fed well, there would be no confusion. No failure of conviction. The conscience would be at rest. If the doctors and nurses just did their job vis-à-vis the bullet hole . . . . If the Guards could arrest the one who had shot her . . . . A snifter would help make her magnificent again.

Magnus capitulated. 'I'll ask the nurse.'

He was glad to get out of the ward again, if only for a minute. He didn't approach the nurses' station directly, but lingered in the corridor. For some bizarre reason his arms seemed too long. The sight of a half-empty box of chocolates made him want to throw up. No – it was the smell. He could row down that corridor on the thick air with his long arms. Even now, he could feel himself manoeuvre in the current: left forward stroke, right reverse stroke.

'Excuse me, nurse . . . she wants a drink. My mother, that is,' he said, pointing.

He went back into the ward. Where was his father? Was he just sitting in the car? He should have been there to deal with this, sheltering Magnus. Magnus made the mistake of venting his frustration on his mother.

Predictably, Stella complained about his father. 'He sleeps when he should be awake to the world,' she said. 'When he should be living. When he's awake, he creeps around the house. He stares into the wardrobe. *My* wardrobe.'

'Why would he do that?' Magnus asked, without much conviction. He was feeling a little dazed himself. Stella continued with her agenda.

'I tell him not to stare into my wardrobe. When I rouse him out of his chair, I can see the little beady eyes darting about to see what there is to be avoided.'

'Really. And what could that be, I wonder?'

'Then, he goes off creeping, and when he's finished creeping about, he wanders off into open spaces, where boys play football.'

'He wants to play football?'

'No-o-o. He just stands and looks about. I've seen him. I'm on to him. I wouldn't be surprised if he goes missing.'

'Don't say that.'

'Oh, he'd be brought back eventually and have nothing to say for himself. Not a care for the worry he may have caused. We'd be none the wiser, except – I'm on to him. I know what he's at.'

'Ah-h . . .'

'"I'm on to you," I tell him, but it's useless, of course. He just continues with his act. And now, I'm in here.' She was trying to establish a clear connection between her medical condition and her husband's waywardness by rolling her eyes about the ward with bitter fortitude. 'I'll not be here for long,' she assured Magnus, and in that assurance there was a firm allusion to his responsibility in the matter. She emphasised this with a cozy deflector: 'Are you here to get in the way?'

'No,' he replied patiently.

'Just wandered in, did you?'

'More than that, mother . . .'

'Just like your father.'

She was complaining to Magnus about Edwin, but really, she was railing at her own sorry state. That much he readily grasped. The weight of all her days wasn't sitting right. So much that mattered had gone without due acknowledgement, without her fully drinking in the consequences. This was a time for self-knowledge, for priorities that could be called absolute. A time to ignore illness and decrepitude.

The confusion had given way to a new alertness. All of this was ordinary, she had decided. You only had to look out the window: how ordinary was that, with the trees, the rain, the parked cars, the skinny lamp-posts nodding in the wind. And throughout the entire hospital building – all this effort. Every class of person turning up to attend to those marooned in a bed. She was being cautious in her toughness, not fretful. Everywhere there were people with true resilience. She was up for it. Big things happened to human beings, often not of their making. Toughies were used to that. The rest of us could only make pathetic announcements.

'Did you kiss your father?' she asked Magnus, as though she were a barrister who, of course, already had the answer.

'I did,' he replied self-consciously. 'On the forehead,' he added, as though there might be some confusion.

'Do that when he's dead,' she said. 'Don't do it otherwise. It will only upset him.'

'And why is that?' he asked. The words came out abruptly. They went against his own rapid counselling. Was she saying the old man was sick? He was going to die? Her cold concern seemed genuine; might even have been carrying a flush of panic.

'It never worked for me,' she said, referring to the forehead-kissing. 'He never liked it.'

What was this? Did she want to kiss her estranged husband on the head? Do it better than her son could do it? Do it in such a way she could say to Edwin: I know you don't want me doing this, but I'm your wife?

Magnus felt a little surge of panic himself; a sudden rush of guilt. He should have stayed longer with his father. Should have held his hand.

'Don't mind me,' his mother said. Not in the usual callous tone. Something short of that.

He imagined her death, which was a bit of a well-worn luxury, and only a little terrifying in its detail. 'All right, then,' he said, replying to her rhetorical remark. 'I won't.'

She liked that. It was familiar.

'Where have you been?' Magnus demanded. 'Sitting in that damn car?'

His father held up the bunch of flowers he had bought, though he knew this did not explain his reticence.

'You didn't prepare me for this,' Magnus said with a sharp jerk of the head in the direction of his mother's bed.

'It's the end again,' his father said wearily. His gaze wandered up the walls and tracked the course of thin oxygen pipes. 'They kill you with how things should be,' he said of the women in his life. His tone was self-mocking, designed to offset what little he could of his son's shock. He offered a quick, hopeful smile, but really, his face was marbled with anxiety.

'Did she tell you she'd been shot?'

'She did, son.'

Magnus nodded, and his nodding became forgiving. He embraced his father. It was an awkward action, but they fitted better than either man anticipated. 'I shouldn't have brought the dog,' he said, as if to affirm that he had turned out fully and unconditionally.

'I don't know what I was thinking.'

'You left a window open?' Magnus.

'I did.'

'Well then . . . '

'I'm glad you're here, Magnus.' Edwin left a brief silence, then added, 'I must get it a bottle of water. I passed a machine,' he said, looking back down the corridor towards the stairwell.

Was there anybody else Magnus knew who, without malice, referred to their pet as 'it'? This was what came from years of living with Stella.

They entered the ward. Stella was in a deep, stuporous sleep. The bunch of flowers got put into an adjacent sink.

When Magnus saw that his mother was stirring and might wake, he withdrew from the ward again. Told his father that he would go down to the car and check on the dog. He was under pressure at work and the trip from London had drained him. He found himself lingering in the main concourse. Did he want a coffee? Should he just sit somewhere? The dog could wait. It was what dogs did.

A man approaches with a rhythmic sway. Not drunk, but at sea. He's dressed in good clothes but they are threadbare and dirty. His shoes are worn down. One is split. A Caucasian made berry-brown from sleeping it off in the midday sun. Skin lined from smoking. One hand is shaking in its sleeve.

Closer now, the expression on his face tells Magnus there is so much in this world that no longer interests him. But then, something happens. His expression changes when he locks eyes on Magnus. He smiles. The hand stops trembling. He slows gracefully to a halt, seems to genuflect at Magnus' feet, but freezes before his knee touches the ground.

He pats his extended thigh and quickly pulls a bandana from around his neck. 'Shoe-shine?' he enquires. The voice is rich and soft.

'No thanks,' Magnus replies automatically.

The man draws his bandana back and forth across his thigh to show how thorough a job he would do.

'No thanks, anyway,' Magnus says.

The man holds his stooped position. Keeps eye-contact. Keeps his teeth showing. 'You going to the chapel?' he asks.

'No,' Magnus says, 'just making my way out.'

'I could get you there. I could help you. I don't mind hanging around. I can pray.'

This is like being spoken to in Italian, Magnus thinks: he feels sure he can understand what is being said, but really, he doesn't. He feels a sudden absence, which he fears will be permanent.

The man turns ably to one side, into a crouch, and pats his back. His jacket and shirt collar are riding up around the nape, as though he sleeps on a crane hook. 'Hop on,' he says in the same mellow voice.

Magnus responds with a nervous little laugh. This is a strange day, indeed. It is the softest pan-handling he has encountered. He feels he hasn't got the tone right for the moment. It makes him realise how stiff he is; how wound. In any case, the man goes on his way before Magnus reaches into his pocket. He's failing to connect. That's what's happening at work. Hence the continuous pressure. Opportunities are being lost. This is a bizarre poke in the ribs.

He watches this raggedy man shamble towards the self-service café, where he approaches a security guard on his break who doesn't want to know. Magnus watches the shaky hand in the sleeve. It seems to be searching for it-doesn't-know-what.

Magnus stands in the middle of the concourse for some time, blinking in a shaft of Indian sunlight that is bound to disappear at any moment. He imagines being soothed by the relative quiet in spite of the size of the place and the amount of pedestrian traffic.

Eventually, a hospital porter approaches. Magnus observes the man from some distance off and notes that he makes a clumsy detour to present himself and ask if he can give directions.

'My mother is dead,' Magnus says. The lie just tumbles forth. He wants to try it out. See how it fits in the world.

'I'm very sorry,' the porter says.

'I know,' Magnus replies, and hangs his head as the man lopes away reverently.

There is something wrong with one porter leg, Magnus notes.

The sunlight fades. Magnus walks on towards the entrance, the car, the sleeping dog. Without knowing why, he tries a bit of a limp, but it is gone by the time he reaches the swing-doors. A misty rain begins to fall.

CHAPTER 3

Edwin with His Son, Magnus, on a Bullet Road

Change is coming for the Sparlings. The fourteen-year-old Magnus can feel it. He accompanies his father to the Munster and Leinster Bank to change Irish pounds into US dollars. At the counter he watches Edwin formally receive the count-out and then sign traveller's cheques with his fountain pen. This is all tremendously reassuring, and traveller's cheques are exotic. He contributes by noting they should pack a bottle of ink.

In the taxi on the way to Dublin Airport, Magnus tries to occupy as much of the back seat as his father. He wants to see all his father sees, but the seat springs are weak and the stuffing has sunk to the frame-plate.

Edwin Sparling politely makes it clear to the driver that he wants minimal communication with him. Magnus knows to smile, be happy and be quiet. Magnus studies his father as they bounce. He sees that his father wants this journey to be a period of transcendence, but the taxi driver talks regardless. Magnus wants to tell the driver how delicate the situation is, and for him to shut his hole. But Magnus says nothing. His smile begins to ache, but he wants to be smiling.

Is it good or bad to be born and to live in Dublin? Magnus can't say, but the streets pass through him, their sounds, theirs smells, their structure. His father is not fixing on the adventure ahead, but seems instead to be taking in the sights in case the plane crashes. This gives him a curious twitching of the nose. The twitching, Magnus thinks, has to do with concentrating, with his father keeping his nerve.

Stella, Magnus' mother, doesn't think this trip is wise; doesn't think it is worth it; thinks it is a mistake. Edwin had listened to her patiently, had then informed her that he was taking Magnus. Stella had wept. *What is she crying for?* Magnus had wondered. They were going on an adventure. She could have come to America if she'd wanted. If she wasn't too busy.

While Edwin queues at the check-in desk, Magnus wanders in the concourse and wishes his father had told his aunts what they were doing. Charlotte would have made Stella come to see them off. Aunt Maureen would have given in and come too. It would have been a blast to have the three sisters there, all wavy and laughing and teary, and full of chatter, because of it being an adventure.

The airport is familiar. It has important standing in the wider family. Sunday dinners at the zoo have been trumped by dinner at the airport. Stella, Edwin and Magnus. Aunt Charlotte often comes, and sometimes Aunt Maureen, though she is never comfortable with it. She had enjoyed the expeditions to the zoo, but had to be coaxed. She prefers the zoo to the airport, though she thinks it's uncouth to eat there.

Everyone knows Stella is in her element at the airport. Hostesses are glamorous, but she cuts a more striking figure than any of them crossing the concourse, in her high heels, half a step ahead of her sisters. Edwin gets pleasure out of letting the sisters on. He holds Magnus back as though some lesson is to be learnt. 'She's a mystery, your mother,' he says, as though there is no mystery at all.

There are jet planes to watch, and Stella to be seen. The meat and vegetables are usually cold, but the gravy is hot. Stella will swing her legs out from under the table and cross them with extraordinary ease, though in Magnus' estimation it has to get sore leaving them out there as long as she does. On one occasion, Charlotte balances her teacup on Stella's knee. It is meant as a joke – Magnus and his father laugh, even Maureen titters – but Stella doesn't like it.

Now, this airport scene is eclipsed by a new association. Father and son's expectations soar with the jet, up through the puffball clouds and into the blue. Twenty-five minutes later, they make a steep descent through a sheet of white onto the runway at Shannon Airport for the mandatory stopover. This presents as an affront to their high spirits. Edwin buys Magnus a Babycham at the bar of the duty-free hall. Though it is still morning, he treats himself to an Irish coffee – which was never his drink.

Two hours later, Magnus is eating his dinner over the Atlantic. As soon as he is finished, he swings his legs into the aisle and crosses them. His father doesn't seem to mind. Doesn't seem to notice, actually. It is an air hostess who smiles and says 'Excuse me' and waits for Magnus to swing them in again.

'You made short work of that,' Edwin says, nodding at the boy's tray. Evidently, he is relieved Magnus has not lost his appetite.

'It was very lovely,' Magnus declares, thinking it is important to be absolutely clear with his opinion from this moment on.

Father and son change into their best clothes in a toilet at Los Angeles Airport. Good Van Heusen shirts, new Clarks shoes, ties bought in Switzers. Edwin puts on a dark mohair suit, and Magnus a light sports jacket, also from Switzers. They have v-neck pullovers in case the nights are cold. These form the top layer in the grip-bag Magnus is carrying.

'The stripes go in a different direction on an American tie,' Edwin declares, to make the wearing of a tie more palatable. They both have striped ties. 'I wonder will anybody notice the trouble we've gone to?'

'They'll notice, all right,' the smiling boy says.

'Good.' Edwin says they might drive the distance and go straight to the house.

'Do I have to wear the tie?'

'You do.'

'The trousers are bad enough . . .'

'Aren't they flairs?'

'Yes, but . . .'

'Didn't *you* pick them out?'

'Because you made me.' His mother was a good judge of what he should wear. She knew about men's fashion – even fashion for teenage boys – but she didn't get to approve this outfit, because she wasn't told about this trip in advance. She was staying with her sister, Charlotte. Or was out with other men.

'We're ready for anything, the two of us,' Edwin says. They are looking each other over as they cross the airport concourse. Magnus has already taken off the sports jacket and has it on a crooked finger at his shoulder. 'I'm *not* wearing the jacket.'

'You don't have to,' Edwin concedes. 'Just have it to hand. That, and your pullover.'

His father has bought him a diver's watch, which he likes very much. It has to be seen at all times. Magnus also wants people to see his identity bracelet, which has his Christian name engraved on the inside.

Like many Irish of his generation, America holds a fascination for Edwin, but it is not his spiritual home. For Magnus, he is sure, it will be different. The hiring of an American car to drive several hundred miles is a dreamy affair. Edwin loves cars, though he is never a bore about it, and never boastful. He claims to know a lot by the sound of an engine. He is an old-school professional gent for whom motoring is part family conveyance, part lifelong personal hobby. He has never driven in right-hand traffic before, but he knows what he is doing. He wants to drive a stick-shift convertible, but the only convertible available at the airport today is an automatic.

The car is handed over by a tall black man in a pressed, short-sleeved shirt. He has a name-badge. Preston Jones. Magnus memorises the name. Preston holds out a clipboard to Edwin: sign here for the insurance; that's how much gas there is in the tank. He hands Edwin the keys. Thank you, sir. Edwin is smiling, too. He can't get over himself.

Edwin has never driven an automatic, but you wouldn't know it to watch him drive the tan-coloured Buick with white convertible top out of the wire compound.

'Now, Magnus,' he says, 'when we get out on the highway you are to look for signs for Bakersfield.' He speaks with the authority of a driving instructor, but with obvious pleasure. Magnus knows his father has the route planned, but wants to include him from the outset. An American wouldn't know my dad hadn't been in America before, Magnus is thinking. Preston Jones didn't know, he is sure.

They head east from the airport, avoiding central Los Angeles, then north towards Pasadena. They aren't here to see Hollywood, to visit film studios and tour the houses of stars. That has to be firmly acknowledged. It is simply part of the extraordinary route to Edwin's birth-mother. To stop to make a little holiday, to alter the purpose even for a short interlude, would be bad karma.

They don't expect to see a film star or famous musician in their auto or coming out of an expensive shop. Nor do they think they will see a scene being shot on location. Nor do they. They do, however, drive down streets lined with the very tall palm trees that Magnus recognises as featuring on the LP label of Warner Brothers.

Monkishly applying themselves to their mission empowers them, they believe. Edwin promises they will drive around Hollywood and act like a pair of swanks, as he puts it, on the way back.

They have put on too much suntan oil. Too much suntan oil makes you go orange, Magnus tells his father. It certainly makes his hair stick to his forehead. For Edwin it just blends into his hair oil. Edwin seems much better adapted to the climate than Magnus. How is that? Magnus knows that he should study his father more closely then he has ever done before. This is a momentous trip and there is a lot to be learnt.

There are dentists and opticians with their offices in skyscrapers. Downtown, that is. Undertakers, too, perhaps. And whores. They can be anywhere in every city and can also be found on some ranches. There are definitely orgy clubs in Los Angeles. Magnus has been told as much by Taaffe, the school rebel and sometime bully. He wonders does Edwin know that. The whole floor is a mattress. Taaffe had said it is best to keep your socks on, though he didn't say why. Some of the places have pools with submerged seats where they sit naked. In America women who sit in such pools go to the shops wearing no knickers. You won't be able to tell where these clubs are by just driving down the street. But you will see whores on Sunset Boulevard. Whores on Sunset Boulevard wear knickers, but only because it gets cold at night. They'll show you their knickers if you ask, and you won't have to pay for that.

On a straight stretch out on the highway, Edwin takes his hands off the steering wheel for a moment. He says it is to check the wheel balance, but really, it is for the excitement. Magnus had not seen his father do such a thing before, but this is no ordinary journey. He is thrilled, but feels safe because he knows his dad to be a cautious man and a good judge of margins of error.

'Can we put the roof down?' Magnus asks.

'Yes, we can. You find the switch,' Edwin says, knowing right well where the switch is located.

Magnus lets down the roof. 'We could have the radio.'

'Let's have it,' Edwin replies.

Magnus turns on the radio. It is tuned to an evangelical station. They listen for a moment. In the peaks of this particular homily, the preacher-man is presenting as heartbroken wailer. He makes the name Jesus very long on the airwaves. In the troughs he seems to be sorrily mumbling wartime code. Attack the bridge tonight. The Yanks are coming. Magnus rolls the knob and immediately hits a smooth twanging rock. He gives a little squeak of delight. They are in the land that makes this music.

'Will we have some jazz?' his father asks mischievously.

'No, dad.' But he rolls the knob until he finds jazz. Then, there are high-energy commercials to which they both listen intently. Magnus had been wanting his father to buy a Ford Capri. It's a car with a rev counter – that's rare – and it's a coupe. It's a good time to remind him, and so he does. Edwin says he just might, smiles, and puts on a spurt of speed.

He is his father's companion. They are on a mission. They are travelling in a fast convertible across a stretch of America. It doesn't get much better if you are a fourteen-year-old boy.

Edwin doesn't drive directly north on the main highway to Bakersfield, but turns off at Santa Clarita on a route that takes them through part of the Mojave Desert. Then, they cut back through the mountains. It is cowboy desert. A cowboy desert with this bullet road running through it. 'I know this place,' Magnus wants to shout, but he doesn't want to make his father jump. He opens his mouth to take it in. Lets his mouth fill instantly with hot, dry air. He lets out a yelp, when really, he wants to shriek. Desert dust hitting the back of his throat does this.

Magnus finds he can't take in the experience just yet. His father has him on edge because his father is scared to be doing what he is doing.

Can they go to Eureka Dunes, Magnus asks. The sand dunes boom there. They make an eerie and fantastic sound.

It is much too far away, Edwin tells him. Magnus needs to remember the scale of this continent, and the vast distances, place to place. They are only making a modest detour here and yet look at the mileage.

Magnus shows his father a picture in their guidebook. Buying the guidebook was OK, having it with them in the glove compartment with the bottle of ink was OK too, but Magnus knows his father is uneasy with any reference to it because that somehow detracts from their quest. Eureka Dunes, however, is important, Magnus has decided, and in a strange and secret way may be part of his father's salvation. He will not say this, be he must make him want to go. 'There they are,' he says. He holds the map so his dad can see it. He points to Death Valley, runs his finger back to where they are currently. 'Look, we're just here . . .'

Edwin laughs, which offends Magnus. 'That's much too far, son.'

Ranging in Eureka Dunes, they could be sure, would be special. A visit to the blood-mother might not. It might turn everything bad. Magnus folds the map the wrong way, stuffs it into the pages of the guidebook, throws the bundle onto the back seat. 'Can we stop here to look around?' he asks resentfully.

Magnus doesn't really want to stop in this place, and Edwin wants to make good time. Edwin will only slow down. 'Look at that,' he says repeatedly, pointing with an open hand. 'What do you think?' Magnus, he sees suddenly, is so very nearly not a boy.

They'll pull in further up the road, Edwin promises. He wants to inspect the Los Angeles Aqueduct, which they will cross on the near side of the mountain range. Why, Magnus asks. Why look at something like that. He doesn't really want an answer. He just wants to register a protest. It is a great engineering feat, his father tells him. Later, they will find a nice spot in the mountain park he's marked on the map.

'There's two aqueducts, actually,' Edwin informs him enthusiastically. 'What do you think?'

Magnus doesn't think anything much about aqueducts, so he says nothing. He wants this floating to go on for days and nights. Wants to cut across the open desert, but at speed, then stop to explore without any explanations.

'There were all sorts of scandal associated with the project,' Edwin says, 'but what a feat.'

It annoys Magnus that his father has read up on this stuff and wants to revel in it. Weren't they only allowed the one mission: to meet the blood mother?

Only after that encounter could they make another plan: wasn't that what his father had insisted?

'If we get our business done and get back on the road early,' his father says, reading Magnus' mind, 'if we don't waste time, we might take another detour. We might just have enough time for the Hoover Dam.'

Will we be able to go straight there, Magnus wants to ask. He means drive a straight line and at high speed. But he doesn't ask. Though he would like to see the Hoover Dam, he feels he should offer no encouragement. He has settled for the raid on the blood-mother. If there is anything after, it should be Eureka Dunes. 'You mightn't feel like it,' he says, trying to be generous.

'We'll see,' Edwin replies softly, and builds the speed at which they are travelling.

Magnus likes to see the miles clocking up. He makes regular checks with the counter. Racked by tremorous anticipation, Edwin, too, watches the mileometer. Their displacement brings long, expectant silences between father and son as they drive through the landscape. This is a sacred, ghostly adventure, and both are incredulous when they consider their action.

They don't stop to inspect either of the aqueducts. That Hoover Dam slips out of reach. Eureka Dunes may as well be on the moon.

Magnus consoles himself with the smooth hiss of the tyres on the highway, the soft, fast ride that lets him slide his eyes along a distant saw-tooth ridge of pine-covered mountain. This expanse, these scenes, have always been in him. Like Dublin rain.

'Look at that, dad,' he says, putting a finger out against the blast of oncoming air and tracing the jags. 'You could tear off a piece of sky if you could reach.'

'Oh aye.' Edwin doesn't know what his son is talking about, but Magnus is content to let his father be distracted. He tries to read the music of these continental lines. What he hears, he will remember forever.

These are big trees, but nothing like as impressive as what is further north, he knows. These woods give way to ridges that are bare, but beautiful in the smoky-pink evening light.

'The trees,' Magnus says, turning his head as they slide behind. He leaves his arm extended in the air-stream. 'The jagged trees. You could rip the sky on them.' Now, he's feeling a little foolish for repeating himself.

'Sugar pines, I think,' Edwin says, surprisingly.

They are both high on excitement. Why should he feel foolish? He gladly repeats the name. 'Sugar pines.'

'I might be wrong,' his father adds with a careless grin.

Magnus opens out the map to measure again the distance to Eureka Dunes. At the point of having one quarter of it spread, the map blows out of his hands and the whole of America takes off back down the road and up into the air with an enormous leap. Edwin's first reaction is to slow and prepare to stop, but then he lets out a cheer and drops his foot on the accelerator. Magnus struggles in his belted seat, manages to get on his knees to look back into the sky. It isn't good to be a clumsy companion, but he sends a giddy cheer after the tumbling sheet of paper.

They're burning, Edwin realises. He lets up the soft roof.

Magnus wants to pee. Up ahead there is a large shopping mall on a spur from the highway. They pull out of the flow on a long, slow bend that leads to a vast car park. Edwin doesn't want to delay, doesn't want to be slowed by air-conditioned interiors and easy buying. There are woods on one side of the complex. Densely packed, tall, skinny trees. There is no fence, no boundary other than the curb and the first line of trees. Edwin pulls the Buick in alongside the curb.

'You can go in there, Magnus.'

'Are we not going into the shops?'

'No. We haven't time. You go in there and I'll get us some sweeties.'

The use of the word sweeties – that offends Magnus. Sweeties are a bribe for kiddies. Still, he takes account of the fact that his father is confused by generations, never mind his son's true age.

'All right.'

'I'll get us something American.'

Well of course he is going to get them something American. Magnus is used to seeing his dad being distracted in the presence of Stella, especially when they are dressed up and in the company of others. Was the confusion spreading?

Edwin pulls away in the tan-coloured car. It is a strange sight. There has to be a thrill to being abandoned, albeit temporarily. This is what bubbles under Magnus' ribs, as he steps through the coarse yellow grass.

As soon as he enters the woods, the air about his face is cooler, but no less dry. The sounds from the parking lot instantly seem uncannily distant and exotic. The ground is relatively even, but he advances cautiously. He is embarrassed to be observed from any distance peeing, so he intends to go deep. He descends into a hollow. He has an urge to explore as long as he dares. Content to be away long enough to have his father worry. Magnus' sweeties can melt a little on the front passenger seat.

Eventually, Magnus does stop to pee. When he is finished, he leaves his penis out for a time and stays perfectly still because it is a nice thing to do.

He puts his hands on his hips and studies the tree canopy. When he hears a flurry in the bushes some way off, he nips his skin on the zip of his trousers tucking himself in. At the end of the hollow, something comes out of a thicket and quickly comes at him. It is fast and low-slung. It is a hunting dog. It behaves like no dog he knows. It freezes suddenly and modifies its breathing to recoup moisture dripping from its tongue. It is giving Magnus' position. It is waiting for an order. To attack. To retrieve. The lone hunter does not come through the thicket, but around it in a wide arc, appearing silently with rifle at the ready, a sure-kill distance from the spot where Magnus stands. Magnus knows not to make sudden movements, even now that man and dog have seen him. It seems incredible to the boy that they are less than a thousand yards from a shopping mall, but here is this man in camouflage with a dog, out for killing.

Magnus waves at him, though it presents as a wildly exaggerated gesture at this range. Suddenly, the dog is at him, sniffing and whimpering. The hunter stands motionless and staring, for all Magnus knows, sensing with the hairs on his ears the vibrations of animal movement in another part of the wood.

The hunter makes a kind of hiss-whistle that immediately brings the dog to heel. He then gives a slow jerk of his chin – which Magnus thinks is either to indicate that Magnus is lucky he hadn't been shot, or that he should now run for his life. He doesn't know which. Though his heart is pounding, Magnus maintains eye-contact. Man-eyes and dog-eyes are indistinguishable.

'Nice dog you have,' Magnus lies with a clack in his dry throat.

The hunter says nothing. Just stands there and waits for the boy to get out of the woods – which Magnus does with an initial bolt that startles all three of them. He springs from the tree-line so quickly that he is nearly knocked down by a slow-moving silver Mustang.

A hunter with his dog in the trees beside a shopping mall. It is more incredible to Magnus now that he stands out in the open.

He might have been shot dead, or killed under the wheels of a car, but America has spared him. Edwin is waiting anxiously in the wrong place. Magnus finds the car by running two sides of the perimeter of the parking lot.

'Where were you?' Edwin demands, even before his son is properly in the passenger seat.

'I was where I should be. I was back there. Where you left me.' The alarm in his voice is unmistakable.

'This was the spot,' his father insists.

Magnus comes back, but suppresses his alarm with a kind of trembling wonder. 'You weren't looking out for me,'

'Your fly is open. For God's sake, Magnus . . . '

Magnus tells his father nothing about the hunter and his dog.

Their route takes them through Woody's Peak. The way is well signposted. There is a large car park with heavy wooden picnic tables and barbecue grills. They are on a rock-pile with the Los Angeles Basin behind them and the San Joaquin Valley ahead. There aren't many cars or camper vans. It is a working day. There is a thick heat haze and no wind to speak of. Edwin pulls over, away from the picnic area to a spot that would have offered a spectacular view ahead were it not for the conditions. He switches off the engine and throws his arms along the backs of their seats.

'Smell that,' he says.

'What?' Magnus asks. Are there sausages and rashers cooking?

'The high mountain air.'

Magnus can't smell it. It's a phony remark as far as he's concerned, but he knows his dad has planned to say this, and that he should go along with it. He draws a deep breath.

'There could be bears,' he says with a casual exhalation.

'You might be right,' Edwin replies, humouring him.

They are getting to their picnic when a funeral party comprising a hearse and one limousine rolls up the final stretch of incline, circles and pulls in to the shade a short distance from the Buick. These cars seem to function without engines. There is just the sound of their tyres on the gravel. They stay in convoy formation. People get out. Family stand about with rounded shoulders looking well-scrubbed and dazed while the limousine driver goes to the boot and takes out two baskets of food, a collapsible table and six folding chairs, which he sets about arranging. The two hearse-men get out and stand respectfully by their vehicle with their hands behind their backs. They gaze at the rock formation. Their hearse is still shiny in spite of having a layer of fine road dust. It has a matt hard-top with slender italic 'S's in chrome on either side. Magnus wonders why anyone might want to pretend the vehicle is a convertible, like theirs. It has a light-fixture on the roof, just above the windscreen, that is like a police set, but it is purple. This is a good idea, Magnus thinks, though he can't think why. It is a sleek modern hearse, but there is a wavy pelmet with tassels in the rear compartment. It sits heavily on the ground. The casket looks like it is made of bronze. Both hearse driver and mate are allowed long hair under their caps, one thick and curly, the other fine and straight. The limousine driver has short hair, but a heavy blond sweep across the forehead. Their glowing white shirts have extra-long collar tips that reflect light onto their tanned chins and make them look like film stars.

Something comes over Edwin. It is as if the party has pulled over on his account. Magnus sees that his father is mesmerised and that bizarrely, he wants to connect with these people. It is strange to see a hearse with an American casket with a body in it, and the relatives having a sit-down picnic on the side. Magnus wants to gawk, but his dad wants more. He can only assume it has to do with his anxious state of mind, and the heat, perhaps. It might be different were they able to see for miles and miles.

In the event, Edwin only has to make a token move in their direction. Magnus tries unsuccessfully to hang back. He wants to hear the worst. A middle-aged woman makes it easy for Edwin. It is as though she is expecting to engage. 'Are you going to Los Angeles?' she asks.

'No, we're visiting relatives in Bakersfield.'

Edwin hides his disappointment that there is no positive spark of recognition, no show of interest in the town of Bakersfield.

'We're burying Walt in the family plot.'

'I see. In Los Angeles?'

'We'll have a service down there, then he goes in the family plot.'

'Well, that's as it should be, I'm sure.'

'I don't know,' she says.

They move towards each other, in a penguin waddle. Now they stand forming a wedge and facing the hearse, but not looking at it directly. Older people do this positioning thing, Magnus notes, especially in public. Other people in the park who have noticed the hearse come into their midst, but they just look for a brief moment, and make a point of not being bothered. It is their way of showing respect, Magnus supposes, a way of not making a spectacle of it. He thinks again about his own ancient American blood-relative.

Is she rich, he wonders? Has she liver spots and skinny brown arms? Does she wear a white turban, big sunglasses and sneakers? Does she still get into a swimsuit? *She* might be a spectacle.

'Walt is your husband?' Edwin asks.

'My brother. He was only sixty-two. Only sixty-two.'

'Oh dear. I am *so* sorry.' This stopover seems to have a ceremonial character to it. The family is taking in the scenery in a most deliberate manner. Edwin wants to show empathy. 'He was a man who loved the outdoors?' he ventures.

'Oh yes.'

He worked as an engineer, perhaps? He is an architect himself, he informs her. He and young Magnus have crossed the two aqueducts, of course. What a marvellous feat of engineering.

No. The deceased wasn't an engineer. Walt was a margin clerk in a firm of stockbrokers. He retired early, came up north, got himself a place, bought a gas station just out of town.

'But he liked this place?'

'Oh yes.'

Walt's father had a ranch but he lost it. Left Walt just a pair of shoes and his cufflinks.

'Oh dear.'

'But Walt made good.'

Edwin was sure he did.

'He married her.' She points.

'Ah. I see.'

'I'm his sister,' she repeats.

Edwin doesn't ask what the father left Walt's sister.

'You can say something to her if you want.'

'Well . . . yes. I will.'

'Walt would like that. He was interested in buildings.'

'And he liked coming up here.'

'Oh yes.'

Edwin doesn't really want to speak to the widow. Doesn't want to intrude. She appears sedated, set on her course in a confused manner. 'You live up north, too?'

'We don't live anywhere near.' Again, she points, this time to a shiny-headed softie bursting out of his dark suit. 'That one's my husband. We live in Louisiana. He's from Baton Rouge.'

'Baton Rouge?'

'You know Baton Rouge?'

'I know the name. I know where it is on the map.'

'We don't live there.'

Edwin doesn't ask where she and her big husband live.

'We're in transport.' She says this because the stranger has told her he is an architect. It's only polite. 'You want to join us for food? We got lots of food.' She makes a gesture and shuffles the short distance to the family group.

'That's very kind of you,' Magnus hears his father say. He can't believe it. What is his father at? Does he have heatstroke?

'I'm Edwin. This is my son, Magnus.' Edwin pushes him forwards with a thumb in his back. They are introduced to the other strangers. They even shake hands with the undertaker people.

'And that's Walt,' Walt's wife says, pointing.

Magnus blushes, and squirms in his pants. The whole experience is excruciating, but the food is nice. All sorts of sausage, and salads with fruit instead of a hard-boiled egg. He would have liked a hard-boiled egg, though.

He has to listen to his father ingratiating himself with Walt's people. He has to watch him act like some weird ambassador man. You're from Ireland. Oh my. The big shiny man likes the Buick. He leans on the bonnet with the tips of his fingers looking like he might make an offer on it, but no. Walter's convertible is in back of the gas station. This man will be getting that.

When the picnic things are packed away and it's time to leave, sister links arms with sister-in-law for the few steps to the limousine. Nobody thinks to say good-bye to Edwin and his son, who have drifted back to their rented car. All of a sudden Edwin feels compelled to move on.

'How are we for time, son?' he asks, distracted, as he searches his trouser pockets for the car keys.

'I don't know,' Magnus replies sullenly. He feels he has been deprived of some wider, indefinable experience.

'Now remember, you're in charge of map-reading.'

'Just follow the signs,' Magnus says, throwing himself into the front passenger seat. 'Just go straight.'

'They were nice people,' Edwin says, turning over the engine.

'I suppose.'

'It's sad about Walt.'

Magnus doesn't like his father's tone, which seems to suggest the dead man is an old family friend. If this is meant to be some sort of lesson about it being OK to be upset, Magnus doesn't need it. 'Do you think if they left him in this place the bears would eat him? A bear could break open that coffin easily.'

Magnus sees by the way his father's face flushes as he laughs that he thinks this is a boy's way of coping – which only adds to Magnus' annoyance.

'Hey,' Edwin says, 'we still have those whopping sandwiches.' He tussles Magnus' hair and reverses the car in a wide arc. Before pulling away, he makes a gesture that is half wave, half salute, but the funeral party is already driving across the car park towards the Los Angeles Basin. People raise their heads to observe. Children pause to watch the dead man glide. Looking back, Magnus sees one man raise his straw hat into the haze before they slide off the mountain.

CHAPTER 4

Father and Son Visit the Bloods

'Who knows where we'll be staying tomorrow night,' Edwin says, as though he had no influence in the matter. There is a trill of nervous expectation in his voice.

'But we know we have to stay *somewhere* around here tonight,' Magnus replies. He means to be helpful. He wants to be a better companion. 'We might have to sleep in the car,' he adds, with a dart of pleasure.

'We might,' Edwin replies, going as far as he can to meet his son's excitement.

Their bodies are resisting the time-change. They're both extremely tired. The crisp, clean beds are enormously inviting in the plain hotel Edwin chooses. It is reassuring that there are a hundred or more identical bedrooms in which others might be settling.

They have brought pyjamas to America. Weren't they going to sleep in their underwear, Magnus wants to know, they being in America and being man and boy without women? It's good to have pyjamas and not wear them, even if it gets cold in the night. You are better wearing a pullover, jeans and socks under the covers if it gets icy.

His father tells him he should wear the pyjamas. He is unusually insistent, so Magnus doesn't argue. Edwin is already wearing his pyjamas, to hurry the morning. He moves around in a manner that suggests he doesn't expect to sleep, in spite of his exhaustion. He is in a worry daze.

Magnus shambles into a corner, puts on his pyjamas, folds his clothes neatly and puts them on a chair. His father seems not to notice. Magnus takes this as a sign that they both have been fully taken over by the blood world – whatever that involves.

There is the smell of paint. The hotel interior is being painted while patrons sleep. Edwin and Magnus see no painting being done, no painters' truck, no painters.

When they come blinking out of the Silver Rails Hotel the following morning, Magnus' father is full of phony confidence. He turns the key in the ignition and revs the engine to make a loud and unnecessary noise. He drives off in a particular direction without consulting his map-reader. He turns down a back street with an impressive sweep of hands about the wheel. It is a spontaneous act. Another little demonstration of bravado.

'What's down here?' Magnus asks.

'Who knows,' his father replies, flashing him a bright smile.

Magnus is excited. His companion status is secured. 'But where will it take us?' He is hoping for the same answer, and gets it.

'We're exploring.'

'We are.'

'We have the time.'

'We do.'

'We'll work in blocks.'

'You're turning American.'

'You think, son?'

'Cool.'

This first stretch takes them past the rear entrances to a line of restaurants and bars interspersed with painted brick walls. Big wooden poles supporting heavy black power cables pass, each with the same air-thud. There is a smell of cooking fat and stale hops. This might be the sort of street where an orgy club would be located, if they have orgy clubs in Bakersfield.

'One cat, two cats . . . ' Edwin counts out.

'One dog . . . ' Magnus calls.

'Where?'

'There.'

'Two cats, one dog . . . ' his father confirms.

They cross a junction with a dip that makes the car bounce, American-style. The back street gets narrow. There is a cluster of dumpster bins up ahead. One is partially blocking the way. Edwin slows and stops.

'I'll get it,' Magnus says, and springs out to push the bin aside. His father blows the car horn mischievously. 'Get a move on, boss,' he shouts.

'Yes, sir. Right away, sir,' Magnus shouts back. Is this really his father? The boy puts his shoulder to the dumpster and pushes. It is very much heavier than he expects. It won't move.

Edwin blows the horn again and gives out with a snuffly laugh. From behind the bins come three shabby men. Two black guys wearing filthy hats that shade their eyes, and one white guy eating from a chicken carcass. This last one has jet-black oily hair and a bottle swinging in his jacket pocket. They are around the car suddenly, shouting and catcalling and pretending to be friendly.

'Hey, hey, hey. What's with the horn, mister?'

One leans right in under the canvas top. He does this without knocking off his hat. Another sits up on the bonnet and drums his fingers on the paintwork. The third, the one with the carcass, swings around the front passenger door Magnus had left open and sits in the seat. These are not cocky teenagers. These are not young men. Edwin engages these men's eyes for no more than an instant. He blows the horn again and beckons for Magnus. He pretends he is furious with his son.

'Give us a hand,' the boy shouts, not reading his father's signal correctly. He knows these guys aren't kitchen porters. He knows they are down-and-outs. But Magnus wants to show confidence too.

'You want help, son,' the one on the bonnet shouts in a hoarse voice. 'We'll give you a hand, won't we?'

'We will,' says the other, putting a hand on his hat and nodding. The two go to help with the dumpster. The third sucks on a chicken bone. He frightens Edwin with his yellow teeth and greasy lips. Edwin lets out a nervous laugh.

'What's funny?' the man asks, with a quickness that sends a shiver through Edwin. 'You're disturbing our lunch, that's what.'

'You shouldn't be in here,' Edwin says stiffly. 'You should get out.' He calls again for Magnus. This calling is meek.

'Get back in here, Magnus,' the chicken-man echoes with a shout. 'You get back in here right now. We'll take care of that.'

But Magnus is glad of the push coming from the two black men in hats and wants to be part of it.

'Strong little fella, ain't you?' says one without malice.

'Yeah, thanks,' says Magnus.

'But you got to unlock the damn wheel,' the man says, and does it himself.

'Oh . . .'

'There, see?'

The dumpster moves with them now.

'Thanks a lot,' says Magnus, giving it his all from the shoulder just to confirm that he is, indeed, a strong little fucker.

In the car the chicken-man puts out his hand for money. 'There now . . . whatever you think it's worth.'

Edwin struggles to pull a note from his trouser pocket without bringing the folded bills into the light. What comes out is a ten-dollar bill. The man takes it and it disappears instantly. 'Thank you, sir.'

Magnus comes running back to the car. The carcass holds no more interest for the chicken-man, but only because he has stripped it bare. He puts it on top of the dashboard and climbs out. 'You get in there and you listen to your daddy,' he bawls, mock-scolding the boy.

'Yeah, OK,' Magnus replies with enthusiasm. He jumps into the seat, ready to fulfil his duties. 'Ugh, what's that?'

'Shut up,' his father barks. He drops his foot on the accelerator and swerves around the men. They wave and holler and make obscene gestures. Magnus thinks the single fingers they jab in the air are altogether more impressive than the two he holds aloft. 'You should have come when I called,' his father says in a choked-off cry.' He points to the remains of the chicken. 'Throw that out,' he orders, as if Magnus is responsible for putting the filthy chicken carcass there on the dash.

'I can't.'

'Do it now. Throw it out.'

Magnus throws the carcass into the street. He can't understand why his dad is so upset. 'They weren't going to do anything to us . . . '

'How do you know?' his father cuts in with an angry rattle. 'You don't know, do you?'

'Well, they weren't . . . '

'That's not the point. The point is, you didn't do what I told you to do.'

What has spooked him so much? Magnus wants to know. 'Sorry,' he mumbles, looking at the greasy mess in front of him.

'It's all right,' Edwin says when it is too late, when he is calm and they are again driving on the main thoroughfares. 'Just listen to me,' he adds, in his most reasonable voice.

Magnus nods without rancour.

'We have to be smart, don't we, son?'

'We always have to be smart, dad.'

'We don't always know what the ground rules are, do we?'

'No.' Magnus sees that his father is fretting, and he wants to say that it is wise to be cautious, particularly when a person is in town visiting a blood-stranger and liable to be jumpy. 'You're right,' he says, and nods again.

'Where are we now?'

'I'll get the map.'

'We've plenty of time.' Edwin says this as though his nerve is about to give out. Magnus is quick to get the guidebook from the back seat, and locate their position.

It is the last in a line of block and plaster houses that are painted either white, or soft pastel colours. Hers is powder yellow. This kind of house Magnus associates with pictures he has seen of the suburbs of Los Angeles. Next to hers, and on down the street, the houses are older wooden structures with modest porches that are mostly well kept. They have found the street easily, and there is plenty of curbside parking to be had. There are evenly spaced mature trees, all of the same species, all of them thick-leaved and jaded. Some kind of gum tree, Magnus speculates, that nobody climbs.

They pull in under one tree a little way up from the house. It is a quiet neighbourhood. There is just the sound of children playing in back yards and driveways. There is a young woman bouncing herself on a heavy chicken-wire fence. So far as Magnus can judge, she is too old to be doing that sort of thing, but this is America, and he likes the way she doesn't care he is looking at her. She pushes herself off the wire mesh with her shoulderblades. She has a steady rhythm going. Enough to spring on any passerby. She's waiting for her tough boyfriend, Magnus supposes, and speculates that she knows his real grandmother, doesn't like her, thinks she stinks.

His father is going to go straight at this encounter. Magnus can tell. After all, he's been waiting all his life for it. Every single living moment from birth. The look Edwin gives his son now is to say he's going in by himself. Magnus doesn't read it. He wants to go with him. You can get strangers in America talking if you put out your hand for them to shake and you show them you aren't a toughie. He can make sure his dad doesn't come across as a toughie.

The blood-relative's house, just beyond the wire fence, has wooden shutters with inset venetian blinds. A screen that looks like a nylon stocking stretched on the hall door. The porch has a lot of big-leaf and spiky shrubs around it. There are three steps up. The middle step has the number painted on it, in case a stranger can't read the number on the door perhaps. The digits on the door ascend diagonally and are in italics. Magnus knows he should take it all in. It will be important later to recall the details for his mother.

It is calm. An elderly woman suffering under the weight of her bags in the heat pauses near the bouncing woman, whom she ignores. She raises her chin to take the slightest of breezes full on the face and throat, but then she turns and fixes her gaze on the new arrivals in their car. She picks out Magnus with a look that tells him she knows what is about to happen, and that she has something to say about fucked-up families that is harsh but truthful.

'You stay here, son,' Edwin says. His getting out of the car sends the heavily laden woman on her way even before Magnus can offer her a quizzical expression.

'I will, dad,' Magnus replies. He doesn't want to, but he stays. He knows the blood-mother wouldn't be buying his dad back today. This is only a visit. A chance to say hello and see if there is anything to like. To see what she can give. Magnus' mother couldn't grasp that this was the purpose of their visit, Magnus had decided, and that was why his father had taken him as companion instead of his Stella.

Edwin is thinking he has brought Magnus to teach him courage. Some measure of courage could be taught, he was sure. Courage needed to be asserted in this family. A person needs to take action in this world, however clumsily. It is normal to feel disinclined, as he does now, walking up the garden path. A person needs to make a plan. Carry it through.

But Edwin must admit he has brought Magnus for selfish reasons too. The boy, he knows, will be made the centre of attention if introduced. He will introduce Magnus if he needs to deflect unwanted sentiment or to demolish any base purpose that might surface. He can keep his blood-mother in check with the merest glance at his son once he has brought him in.

Magnus can't see much of the encounter on the doorstep, just a silhouetted figure of a woman with her hair permed, no turban. He sees her stepping back into the hall, and his father standing squarely, but reaching to get in a good handshake. There is then a rough hug. Magnus can't get it all because of the greenery. They come in and out of view. She is so much smaller than his dad. Perhaps that is why there is some rocking from side to side. The hug doesn't last long, and there is a release that works on a spring.

His father is then admitted to the house. Magnus gets out of the car and goes to see what he can see. He's content, remember, so what can go wrong? As if to prove the point, he offers his hand for shaking to the bouncing woman, but she just turns her head to one side and maintains her rhythm.

Magnus goes straight to the house. Perhaps what he hears is the sound of a lawn sprinkler he cannot see, or a large insect that has flown in from the desert. God is watching from the bushes. The sound is God sucking air in through his teeth.

Magnus crosses the patch of tightly cropped coarse grass, leaving footprints a shade darker than the intense plastic green of the whole spread. He steps into the deep, defensive flowerbed that skirts the house, careful to avoid the clusters of cactus spines. There is something under the living-room window that has two-lobed leaves, which, to Magnus' nose, smells of exotic piss on a rope. He is good at snooping. Light on feet that most often take him to the right place at the right time. He is alert to whatever might be underfoot; also, to bars of light and shade, and to reflections. He is capable of remaining perfectly still for long stretches. He can stifle a cough or a sneeze, even with God watching, and dry, hot-rope piss-air filling his nostrils.

He watches his father with the blood-woman through the open blind slats. He can't make out what is being said. He tries to read the situation beyond what he knows is occurring. He sees his father touch her hair, and her reach to his hand, either to feel it or move it away, Magnus isn't sure which. In any case, his father takes his hand back.

She doesn't know what to do, and that serves her right. She has her face close to his, then she pulls back, then she goes in close again. Magnus' father doesn't like the unpredictable moves.

This is a special moment, Magnus knows, but special doesn't necessarily mean good. His dad is looking for an explanation. Doesn't she get it? She is allowed to cry, but is required to speak. She is old, but that is no excuse. Old people should be made to talk.

Obviously, she is no good as a mother, and has always known that. Obviously, Magnus' dad knows this, so he is really here for an important discussion about things she should know and he can tell her. When that is finished, he and his dad can sigh heavily, maybe even laugh, then go and have a holiday with the time that is left. She might visit them in Ireland one day. She might get on with Stella: his dad should tell this old woman that Stella is very sociable and likes to laugh. Magnus will never have to call this one 'granny'. If they don't get on with her on her visit, she can be easily kicked out.

'And how are your neighbours?' she asks. 'Those three lovely girls.'

So considered is the tone of this question that it carries undue weight.

'Only Charlotte lives there now,' Edwin replies. 'The only one left in Wicklow now.'

'The only one,' Irene echoes. This news breaks some intensely delicate connection.

'But I married one of the Dooleys,' Edwin adds urgently, and her face lights up. 'I married Stella.'

'Stella,' she repeats, sending the name out a short distance. Though she cannot remember which is which, she remembers the sisters were all attractive and bright and attentive, and in their way angels to her. 'Well now, isn't that a marvellous thing.' Her eyes fill with tears for all that has been lost to her.

After all the years that have passed, she cannot bring herself to ask about the Sparlings. Edwin realises that news of them will have to be volunteered, so he gives her a brief account of his adoptive parents' lives lived out on their farm. He laments the razing of the mothballed house. Burnt down by children, the Guards believe. He will choke if he talks at any length about his beloved adoptive parents in this company. For a moment his mind's eye is dazzled by the reflective shimmer coming from the little reservoir of rainwater in the bottom of the glass mantel of the lamp above the Sparlings' hall door. It has caught the early-morning light. Surely this cannot be a real memory, and yet it is the root of his being. The cat is drawn to the play of light on his infant face, the cat makes him cry and the door is opened. His birth-mother is Roman Catholic, the Sparlings Church of Ireland, but this transient bathing in light is his true baptism. For the good thing that this baby is he gets one kiss, but it is from all humanity.

The Dooleys were going to buy the Sparling house, Edwin tells Irene, but it never happened. 'There wasn't the money,' he explains, and in any case, who would work it?

'Ah,' she says, pretending she recognises that in the end something had been satisfactorily resolved, but Edwin sees that the report of these changes makes the old woman shrivel. 'Stella,' she repeats, 'yes, I remember her clearly.' He sees she is lying. The faces of angels are virtually indistinguishable.

'Did you ever wonder?' Edwin asks her. 'About me,' he feels he should add. His neutral tone sounds absurd to his own ears, but that is to be expected.

She cannot find words. Her lower lip begins to tremble. She looks away as she nods. But then, she re-engages. She re-engages because she hears her husband's heavy footfalls. She had somebody to introduce.

An older man enters the room. He is introduced as Ned, Edwin's biological father. A shiver runs through Edwin. The hand that is caressing his heart squeezes harder. The biology that connects him to this woman has a power that needs to be diminished, if not reduced to a simple acknowledgement of a life-long separation. He has made no allowances for being outnumbered.

They must begin again. Irene draws back her tears. She and Ned strain to see what they have made. They look to each other to signal that they could have done no better for him. After they have done this, they force quivery smiles through tight lips, shake their heads, let their eyeballs swell in their sockets, to signal to Edwin that they are well pleased in him.

Magnus anticipates that his father might glance in the direction of their hired car, might do that irregularly. Accordingly, he is careful with his positioning and his cover. What he fails to anticipate is the sudden move to the window of this second entity – perhaps in response to something his father is saying, or to get as far away from him as the room will permit. In any case, it is this shambling stranger who spots Magnus in the flowerbed. Edwin is forced to identify the interloper as his son. The blood-mother is frightened. She pushes in clumsily to look. It is she who pulls back the shutters on their hinges. She smiles with alarm and wiggles her fingers. This produces a momentary buckling in Magnus' chest.

She beckons like a mad witch. God holds his breath.

CHAPTER 5

Edwin's Blood Parents

The woman treats it as if Edwin had been keeping Magnus as a surprise. The boy is a bonus. A precious glimpse of Edwin, aged fourteen, as well as a crowning glory.

'Magnus, this is your grandmother,' Edwin announces formally. To Magnus the words sound absurd. 'Grandma Irene,' his father adds, making the introduction more absurd. And now he, Magnus, is the centre of attention. This is some kind of cruel punishment for snooping.

Edwin lets out a gasp of anxiety, but only because his son has been brought in earlier than he had planned.

'He's a young *man*,' Edwin's mother marvels. 'He's a beautiful young man.'

Irene, Grandma Irene, Ned: the names mean nothing, and Edwin and Magnus are strangers to them. That is the single, incontrovertible fact to provide any comfort. Magnus doesn't want this old woman fingering his hair, so he moves his head to one side and she immediately desists. She keeps smiling at the little saviour and repeatedly makes encouraging by-play with a range of exaggerated facial expressions. Some of this catalogue Magnus has seen on the faces of his great aunts.

'Look at him, Ned,' she says to the other blood. 'Wouldn't you be proud. We *are* proud, aren't we, Ned?'

Craggy old Ned isn't sure, but nods without hesitation. 'Yes. Yes, we are.' Ned can say no more for the present because he is afraid. Afraid for his wife and for himself. It had been a regular day until the doorbell rang. Terrible things happen on regular days, and he counts himself a man who has had his share of good fortune and might be due some bad.

Magnus smiles, puts out his hand for shaking, says nothing, which confuses the Ned man and makes him shake the extended hand with an aggressive jerk.

Magnus manages to say nothing again. He looks to his dad to register his alarm, but his dad chooses to ignore this connection.

Edwin has no vision beyond this point and vision is suddenly required. He is shocked, even appalled, to find that she is still with the man who impregnated her, the man he simply cannot bring himself to acknowledge as father. But why should he be appalled? He doesn't know. There is no mistaking the family likeness. Ned is killing, and now, suddenly, Edwin can't bear his mother's fawning.

Magnus sees her put her hand on Edwin's chest momentarily, sees her take his arm and hold it a little longer than before. She wants to touch him. Does it feel good to be touched by her? Magnus can't tell from his father's reaction, though he can see plainly his father is uneasy about touching her.

'When you came back to visit . . . ' Edwin says with great deference.

'I never went back,' she replies with a sweet-old-lady shake of her head.

'But this is how I found you,' Edwin continues, with the same deference.

'I didn't go back to visit.'

What she means is that she did not go back to visit him. A flat denial she thinks is best.

'The Dooleys,' Edwin says, 'my wife's family, Stella, Charlotte and Maureen . . . . You talked to them.'

'No.'

'You told them a little about yourself. Before you went to the Garda station,' Edwin persists in the same mild-mannered way he employs when testing a point with a site manager or an official from the department.

'I'm glad you're here, Edwin,' she says. His name doesn't sit well with her. It makes her declaration of gladness sound formal and insincere. She can see he is an intelligent man, a man of good judgement, and she wants credit for this observation. She is desperate to deflect his line of enquiry. 'We're both glad, aren't we, Ned?'

Ned agrees that he, too, is glad. The exchange lurches back and forth. Greetings are repeated as declarations of shock. It's to be expected. 'It's lovely to meet you, boy,' Ned says. He wants his son to know there will be no talk of regret from him. Belatedly, he steps forward and places both hands on the caps of Edwin's shoulders, then, in a strange automated fashion, transfers this arm's-length embrace to Magnus. 'Lovely to see the both of you.'

Do they talk to themselves in these accents? To Magnus' ears their Irish-American accents seem put on, a disguise. The Ned man's skin is too shiny for an old man. His teeth are too small, too ridged and yellow, and his voice not wide enough in the mouth to be a proper American, which is what he is pretending to be, right? He's afraid, but not afraid enough. Happy, but not happy enough. He wants Magnus to cut his hair. Magnus can tell.

'Lovely to meet you, granddad,' Magnus says. He knows this will stick it to him, but it will also embarrass his father. There had been no instruction on the use of the term; no guidance. Magnus is there to help. He has been brought in from the front garden. This is helping. There is a queue of Magnuses wanting to get in on this, each one less intimidated than the preceding one.

This woman had promised God that she would one day look her grown son in the eyes directly, acknowledge the birth, admit to abandoning him. But not now. Not in this moment. And still, she gropes. She takes Edwin's arm a second time. She squeezes hard. She seems to want to lead him to Ned, but neither man is willing.

This *is* the moment. There is nothing bewildering about it. God has delivered Edwin here. She must make it work and she must glory in it and ask forgiveness. She must demonstrate that she is old and useless, but will stand as firm as she can on her quaking legs and properly receive him.

Edwin sees she is afraid for Ned. He concludes she has always been the stronger of the two. Ned does not know how to conduct himself and will not hear God's voice. He might get angry. It might break him.

Irene reaches for Magnus to try to gather him in, but he, too, is unwilling, and he makes this clear by stepping to one side.

Why did she come back to the house in Wicklow? Edwin wants to ask again, but doesn't. Had she come to spy? To talk? To seek forgiveness? To look for help? She did none of those things, according to the Dooley sisters. Edwin has a sudden lack of heart. Let her be dumb on the subject, he decides.

Stella understands better than her husband the rituals of life. Edwin wants Stella here with him now, so that she might see he is not without good judgement. Just short on nerve. He resolves to fully report this moment, in spite of her opposition to the reunion.

Edwin sees family photographs on a sideboard and on the wall by a large desk. He quickly calculates how long after she had given him up she gave birth to her two other children, smiling out of these frames. 'You've a lovely house,' he says. He wants her to offer a tour. He wants to see her other children's bedrooms.

She sees him taking in the photographs. She rushes to meet his cloudy gaze with a few rudimentary facts. 'That's Sean. And that's Angelica. Grown up, they are.'

Edwin is giving out with exaggerated facial expressions of appreciation. 'Sean and Angelica,' he echoes. He can't concentrate now that he has to look out for Magnus. Can't properly drink in the bitter-sweetness and the oddity, as he wants.

Edwin has brought on this collision. He is driving it still, closing some physic circle, as he thinks. At his age, how can he have made such a miscalculation? he asks himself. From the outset he secretly thought it might well be a mistake, but still, he is hoping to be contradicted. That's how these things work, isn't it? A new chemistry gets discovered in a cautious man. It is right that he should be somebody's child again. He isn't here for a social visit. This is the science of genes, and applied mechanics of the heart. He needs to tune in again, and quickly.

What is she saying? Does Magnus like maths? Can he paint and draw? Is he good at sports? In her day she was a good runner. She was good at French, too, but has lost it. Where does he go to school?

Good God.

Magnus thinks his father is standing too close to the woman. Letting her see that he's fretting. His father wants too much to please. What Magnus does not grasp is that his father wants to smell his mother's skin. Wants to see if at some primitive level he recognises her. He hasn't found that recognition in her voice.

Edwin ascends the staircase with hunched shoulders. Why does he hunch his shoulders? Magnus wants his dad to bait the woman. It's all too proper. The blood-father should get a punch in the face right now.

Edwin sees the bedrooms of his remote siblings. It is Magnus who is told that Sean and Angelica would be honoured to have him stay in one of their rooms. He can come to visit in his summer holidays. Will he tell her again which school it is he goes to? Magnus tells her. She doesn't disguise the fact that the answer means nothing to her. If he comes to stay, Magnus will meet her grandchildren – *her other grandchildren.*

Magnus' expression strongly indicates that he is not interested, but this has no effect. Irene is proud of the hand-stitched American quilts she has on their beds. Antiques, she says. Magnus' hunched father steps forward to feel the quality.

All the years of his growing, Edwin has dared to wonder if his biological parents are both still alive and, if alive, are they in rags? This has been a lonely wondering, bereft of emotional charge. Now, he sees that they are alive and not wanting, that they are still together, and with other grown children, this wondering turns to compassion. Compassion for himself.

'Sean is in the navy,' she says suddenly and directly to Magnus.

'He ships out of Seattle,' Ned adds. Sean loves the sea, he says.

'We don't see him much these days,' she says. 'We were up to see him before Christmas. We had a picnic. They set us up in the gymnasium. We have the picnic in the gymnasium when it's too cold,' she explains.

'The weather got bad real quick that day, didn't it?' says Ned. 'They made an announcement over the tannoy. A big front coming in. So we didn't stay long. We drove straight back down, didn't we, Irene?'

'We do family picnics year-round,' Irene says. 'We do, Magnus. Even winter.'

There is something about this storm picnic in the navy gym that intensely annoys Magnus, but even before he can curl his lip his father comes in –

'And Angelica comes along?'

'Oh yes,' says Ned – which is clearly a lie.

'When she can,' Irene adds. 'It's a long journey for her. We talk a lot on the phone.'

Edwin and Magnus must both come to visit when the children are in town, she says. She and Ned will look after them. Edwin feels sorry for her in her state of panic, making promises to strangers, but this he has anticipated. He calls her by her name, not by the term 'mother'.

'We will, Irene. We'll both visit.'

And Magnus' mother? Where is she?

She is in Dublin, Edwin replies simply.

She must come, too.

Magnus pulls a face that makes it clear his mother will not be interested.

'You come and help me get the tea,' Irene says, and she leads Magnus into the kitchen. She wants to take him by the hand. Wants to take her grown boy, Edwin, by the hand. God's mercy grants that she might use Magnus as her bridge, but Magnus awkwardly puts both hands in his pockets.

'Don't you drink coffee?' he asks her.

'Oh, we have coffee, if you want coffee,' she says.

The placement of objects in the house had meaning Magnus cannot decipher, except that he knows it had something to do with being found to have a whole, self-sufficient life. This includes having a cake on the kitchen table, there in its entirety, ready to be eaten. It is sitting on a plate, white-topped, like the convertible, with a big silver knife to one side.

The two men stand in the living room. 'It's good that you're here,' Edwin hears Ned say. Hears him say it rather than sees him say it, because he is still looking to the kitchen.

Magnus doesn't hear his dad say that there is no explanation sought (though it is desired). That there is no bad will (though there is great hurt). Doesn't hear Ned say that what he and his wife see makes them very proud. Doesn't see the clumsy attempt at an embrace. Doesn't hear Ned ask his Edwin what he does for a living. Doesn't hear Ned weep when his dad tells him he is an architect.

Magnus watches his grandmother intently as she moves about the kitchen in some kind of old-woman ritual. He thinks she might be praying under her breath. He and his dad are related to all of this. He's taking it in, but he is sure he will forget it all.

Edwin comes into the kitchen. He can't bear to be in the same room as his father. But Ned-the-father follows. There are too many fathers.

'I nearly got shot by a hunter,' Magnus blurts out.

'Did you, dear?' Irene says with a melodramatic intake of air. 'In Wicklow, was it?'

She isn't listening. Magnus thinks she hasn't been properly listening to his father, either. 'No. Here, in America.'

'A hunter, you say?'

'Yeah, he came after me with his dog. It was in the woods by a shopping mall.

'In the woods?'

She is a stupid old cow, maybe.

Edwin finally wakens to the story. Sees how anxious Magnus is. 'Fine imagination you have, son. Fine imagination he has,' he echoes to Irene and Ned.

'I didn't stay in the woods,' Magnus continues, more insistent than before. 'I would have been mad to stay in the woods.'

Now Irene scoffs and gives a friendly wave of her liver-spotted hand in front of her face. 'I'd say you're always up for mischief.' Her accent is suddenly more American than before – entirely American, as Magnus reads it. 'This boy is blessed with adventure,' she declares to Ned, conspicuously playing along.

'He certainly is,' Ned replies. 'Go on. Tell us what happened. What a boy,' he exclaims.

Magnus can't believe his ears. These are definitely phony accents, he decides. Getting choky has got them migrating in the wrong direction. Maybe it's a way of keeping a distance, of keeping strangers forever strangers. That's good. He'll carry on with his story directly, because it's the smart move.

'The hunter and his dog came out after me. I lost them in the shopping mall.'

'What a boy,' Ned exclaims.

Irene has paused with her ritual movements. She steadies herself now to address him formally in front of Edwin. 'Magnus, what do you want to know about me?' She is acting now as though she and the Ned man have been expecting this visit and have had a long time to contemplate.

Magnus shrugs. 'Ask my dad,' he says, as though his father is in another place.

'All right,' she says in a confidential tone, 'if you say I should, I will.'

OK. So maybe she isn't a stupid old cow, but this Ned man leans against his wife. Magnus thinks he looks like a child leaning against his mother's leg. He knows this must be some kind of primitive display of togetherness, but it spooks him. What must his father think? Might he perform the same action? The trouble this could bring.

Magnus can't take his eyes off this weld. Look at that, he wanted to whisper to his father. My grandfather is a primitive. Let's get out of here.

Edwin must fill a hole he cannot fill, but he sees clearly now why he has brought his son. He can hardly credit his own scruples making the boy wait in the car. Thankfully, Magnus has more sense. He has made a great play of his story about pissing in the trees by the shopping centre. Edwin now makes Magnus tell the couple about finding the body on the beach. Makes him tell this story. Doesn't mind being uncharacteristically harsh in his insistence, because it is true. 'You'll want to hear this,' he says to the sprawling wreck that is Ned.

For Magnus it is a terrible betrayal of confidence, but he must do this to help his father. He bitterly gives a matter-of-fact account of finding the body. His father is unbearably attentive and, it seems to Magnus, full of spurious wonder.

The bloods don't know why they are being told this story, except that they are required to recognise in their grandson the same sense of responsibility they see in their son. That, and a healthy respect for the departed.

When the brief telling is over, Irene helplessly makes the same melodramatic noise she made in response to Magnus' story of the hunter and his dog.

'What a boy,' Ned repeats.

Edwin abruptly announces that it is time to leave.

'Oh no . . . ' Irene protests.

'Yes, we should be going, Irene. We're tired. We should be going to our hotel.'

Magnus wants to stay a little longer. There is a strange energy in the house. He has never seen old people so attentive. Though he can't name what it is his father wants, it is clear he hasn't got it, and Magnus feels he should do something to help. 'But we haven't checked in at a hotel.'

'You must stay here, of course,' Irene chimes.

This only makes Edwin more anxious. 'No. I have a hotel in mind. One that's been recommended. We have our plan.'

Magnus sees the urgency. Knows there is no plan from here. His dad is an architect. Can't tolerate the angle of his drawing board being a few degrees out, never mind having no plan to draft. That is a good lie about the hotel, though. The only kind of lies he has ever detected coming from his father are lies that deny his own discomfort. But Magnus wants to stay now. These bloods are scared and are sure to give him and his father a good time. Maybe Ned has shown himself to be a mean and stupid man in the living room. Maybe that's why his dad wants to run.

'You must stay for supper at least, Edwin,' Irene says. She is trying to get used to her son's name. Trying to get it to roll out of her mouth with a proper familiarity.

'Ah, you will,' Ned urges.

'We will, dad, won't we?' Magnus says, though Ned's urging seems deeply sinister.

'You go through to the parlour. Go now, Edwin. Magnus and I will bring in the tea. It is tea you want, Edwin, isn't it?'

'Yes,' Edwin replies. He moves ahead reluctantly. He gives Magnus a hard look as he does so – which is entirely out of character.

'What?' Magnus whinnies under his breath, evidently making the situation worse for his father.

Edwin can't bear to see the shame in Ned's white face. He goes to the window in the living room, points through the opened blinds. Ned shuffles in behind, as he feels he should. 'You see that car . . . the tan and white one . . . the convertible . . . that's what I'm driving.'

'You rented that?' Ned retorts, trying to inject some wonder into his down-beat utterances. 'Well now, don't you deserve it? What is it? A Buick?'

'A Buick.'

Ned makes no reference to the Pontiac, of which he is more than proud. It is parked at the side of the house, at the top of his sloping drive. 'Yes, Edwin,' he says, stumbling over his son's name, 'that's some car you rented.'

'A very smooth drive,' Edwin adds.

'I'll say.'

'Very smooth,' Edwin repeats pointlessly. He wants to bolt, but he can't yet.

The Irene woman loops back. She doesn't want Edwin and the boy to leave. God hasn't done his work. Sean, she says, had to wear a protective leather helmet when he was a small boy. He was forever bashing his head off the table corner, the doors, the banisters.

What was wrong with him? Magnus asks. Was his distant relative defective, he wants to know, but doesn't like to ask outright. He will deduce from her answer.

Sean was a special boy . . .

Oh God.

Sean was a happy, quiet boy often away in his own world, not always pay-ing attention to what was around him. It was as if his daydreaming made his head a little too heavy for his body.

Oh God. Magnus gets her to describe the leather skullcap. When the bloods were living in San Francisco on the top floor of what Irene calls a four-storey walk-up, when Ned was away all day working in the navy yards, she'd have to manage the stairs by herself. That is to say, she had to get Sean and Angelica down the steep flights in stages. The best thing to do, she found, given Sean's condition, was to take Angelica all the way down first, tie her reins to the banister, then bring down Sean. She flushed when she told this. She was proud of her pragmatism. People could thrive on making do. She and Ned did. There wasn't a door that hung right in that house, she says with conspicuous affection. Her firstborn son, being an architect, will appreciate her acceptance of such imperfections.

Magnus doesn't like her depiction. He finds it too intimate. He sees his father give out with a nervous laugh that is meant to be indulgent. Magnus can see that any reference to these other offspring is wounding for him, but doesn't see why. What Magnus now wants to ask is what made her think his dad wants to hear this?

'Is his head all right now?' he asks instead, deliberately cutting in.

'Oh yes . . . '

'Do you still have the leather hat?'

'Somewhere, I think.' His grandmother is at last on to his resentment, and wants to dispel it. 'Would you like to see it – if I can find it?'

'No,' Magnus replies with an affected yawn. 'I can imagine it.'

'I have photographs,' she says.

'I bet Angelica bawled her eyes out at the bottom of the stairs.'

There are more indulgent noises made but really, nobody wants to hear what Magnus has to say on the matter.

Edwin stands with all his muscles taught in his smart suit. Do you go on holidays?' he asks. This must surely end soon. Yes? They do? Where do you go? Do you ever go to Ireland? Have there been family holidays in Ireland with Sean and Angelica? These are good questions, Magnus determines. He is thinking Irene and her stinking old-fuck man can't stand each other. They stay together because of what they have done.

There is no innocence here, Edwin acknowledges, just a dulling of sensibility. Perhaps it is precisely this that he has come for. He hasn't yet stated why he has come. Had she thought about him today, for instance? Or last week? Putting a face on her makes something of this simple enquiry. No hurt, no rage is more remote than his, he wants to say. He is here to remove the humdrum mystery. He will log whatever else she might offer in the way of facts: she had stayed with her husband, who had gone to work in the navy yards, her second son had a heavy head, her daughter could be tethered to the banisters, and such.

The leaving is abrupt. The farewells, brief. This suits everybody.

'You shouldn't have done that,' Magnus says to his father once they are outside. There is a climbing anxiety in his voice. To have been forced to confide in these people is intolerable.

'Do what, son?' Edwin asks.

'Make me tell them about the beach.'

Edwin takes Magnus' arm in a tight grip and swings him face-on. 'But it's your special story. Now tell me, what did you think you were doing in there? You think it was right to just sit down to tea after spying through their window?'

'No. I'm sorry.'

'Have her get cake out when we're ready to go?'

'I'm sorry I ate the cake. I am.'

Edwin lets go of Magnus. It isn't right to manhandle the boy. 'You didn't see *me* eating cake, did you?'

'No.'

'Christ, son . . . '

Magnus is sorry that he had eaten the woman's cake. He makes a noise, a little croak of anguish, then he sticks his fingers down his throat and throws up on her little patch of lawn. He has never done such a thing before, though he knows a teenager can do it, and he is fourteen.

Tea and cake vomit from the heart. He is as shocked as his father, but glad he has done it. He feels faint. Edwin puts one hand to his son's chest, the other to his back. 'Don't . . . ' is all the man can utter.

This Magnus reads as a good response. 'OK,' he replies willingly. Already, he is less fretful. The sweet-sour sickly tang in his mouth steadies his nerve and makes something medical of the situation. 'I'm sorry, dad,' he repeats several times as they move away from the house.

'Don't be sorry,' Edwin whispers in his rage.

They are both squinting in the bright light. They get away from that house. Edwin halts on the footpath. For a moment Magnus fears that because of his throwing up, his father might stop breathing and that the world will end for him. Only the shadow disc around his feet seems to be keeping him upright. But Magnus' fear leaves him when he sees his father take the car keys from his pocket, and he hears them jingle in his hand as he takes a few heavy steps in the direction of the convertible. It is a short distance to the car, but when they reach it something has already given way.

'I'm glad that's over,' Magnus dares to say. Edwin knows his son isn't talking about being sick on the lawn, knows he is trying to sound grown-up. Edwin now seems empty of purpose, but Magnus feels there is a downbeat perfection to their standing on that patch of pavement in their new clothes, standing by their splendid hired car. His father has a wad of dollars in his pocket, all of which can now be spent on them alone. Magnus hopes he has reversed something by putting his fingers down his throat.

Edwin does not declare that he, too, is glad it is over.

'Where will we go?' Magnus asks. He is thinking about the blood-mother with her cold smooth skin and her false-apple-blush cheeks. He and his father now need to get away from there as quickly as possible if this perfection is to continue. 'We could just go for a drive.'

His father stands by the driver's door and hangs his head. Magnus has never seen his father hang his head. He is taking too long to make a decision. It isn't that he is patiently thinking through options. Nor is it an attempt to exercise scrupulous judgement of what had just occurred. It is to do with fatigue. Magnus doesn't get it.

'We could go for a drive,' Magnus persists, 'then have dinner, then ring Mam, then go to the pictures, then back to a hotel to sleep.'

Edwin raises his head slowly and Magnus sees more than killing disappointment in his face. He sees that there is something broken that is unfixable. He sees the rage building again. 'Get in the car,' comes the order in a low, dark voice.

'You need to open it,' Magnus says tentatively, but Edwin isn't listening. He is taking one last look back at the house to see if they are watching. Magnus can give them the two fingers he had down his throat. His father's hurt is enormous, but a gesture might help. With any luck they have seen what he has done on their lawn. He doesn't know whether or not he should feel ashamed of his spying. After all, he has come this far with his father as companion. He needs to know what forces are at work. He needs to be able to offer a response, even if it is just two fingers. If he wasn't meant to be part of this encounter, why had his father brought him here?

'I said get in the car!' his father shouts. The attack in the voice is so unfamiliar to Magnus that he raises both hands in the air, then throws them at his father.

'I can't. Not until you unlock the door.'

By the time he has uttered his protest, Edwin has come around to the passenger side. He smacks Magnus on the back of the head. It is a shocking thing that he has never done before. The expression on his son's face tells Edwin there is no putting this right. 'Sorry,' he says, incredulous at his own action. 'Sorry,' he repeats, lowering his face to make direct eye-contact.

'It's OK,' Magnus says automatically. His father unlocks the car door. Magnus gets into the car quickly. The perfect moment of grace has been blown apart. His head is swimming.

Does his father want to go back in to them? Try again. If he does, Magnus will promise not to spy. He will go in when he is called. Kiss them both without hesitation, if his father wants, and be glad. But he can't find words to express this willingness. 'I'm upset, that's all,' his father says breathlessly, as they drive away.

'I know,' Magnus replies.

Perhaps it is the understanding tone the boy tries to inject that gets such a quick and sharp return. 'You don't know anything.'

'I do, I know,' Magnus insists in a defiant whinny. Lest his dad make him cry with a look, he glares out at the endless row of tidy houses slipping behind them. Takes note of the ascending numbers that are in the thousands. Counts the dogs, the cats, the basketball hoops, ignores the playing children and the snake-hipped girls acting on the lawns, lest they, too, want him to cry.

Perhaps what his father means is that he is only fourteen and can't know what he himself has failed to grasp.

CHAPTER 6

Father and Son Lost

His father drives at a steady forty around the suburbs of Bakersfield. They cross the same junctions two and three times, but never from the same direction. Perhaps the gentle bumps and big turns and the looping promotes quick healing.

The second blood is the problem, Magnus decides. Two is one too many, even if the second is his dad's dad. They are so terribly old. They should have known the bad effect this meeting would have on his dad. His father should never have touched their skin. Touching was a mistake. Magnus knew this from kissing the grandmother woman, and from shaking the other blood's hand. There was acid in their skin.

'I'm thirsty,' Magnus says, as they broadly take yet another shaded corner, but Edwin says nothing in response. He just keeps driving. He drives them into the centre of Bakersfield, then out again. Edwin looks left and right at regular intervals, but takes nothing in. He goes with the traffic flow. Finally, on a straight stretch of road some distance out, he pulls in to the parking lot of a bar, a low, long structure with a tin awning, and neon floating in a black cloud in the widows.

The entrance has heavy double doors with porthole windows.

'Remember, dad . . . ' Magnus cautions, and makes a pulling motion to indicate the swing of this American door.

'I remember,' his father replies from inside his darkness, but pushes without thinking. He opens both doors together, which, Magnus thinks, is a clumsy action for an architect, but then something bad happened.

They sit in a curved red leatherette couch. Nobody else is sitting in the booths. This is a place where men and women like to have their elbows on the countertop. There is low- level inky lighting that gives a blurry sheen to skin.

There is a smell of fried food and pine cleaner. Edwin clasps his hands on the table as if he is about to pray aloud. He appears to be able to lower his head with an extra ratchet on the neck. This is strange. It makes Magnus feel afraid for him. He has not seen his father do such a thing before.

What will he pray for?

Some men adopt this pose when they are going to get drunk, Magnus supposes. He wishes he were older so that he could get drunk with his father and not have to worry. They have loads of money for drinking. Crisp, narrow dollars. He wants his dad to take his thick fold of dollars out and put it on the table. That's what men do in American bars, isn't it, to show they can pay for their drinks?

Edwin does get quietly drunk. From over the rim of his Coke, Magnus studies the tracking of his father's eyes. It's as though he is getting drunk, lost in the jungle. Magnus wills him to speak, and he speaks.

'We'll find a nice place to stay for tonight,' he says.

'We will,' Magnus replies quickly. 'There must be loads of them around here.'

'Do you want something to eat?' It pains Edwin to ask this question.

'No thanks.' Magnus needs to say more. 'It's good to be out of the sun for a while. It's good to be resting.'

It is some time before Edwin replies. 'Never mind,' he says from a great distance, nodding his head. 'Never mind,' he repeats, and continues to nod to make a little lullaby of it, which is a bad thing to do in any jungle, Magnus thinks.

When they leave the bar and walk out into the parking lot, Edwin gently bounces off one of the few parked vehicles, as if cocooned in a thick layer of angel feathers.

'This one,' Magnus says, putting his hand on the door handle on the passenger side.

'I know,' his father says, showing great patience. 'Ours is the only convertible.'

'Is that a hotel over there?'

His father shades his eyes. 'Don't like the look of it. We'll go out further.'

The roof is let down. It seems to be the thing to do. It makes a grinding noise. It is a relief for both when they get out on the road. They hear a train horn sounding at regular intervals, but they can't see a train. It's beyond the horizon. They keep pace with it across a great tract of landscape. Magnus fancies this is what makes his father's driving flawless for the first stretch. That distant burr repeating.

Magnus thinks about the encounter with his blood-grandmother. Tries to formalise his record of it. He knows he should be generous and forgiving. He had felt for the old woman fumbling in her kitchen, trying to put the world right with her tea and her cake. In an instant, trying to express great sorrow and great happiness. It was her moment of truth. And his dad's dad? What about him? He and the blood-mother had prayed to God for their baby, perhaps, and then gone and had two more. Then scalded the teapot and sliced the cake on her best china when their abandoned son showed up.

It is only when his father goes to cross against oncoming traffic that he makes a slight misjudgement and they have a near-miss. Then, there is a different kind of horn blast.

There is a short piece of all-weather indestructible carpet outside the Providence Motel reception that impresses Magnus. It is cherry red. He knows they have this stuff in front of some hotels, casinos and the Little Chapel of Love in Las Vegas. He's seen it in films. Now he knows some motels spread it, too. He pitches his feet hard into the pile for the three strides it takes to cross it following his father into the foyer.

The motel is a two-storey affair. The upper floor has an exterior balcony that runs the length of the building. They are put on the ground floor. They go back to the car and float it down to the space outside their door.

Inside the room, the bed clothing and curtains are starched and thin. Brown, orange and white. There is a smell of stale cinnamon and old wood varnish. The television set is an enormous box on skinny metal legs. There is a king-sized double bed with a single alongside it. The sheets are pulled so tight they will have to lift the corners to release the tension before either of them can get in. Through a narrow doorway they can see that the shower is shabby, but clean, the porcelain chalky and bone dry.

'Go in there and wash yourself.'

'But I don't need to.'

'Do as I say.'

Magnus goes through the motions. His father sits on the end of the king-sized bed. He scarcely makes a dent in the mattress. Even when he presses down on his thighs with both hands and hangs his head. It is the black magic of melancholia that often goes unnoticed.

Magnus opens the map section of their guidebook on the bed beside his father and studies it, hoping it will engage him, too. He reads aloud names of places that mean nothing to him or his father, but their sound is reassuring. There is a phonebox in the middle of the desert. 'Do you know about it, dad?'

His father tells him there are probably many such phoneboxes in remote spots by the side of the highway.

'But this one is absolutely in the middle of nowhere,' Magnus insists. If they pass it, they will certainly have to stop and make a call. They can ring Stella just to shock her. To get her annoyed. To make her anxious, in a good way. 'She won't believe where we are.' He will tell her it's all falling into place. All going according to plan.

Edwin is tired and distracted. He barely acknowledges his son's words.

Magnus gets up to investigate. The neon sign outside is good. So is the slide-in cinema lettering they use to make messages. They'd already seen some that were messages from God, but mostly they give the rates and special features. Apart from the neon and the cinema lettering, Magnus doesn't like the place, and neither does his father, though he says he does. It is occupied by suspicious people. Next door they have a camper van. Why are they staying in a motel when they have a camper van? There are very fat people on the other side. Magnus hears them running a bath. How can either of them get into a bath? This is an unhappy place and everybody knows it. The Gideons Bible in the Sparlings' room has page corners turned down and grease stains that have seeped through page after thin page. Chicken fat, Magnus thinks, when he sniffs it.

'Can I keep this?' he asks, holding up the book.

'No, you can't. Put it back where you found it.'

And another thing, the car his father has hired might be stolen. You can easily steal a convertible in the night. This is where you'd stay if you were a trans-continental truck driver and, like the owners of the camper, you don't like the bunk you have at the back of your driver's cab. Or if you want to have sex with somebody who has to keep it a secret, which makes them unhappy in a content sort of way: Magnus knows this from studying his mother. American men don't dare wank in here because some of these rooms have hidden cameras. He wonders if this room has a camera, and if it does, do they see how upset his father is? Do they see him weep? Well, of course they do, if there is a camera.

Magnus bounces on the single bed without much enthusiasm, then he looks again at his father. 'Will we ring Mam from here?'

'No.'

'Will we go for a hamburger and chips?' He isn't hungry, but he thinks it is a good idea if they aren't going to talk to his mother.

'Not now.'

'I might go exploring.'

'No. Not around here.'

Magnus gets off the bed and switches on the ceiling fan. He stands staring at it. He wants to show his father he is fully prepared to embrace the whole experience. 'Will I turn on the telly?'

51

'No.'

'I want to turn on the telly.'

'Don't.'

'I'm going to sit in the car, then.'

'What do you want to do that for?'

'I want to listen to the radio.'

'Go and sit in the car, then.'

'I need the keys.'

His father gives him the keys. 'Just for a while. I don't want you running the battery flat.'

The bloods had been bad to him. It was God's fault, really. 'Then can I watch the telly?'

'We'll see.'

Magnus spins the car keys on his finger. 'She was a cow, wasn't she?'

'Go and listen to the radio.'

Magnus feels he should stay with his father. He is afraid for both of them. He sways a little from the ankles, waiting for some kind of reassurance. Edwin raises his eyes and makes a pretend smile for his son. This is confirmation that Edwin, too, knows the motel is a place for unhappy people, Magnus decides. That is why they have pulled in here.

Magnus slouches to one side, ready to leave the room, but his father catches him by the wrist and does an odd thing. He turns him back and shakes him by the hand. It is a firm, deliberate shake. Magnus doesn't know the purpose of it, but in the moment he feels his father's hand working as a transformer. He understands this handshake to be a way of passing great strength or great hurt.

When it is done, Magnus goes out to the car.

It is strange to be bouncing on a lousy motel bed in the middle of the day pretending it is time to sleep. When there is still a smell of bacon and syrup on the porch.

Magnus feels compelled to look in the windows of his neighbours. Were they stuck inside, too? There is nothing happening on one side, and their camper van has gone. Perhaps they have taken off without paying. The fat people are lumping about. She is waddling in the middle of the room with one shoe on, annoyed and bewildered. He is looking for the other shoe to put on her foot – so they can go and get steaks, maybe, and a mountain of waffles.

Magnus has a strong urge to knock on their window and give them two fingers for no good reason, but he resists. He gets in behind the steering wheel of the Buick. The vehicle seems to have grown bigger just sitting idle in front of the Providence. He turns the key one-quarter and the radio comes on. The accelerator and the big brake pedal sit comfortably under his feet. He adjusts the rearview mirror so that he can see the traffic whizz past on the road. He sees his fingers reach again to the side of the steering column and turn the key further in the ignition, and he hears the engine start. The action has everything to do with what has passed through his father's hand into his.

He settles in the seat, puts the gear in reverse, lets off the handbrake, lowers his foot meekly on the accelerator and slides out of the parking space. He brakes too hard and the car lurches with a little screech from the tyres, but there is plenty of room to manoeuvre. It feels as he thinks it should feel, so he proceeds. He moves the gearstick to 'Drive' and pulls away gently. He doesn't have to cross the flow of traffic to turn in the direction of the desert. Taking the car is a good thing to do. It is the right kind of trouble because he, too, is upset. He will be less upset alone in the desert, where he can speed, and shout, and swear. Then he will drive back to the motel as the sun is going down. He will certainly be missed, but he can say, fuck the bloods, and get his father to do the same.

'Fuck the bloods!' he shouts down at his feet.

The hiss of the tyres seems more pronounced with just him in the car. Other drivers seem to like him and give him extra space. He thinks they might be looking at him because of his age – the ones who notice him at all – but he soon decides that they take a second glance because he is dressed as a foreign kid.

He keeps his distance from the car in front. He tries the horn once when that car peels off, and for a time there is no traffic ahead of him. Generally, he is a responsible boy and is, without doubt, a smart boy. Smart enough to know that being smart isn't everything. Look at the bloods. Look how smart they played, pretending to be just good folk. Magnus keeps a steady speed.

He lets down the roof. It makes a bit of a grinding noise when it goes into the crack behind the back seat. Perhaps there is something unlikely down there. He'd found a corkscrew down the back of the couch at home. Anyway, he will put the roof up again later, when he stops and there is no breeze to cool him.

CHAPTER 7

The Boy in the Desert

Without petrol, the car glides for a short time at the speed of low clouds. The traction in the wheels makes a nice sound. Small stones make an ever more precise impression on the tyres as the coasting Buick slows down. The steering gets heavy.

When the car finally comes to a halt on the dirt track, Magnus just sits and looks across the expanse before him. There are military installations and mines in this desert, but he can't see any. What did his father say: borax, tungsten, gold, salt and iron worked out of the ground.

The clear, clean air sets everything at a precise distance. Colours change across the landscape with an infinitely graded wash. You'd never know they were mining, he thinks.

He gets out of the car by pushing himself through the fully opened driver's window. He doesn't have to get out this way. It's part of being reckless. It is as easy as pushing his head through the neck of his pullover, but the landing is hard. He grazes the heel of one hand in a graceless tumble, but it's a good thing to do on an extraordinary day such as this, particularly if you are Magnus, son of Edwin Sparling, and you've driven out into the desert.

There are no sally rods here to make into spears. Unlike at home, there are fast-creeping things at which you might throw a spear. Dangerous running animals, too. Howling coyotes and sneaky wild cats. He has seen them in Disney films and at Dublin Zoo. There is the tyre lever – he can use that as a weapon. And if he gets really thirsty he can drink the water from the radiator when it cools down. There is a milkshake straw he can use. And he can listen to the car radio as loud as he likes. He can hike to the nearest town when he's good and ready. That is probably where his father will find him and want to make up.

Except it is Magnus who wants to make up. Wants to comfort his father and say fuck the blood relatives. Say it out loud to make his father laugh. Who does that wagon think she is, making his dad angry and saying nothing about being blood? Pretending she is happy, pretending she doesn't know much. And, that fool with her, the blood father. That has to be bad.

The sun has been beating down on Magnus in the open-top car, but now, it has gone in behind a cloud. He stands with his hands limp at his sides, blinking at the horizon. The sensation on his face, he thinks, might be the agitating atoms of air that make everything fresh, make stones smooth, and make a whistling noise in fence wire. It makes Eureka Dunes boom.

His father submitting to kisses on his face: Magnus can't get the image out of his head. It gives him a pain across his chest. His ears ring with their phony accents. He squirms, thinking about the sitting-and-standing business. Magnus' head is bursting with the wrong kind of blood. It wasn't supposed to be anything like this.

The intense smell of the chaparral plants fills his nostrils. He doesn't know whether or not he likes it, but he closes his eyes, inhales deeply, then holds his breath. He hears the whirr from the beating wings of a ruby-throated hummingbird in a stand of cactus columns near by. He decides he will exhale only when that sound has ceased and the bird has settled, but the sound persists and Magnus nearly blacks out. He fails in his challenge and breathes again. He opens his eyes, looks for the bird, but cannot see it. Then, he can no longer hear it.

His hand begins to sting.

The wind ebbs, then drops away. It is flat calm where he stands. The sounds of insects and birds has suddenly dropped away. The ticking of the car engine has ceased. The air seems to be thinning rapidly, to make way for an electric damp.

The sun is low in the sky and is now obscured. Magnus climbs up onto a narrow ridge of red rock and sees the longest land horizon he has ever seen. The convexity of the planet has been blown magnificently flat, making everything wider, deeper, higher than he can grasp. An enormous bank of dark cloud with silver edges ascends the sky. He can see the road a long way in the distance, charcoal black and going straight at the horizon. It will take him hours to reach it on foot, but at least he has a direction. Distant mountains change from blue to black. Cactus columns become silhouettes. The distance between one place and another presents with ever more definition as the colour drains from the expanse.

He can see the sheets of rain coming. There is a flash of white light, like the sweep of a lighthouse beam with a quiver in it. Then there is a tremendous crack of thunder, and raindrops the size of eyeballs. They fall around him sooner than he expects. This is how it feels to look into the future. This is the way to do it.

Magnus is exalted. The feeling will not last, he knows. He is already blanching. He glances at his watch. His father will be going mad with worry.

Magnus lets out a shriek. He doesn't know whether it is the sound of joy or pain, but he wants to be in this coming storm. Wants to be terrified. Wants to be in a glorious hell, then have it pass over. 'Look at this, dad!' he shouts.

When it comes full force, he gets back in the car behind the steering wheel. The car roof won't go up. He turns on the windscreen wipers and roars with laughter. He laughs so hard that when he stops, he feels nauseous and giddy. The rain beats on his head and runs in rivulets down his neck. He wonders are there little holes under the floor mats for water to drain out of the exposed interior. When the rain becomes too much and he begins to shiver, he gets into the car boot and wraps himself in some of his father's clothes. Extra shirts and jumpers not taken into the motel, there in case the weather isn't what it's supposed to be.

Magnus begins to walk when the sun comes up. He is tired in a way he has never been tired. Afraid in a big, dreamy way. He has hot and cold shivers. That makes it easier to resist the urge to run. He intends to walk a straight line in the direction of the road, but the terrain is more uneven than he expects. The temperature climbs rapidly. The heat comes up from the ground as well as beating down from above. His nostrils flare, their lining chafing on each intake of hot breath. He makes a conscious effort to breathe more slowly, more evenly. Too much or too little of this air will cause delirium.

He soon reaches a slot canyon that has been deepened by the torrent. There is no way of knowing how deep the flash river is. He can see no way to cross. His eyes, three-quarters shut against the light, widen now to take in the churning brown water. He turns and runs all the way back to the car. He gets into the open-mouthed boot again. He is going to sleep in this shade, yes. Keep his feet off the desert floor so the scorpions don't get him. He's going to stay calm, and that means be silent. And yes, when he wakes and is feeling much better, the floodwater will have drained off and he will find his way.

To begin with, Edwin doesn't panic when he comes out of the motel room looking for his son. He sees that the car is gone and pretends to himself that he is annoyed. He tells himself he shouldn't be annoyed because Magnus is upset. These are uncanny circumstances. This is America and the car is an automatic. Any young pup can drive it on these roads.

He doesn't go shouting up and down the motel parking lot. Nor does he run out to the roadside. He remains calm. He stands looking left and right, left and right, quietly chanting for his son. He can feel the alcohol being expelled through his pores. Yes, this is some kind of primitive emergency feature of the body that works for moderate drinkers and that is lost to alcoholics. Edwin has been a moderate drinker all his life. This is the kind of trouble that triggers an emergency response in a moderate drunk.

He lets out one shout only when he reminds himself that this is America and anything can happen. The car might have been taken with Magnus in it. Not an auto theft, but a depraved act.

He lets in a more sound logic. Magnus wants to punish him. He has driven the car around the back, or a few hundred yards up the road, and out of sight, just to give his cruel father a fright. Well, Edwin will take that punishment because he is sorry for using his son.

He presses his hands hard to his face and wipes away the sweat and alcohol vapour. He goes around the back of the motel. Then out onto the road. Runs several hundred yards in one direction, comes back, then the same distance in the opposite direction. He paces himself to prove he isn't in a panic. He comes back again. He knocks on the neighbours' door, the camper-truck people. Have they seen his son in the car? Have they seen him reverse it out?

No. They have not.

He goes to the other side. The heavy couple. They haven't seen the boy, either.

He runs to the motel reception. Have they seen the car pull away? Well, yes, they have. The young man was driving. They saw him pull out, but they didn't note which direction he took.

Magnus is in a tight crouch and motionless when he hears the engine of a pickup truck. It is crossing the desert far away, then, suddenly, it is there in front of him and they are standing looking down at him. They can see he is suffering from heatstroke. It is in his eyes, his skin, his breathing. It is on his tongue. He is disorientated but he is not distressed. Nor is he traumatised, though his heart is fluttering. This is curious.

Magnus shades his eyes and looks into their faces.

CHAPTER 8

Magnus with Stella in the Hospital

When Magnus returned to the ward, he found there had been no change. His father was lingering in the corridor.

'Did she tell you she was dying?' Edwin asked, lowering his voice and looking about without realising he was doing so.

'She did.'

'"I'm dying." How many times have you heard that, son?'

'She's been dying for years, of course.'

This comment upset Magnus' father more – which was not the intention. It made him jerk his chin in the air several times in quick succession. 'This is an awful bloody affair.'

'Is this really it, do you think, dad?'

'Who can say? She'll be disappointed if it's not. Disappointed if it is.' He looked at his shoes. Let his gaze go out across the polished floor.

Stella had taunted Edwin and Magnus both with this scenario for a long time now. Her frustration, her dissatisfaction with her lot was mysterious to them, but they had learnt to nod gravely when she came at them with it. That isn't to say that either succumbed. 'You're dying. I hear you,' one might say, just to keep it in check.

'Your mother chose us, son.'

'Chose us?'

'To do this to.'

'You're going to tell me this is some strange manifestation of her love?'

'No. I wouldn't do that.'

'That's that, then.'

'Yes. It is.' Edwin took a moment to go sour on the notion of any belated expression of love and fidelity. 'The bitch.'

Magnus had never heard his father call his mother this in all his life, though he felt comfortable making that reference himself. Hearing his father say it made Magnus laugh – which was not Edwin's intention. Edwin had to catch up.

'Oh yes,' he said with a spluttering guffaw, 'she has us.'

'Speak for yourself,' Magnus insisted. 'Don't include me.'

'If you like.'

'She knows all about you.'

'She has the knowledge,' Edwin declared, putting a certain philosophical inflection in his voice.

'She knows how to torture you.'

'She has the deep knowledge,' Edwin admitted.

'That's what has you bonded. You've given her trouble in the past?'

'I've withdrawn from the field.'

'You've made yourself unavailable?'

'I've gone to another place.'

'Are you telling me you've been with another woman? You've had an affair?'

'No. I'm not telling you.'

'But you have?'

'I've had other company. It's stopped at that.'

Magnus wanted to ask what this meant. Did it mean he had slept with prostitutes, had had one-night stands, or was it more innocent? Was he talking about endless flirtation? It was inappropriate to ask. 'And Stella knows?'

'As you say . . .'

'Fuck me.' Magnus didn't know why he was surprised, but he was. The admission didn't make him angry. In fact, he wanted to reach out further. Even celebrate. 'You want to tell me about it?'

'Nothing would be served.'

Magnus couldn't help himself. 'Do you still see this other woman?'

There was no reply.

'Do you love her, this other woman?' It was not a normal question, but Magnus managed to make it sound honest and flat. However, there was no reply. 'Well,' he said anyway, 'I'm glad.'

Edwin urged his son to go in to the ward by himself, which he did. Stella was moving her lips in and out lazily, like a chimpanzee. Performed without dentures, the action presented as some class of mortality alarm. The tendons in Magnus' neck tightened, but really, he was as much fascinated as repelled. This was, after all, his flesh and blood.

As part of a full reality check, Magnus made a concerted effort to imagine his mother actually dying. To aid concentration, he fixed on a lamp in the hospital car park that was lit in spite of the time of day. This skinny lamp was made fuzzy by the soft rain. That seemed to help. He doggedly went at his imagining, just as she went at her denial. Imagined her leathery little heart boxing her brittle ribs. Her complaining loudly about a nurse or another patient – something ready-made from her pannier of grievances that didn't require effort. He found himself willing on a sudden stoppage. An all-embracing, deadly seizure that produced the final cardiac uppercut. Heard the beady swish of the curtain being pulled around the bed. Heard the light tread of the reverend's feet down the corridor. Saw the undertaker setting to work on her makeup. It took no effort at all to imagine such things, and it did steady his nerve.

He went to the bedside. 'Come on, you bitch,' he said kindly out of his forehead. 'Reach.'

When she didn't reach, he self-consciously put a hand on her cold, skinny wrist. He didn't squeeze. He just left it there a moment, then let go. There wasn't outright denial in this instance. His mother canted her head on the pillow and let her eyes wander, which was an acknowledgement that this was the kind of goodwill gesture that was made on such occasions.

Magnus went out to his father, who continued to loiter in the corridor, and asked him about the pump room.

'She's been on about that again, has she?' Edwin said. 'The pump room. That would be in the maternity hospital. Where women gather when their newborns give them trouble at the breast.'

'Trouble?'

'Pain. They go there to express milk.' Edwin was about to launch into an architect's description of a pump room, but Magnus cut him short.

'There was no pump room in her day, surely? She didn't breastfeed.'

'No. She didn't.'

'Bottle-feeding was the thing then, wasn't it?'

'Yes.'

'So why is she going on about a pump room?'

Edwin straightened his spine and pulled his shoulders back, uneasy. 'She's thinking about you and Florence,' he said. 'She wanted to advise Florence.'

Up to that moment, Magnus thought his father might usefully have accounted for Stella's briefing as nothing more than random rantings brought on by delirium, and might indeed have rebuked him for not being more forgiving. What he saw now was that a ferment of emotions had the old man concussed.

'Your mother kept one of the Cow & Gate tins for the clothes-pegs, remember?' Edwin said presently, as if this non-sequitur was all the proof needed to show that Stella's generation of women trusted in the modern age were extraordinarily practical in their nurturing.

Quite suddenly, Magnus felt his neck muscles relax. The whole thing was absurd, after all. He himself was full of bile and his father was in shock. One way or another, this would all work itself out.

Wouldn't it?

CHAPTER 9

Magnus and Edwin Leave the Hospital

Magnus saw that his father had some difficulty getting into the driver's seat. 'What's wrong with you?'

'My back.'

'What's happened?'

'Nothing has happened. I've pulled a muscle. Twisted something.'

'Have you had somebody look at it?'

'I've been to the chemist.'

'The chemist?'

'To get a brace. It's a brace I need.'

'And why aren't you wearing it?'

'It had to be ordered. I've to collect it. We'll go by the chemist now.'

His father drove with more pronounced actions and gestures than Magnus could ever recall. The pleasure the old man took in motoring was evident, as it always had been, but now it embraced a new and exaggerated zeal for road safety. He drove as though his rehabilitation was being constantly monitored. This was a little eerie, Magnus thought, particularly given that his father appeared to be inviting criticism of his driving. This wasn't in character. Had Edwin made a fool of himself on the road? Had there been an accident?

Magnus was still in a rage. Still feeling put-upon. 'Where were you, anyway?'

'I was there.' Edwin was expecting criticism.

'Eventually. You were hiding out?'

'I wasn't hiding out.'

'You couldn't take it, so you went to ground.'

'*I* called the ambulance.'

'Were you hiding out with Noel?'

'I was at home.'

'She has the DTs, you know that?'

'It's to be expected.'

'She's seeing ten green bottles hanging on the wall.'

'No harm.'

'No harm?'

'It's part of the process.'

'She's talked to the Guards.'

'No, she hasn't.'

'Of course she hasn't. She's full of shite.'

'Best to let that stuff subside.'

'I'm a busy man.'

'You've done enough here, son.'

'You think I should head home directly?'

'I do. But you should know I'm terribly glad to see you.'

Sometime in the late 1960s, Edwin had discovered slip-on boots, which he saw as a small innovation in pop culture and something better than what he had worn on his feet in his youth. He had worn these boots ever since. Brown pairs and black pairs. Always well polished. Otherwise, he dressed conservatively, a professional man of his generation. Quality suits, tweeds and cavalry twill, poplin shirts, braces, a narrow belt substituting at weekends, and what he called modern ties. He owned a cravat, but Magnus had never seen him wear it. And where did he buy the boots these days? He stockpiled. He had several pairs in their boxes. Elasticated boots particularly suited this new style of action driving.

'They asked her if she drinks. "An occasional social drink," she told them. I had to go behind the bedstead and mime like a bloody cartoon character lowering massive imaginary whiskeys.'

'You did well, son. I've no doubt.'

'*You* should have been there telling them.'

'I *was* there. I saw her into Accident and Emergency. I rang you.'

'You got me over to handle it.'

'No.'

'Look, I'm not complaining. I'm under pressure.'

'I'm sorry to hear that. These things never happen at a convenient time. She wanted to see you. Fair enough, I say. She thought – you know – she might . . . '

'Did you think she was finished?'

'I wondered.'

'She's such a liar. They had her age wrong on the white-board. Eight years younger. She lied about that, too.'

'She could take another turn.'

'When she comes around again, she'll be wanting to flirt with her imaginary cop. It doesn't bear thinking about.'

'I'm not thinking about it.'

'Maybe it's a good thing. She might get herself so worked up . . . '

'Stop it.'

'She might take another turn.'

'That would do it, you think?'

'It's the heart.'

Edwin nodded at the fecklessness of fate. 'I'm taking care of myself,' he volunteered. After all, he was worth some consideration, too.

Magnus imagined his father moping in his chair, alone in the house. 'You haven't been taking care of your back. Aunt Charlotte has been in?'

'I've talked to Charlotte on the phone.'

'Maureen is coming over.'

'I've talked to Maureen. She'll be staying with Charlotte. I'll be on to them.'

'They're both in shock.'

'I'm in shock.'

'They've been very good.'

'You can rely on Charlotte and Maureen.' There was a long pause. He seemed momentarily to lose his way in the streets. He spoke again. 'Crisis over, barring another turn.'

'Yes. You're right, dad. Crisis over.'

Edwin put on a spurt of speed on a clear stretch of road. 'I'm quite happy in myself, isn't that ridiculous?' Edwin managed to say this in a perfectly moderate tone.

'Well, I'm glad to hear,' Magnus replied, his rage refreshed. 'And yes, it is ridiculous under the circumstances.'

Normally, his father would have grinned at his civil-service restraint, but today he was grinning at himself in the rearview mirror – which was most unusual. This wasn't the picture of a man floundering.

'I'm weary, of course,' the old man said, in the way that comes to old men.

'I'm not surprised.'

'And this back of mine . . . '

'Couldn't you have gone to another chemist for this brace? There must be plenty of chemists with a stock of braces.'

Edwin studied his son for a moment, absorbing his anger and frustration. A new Edwin was emerging. The last in a finite evolutionary process, but still recognisably Magnus' father. 'I'll go to the chemist where I'm known,' he said.

Parking in front of the chemist was a big production. Edwin punctuated his manoeuvering with a choice observation about his ailing wife.

'Your mother thinks I should be gone.'

'Gone? Gone where?'

'Dead. That's the kind of fury *she* has.'

'You're being dramatic.'

'You witnessed her performance. Have a heart. Stop trying to be fair.'

'Separated. It that not enough?'

'It's a poor second. She'll not settle for that, but it's all she's getting.'

'All things considered, that's a sound attitude.'

'If I were dead, of course, she'd not have a word said against me.' Edwin's arms were climbing one over the other to finish on the steering wheel. 'She'd be singing my praises to all her fancy men, the ones who aren't dead.'

Magnus scoffed. 'You can take great comfort in that.'

'Except . . . she'd need to replace me.'

'Spoilt for choice, no doubt. Even at this late stage.'

'Still, in the end, nobody is replaced.'

Magnus liked this show of battered self-respect.

The engine was finally switched off. Edwin made Magnus wait in the car.

Edwin entered the chemist shop, thinking that only half his brain was fed. The other half was stacked with outsized furniture. Stella called out from behind that pile. 'He's afflicted,' she said repeatedly. 'Afflicted.'

Edwin didn't want to be patronised, or humbled, or born again. He didn't want a jog in any cemetery. He wanted a corset for his aching back. He was a realist, but he couldn't speak out his needs.

The pharmacist was also a realist. She broke off serving a dumpy little woman in a heavy tweed coat, to connect momentarily. She made direct eye-contact. She was used to the sullied luster of old people's eyes. 'Mr Sparling,' she said. 'Be with you in a minute.'

Edwin made no reply. He was wrestling with how best to show that he accepted a corset-fitting. The pharmacist was a caring woman with a gruff manner. That made it easier. He felt he was going up against something. She had married late, Stella had told him. Had put flowers from her wedding bouquet on the grave of her parents.

'Sit down, Mr Sparling.'

But Edwin did not sit down.

'All the good people,' he mumbled, like a dazed mystic.

What was that? Where had these words come from?

Though clearly she had not caught the utterance, the pharmacist gave a sharp, affirmative nod and gestured open-handedly to the vacant chair. 'Please . . . '

'I'm all right,' he replied. He had a strong urge to shout what he had just mumbled, but he resisted, and lowered himself onto the hard chair.

The dumpy woman had the damp little fists of a newborn, and the sheepishness of a poisoner. She didn't like the interruption. She gave this Mr Sparling a vinegary smile.

The pharmacist came out from behind the counter and expertly interposed herself. 'Now, we need to get this right when we buckle.'

'We . . . ?'

'Not too tight, not too loose. Somebody can help, if you'll allow them.'

'I know some rotten people. I don't bother with them.'

The lady chemist was confused, so she said no more. That was the desired effect, though Edwin quite liked her. She didn't sleep much, he could see that. She tortured herself. Edwin swung his head away, found himself looking at his own reflection in a narrow mirror. It was his experience that aging was not an unbroken process, but went in lurches. Relatively small jumps over the entire span, but nonetheless significant. The shunting was more alarming than smooth-rolling, but on rare occasions the lurch was backwards. Only in these modest loops of time was the hard outline of a petty reality blurred and anything seemed possible. The humdrum tyranny of self-doubt was temporarily set aside, and something that he recognised as a lifelong innocence momentarily surfaced.

In spite of the reason for his visit to the chemist, he was in one such loop now. He put it down to the return of his boy out in the car. Nevertheless, he didn't know what it was he should do to show his gratitude.

Edwin got back into the driver's seat with his spine ramrod-stiff. He made a leathery creak when he leaned forwards to settle himself.

'You got it, then,' Magnus said uselessly.

'What do you think?' his father chaffed. 'Sit,' he ordered the excited dog in the back seat. 'Sit.'

The dog licked Magnus' neck. Magnus turned sharply and pushed the dog back onto the seat. It regained its balance almost immediately and licked Edwin's ear. Edwin seemed not to notice. Magnus again pushed the animal back onto the seat. 'Are you all right?' he asked his father. He meant it as a big question.

'I am,' Edwin replied. 'This thing will work wonders, I'm told, if I'm patient. They gave me pills for the pain. I've taken two. I'm already hallucinating.'

'You shouldn't drive.'

'I'll be fine. You're safe with me.' Edwin put both hands on the steering wheel and let out a deep sigh.

'What?' Magnus asked.

'I was just thinking about your mother.'

'Yes . . . well . . . '

'She's been in my dreams a lot recently . . . '

Magnus studied the faraway expression on Edwin's face. He concluded that dreams made a lot of noise in his father's head, but could be readily unforgotten.

'Suppose it goes on?' Edwin said, curiously rotating a finger at his temple, as if using shorthand for being nuts. But he wasn't alluding to mental health. Magnus didn't get that.

'You being the way you are?' Magnus ventured. He wasn't trying to be funny. His father scoffed impatiently and slapped the steering wheel.

'What are you saying to me?'

'What if it just . . . goes on,' Edwin said, his finger now rotating more vigorously in front of his forehead, 'after you're dead. The same stuff, except there's no body. No brain as such, just the stuff of sleep. The dreaming.'

'You think about these things?' Already, Magnus didn't like the subject. Didn't like the use of the word *stuff*.

'I'd be stuck with your mother,' Edwin continued.

Could this be some kind of jaundiced acknowledgement of eternal companionship? Magnus wondered. This line of conversation wasn't good, and could only lead to more discomfort, but he felt it was his filial duty to indulge his father's morbid curiosity, if only for a short time. 'Are you interested in your dreams?' he bleated weakly. 'You must be. Isn't everybody interested in their dreams?' Magnus was getting annoyed with himself.

'She, on the other hand, won't be stuck with me . . . ' his father continued, both hands on his head now.

'No?' This was absurd. 'No . . . ?' he repeated contentiously. 'Were you dreaming before you were born?' This earned a look of derision. 'Then what are you talking about?' Magnus was in no mood to speculate further on the matter. 'You're not going to tell me now you're dreaming up me and my sick mother lying there in the hospital, are you? Because if you are . . . ' He gave his head a sorry shake.

'No.'

'Good.'

'I'm right here with you.'

'Well that's just perfect, isn't it?'

'Cheeky pup.'

Magnus hadn't heard that phrase in a long time. It made him relax a little.

'She'll be dreaming her dreams of choice,' Edwin persisted. 'Fantasy has never been a problem for you, mother.'

It occurred to Magnus that his father was not necessarily predicting gothic nightmares for himself that featured Stella. The after-death dreaming might present as torturous snubs, unrequited affection, unbearable longing from an earlier time. Maybe that was what he meant by 'stuff' continuing. This was the price of consciousness if you were Edwin, husband of Stella, father of Magnus: he should tell him that. He decided to take a run at it: 'Now this isn't very scientific, is it?' he began, po-faced.

Edwin let his hands slide down off the top of his head. They'd been there long enough. In truth, the science angle gave him heart and he swung back. 'There must be some book I could read on the subject,' he said, letting the brightness in his voice thrust out. 'What do you say?'

'Odds are, dad, we're safe and sound.' What Magnus meant to say was that he believed one's experiences were not wasted. Our consciousness gave us a will that would prevail.

'Safe and sound,' his father echoed, unconvinced. 'I won't be looking for a book on being safe and sound.' The brightness remained in the voice, and now registered in the eyes. He seemed to forget that he was behind the wheel of his car and was to drive home, but the corset pinched. 'Bugger,' he shouted, but his curse had soft, dreamy edges.

'I'm driving,' Magnus insisted, springing from the front passenger seat onto the pavement. 'I'll get you home right now,' he said through the windscreen on his way around the engine. At the driver's side, he reached in and took a firm grip on his father's forearm. 'I'll visit her again before I go to the airport.'

CHAPTER 10

Magnus Returns to the Hospital

Full of resentment, Magnus looked at his mother in her hospital bed and summoned to mind the first instance of his parents' mismanagement. They had sent him to school a day late. They had wrong-footed him from the outset. He missed that crucial first day's bonding and was cast as an outsider.

Stella had him dressed in short trousers with turn-ups and straight pockets, Tuff shoes, knee socks and what she called his nicest gansey. She held his small hand in her small hand crossing the yard from the school gate. Birds sang them in, and mocked their lateness. Stella told Magnus it was good to let the other children settle and to appear just before lessons began. There could be no getting back the lost day, but an exceptional boy could make a late entrance and carry it off. Her son could do that. Everybody said Magnus was so like his mother.

At the door she said to him. 'You can put one hand in your pocket, if you like. That'll be good. Not both hands,' she advised. Teacher wouldn't like that.

She brought him into the porch, which was stuffed with children's coats on hooks. She knocked on the inner door and entered without waiting for a reply. The practice was for parents to leave their child here on the first day, to make this the threshold, and to let the child enter the new world guided by the teacher. But it wasn't the first day, was it? Stella walked him into the classroom, stood for a moment and took in all the children as though she were choosing who *she* would sit beside. She was doing it now in a hospital ward, despite her delirium – looking to seize pole position. On this first day of school that wasn't the first day, Magnus saw that she was flirting with the matronly teacher, smiling and flashing her eyes impossibly on his behalf. This was very good or very bad for him – he didn't know which – but in any case, it was unforgivable.

Stella watched while Magnus was seated at a double desk beside a fidgety girl with rosy cheeks and straw hair.

'Now, who's that little girl?' Stella asked from across the room.

'This is Elaine,' the teacher said.

'Elaine,' Stella repeated, as though it were a very special name.

Stella had made a particular effort dressing and making up. Her perfume followed Magnus and the teacher to his desk. He didn't want to look at his mother when he sat down, but he did, and she waved to him. All the children were watching. The teacher nodded meaningfully to indicate that it was now time to withdraw. Stella blew a kiss to Magnus before leaving. She didn't close the door properly after her. It squeaked open on its hinges. Her high heels clicked on the porch tiles, and on the granite step. Their perfectly measured clicking carried all the way across the schoolyard.

Magnus sat perfectly still. He looked straight ahead, at leaves lifting on the breeze outside the window. He kept one hand in his pocket. It was a tight fit under the desk. He didn't move, even when he got a prod in the back of the neck. Little Magnus, already the civil servant.

In the hospital now, he was thinking that his mother's head appeared to be made of lead, such was the dent she made in the pillow. Her eyes fluttered under their lids and sprang open.

'I see you got your hair cut,' she said, completely alert.

'Yes, well . . . ' Magnus had the same short hair he had maintained for fifteen years or more now. He had a standing arrangement with his Ritz Hotel barber.

'Did you cut it?' Stella asked, turning her blank face slowly to the elfin nurse.

'No,' the nurse replied with a professional smile and a shake of her head.

'Are you in Trinity, too?'

'No, Stella,' the nurse said.

'But you smartened him up anyway.'

'He's well turned out, isn't he?' the nurse said, managing to make her words non-flirtatious. She was on a morale-boosting round, so she was prepared to linger a short while.

There was no light and shade in Stella's voice, no irony or significant change in tone, so when she asked Magnus if he was here to give her some of his weed, it had the same spurious credibility as the rest of her mumbling.

'What are you saying, mother?' Magnus' formal use of the word 'mother' was a clear indicator of alarm.

'Your weed. Your college weed. Are you here to give me some?'

'Eh, no.' He shook his head indulgently at the nurse, who, evidently, was going to stick around a little longer.

'I'd like to smoke it,' Stella droned.

It had been a long time since Magnus had smoked anything at all. It was absurd that his mother would want to repeat a one-off experiment from the distant past. 'I don't think you need to smoke weed, mother. You're already there.'

'*You* said it would do me good,' she protested, though it didn't sound like protest.

'Yes, well . . . '

The nurse was enjoying this interlude. 'Are you not comfortable, Stella?'

Again, the face turned slowly. 'He tells me it's good for me.'

'Does he?'

'I like it the odd time.'

'We're looking after you now, aren't we?'

'His father needs a dose.'

'I'll look after *him*,' Magnus interjected, 'you needn't worry.' He was trying to turn this mad half-speed conversation around in a witty manner, but it wasn't working. 'I'll arrange smokes for everybody, but all in good time. How about that?'

'Don't be ridiculous,' his mother told him. 'You won't get him smoking.'

'I suppose not,' Magnus replied, suddenly despondent.

'We'll have it now, will we? We'll see what there is, won't we, nurse?'

'We're looking after you, aren't we, Stella?' the nurse said, leaning in and cocking her head.

Magnus' mother grunted and turned to the wall. 'It's a bloody disgrace, this place.'

'Don't I know it,' the nurse confided in a theatrical whisper, and moved on cheerily.

Magnus thought a moment about the weed he had given his mother to smoke in his college days. The pleasure he had got from giving it to her. He remembered marvelling at the limited effect it seemed to have on her.

Stella had always liked Magnus' boyishness, and his doing boy things to please her. Smoking what she called his college weed was part of that. Magnus looked at her shrivelled hands now. They reminded him of the chicken's feet the grocer kept aside for Magnus on Saturday mornings, so he could pull the bleached white tendon to make the claws contract. The anaemic grocer with the red nose liked Mrs Sparling very much, liked the amused growl she let out when the chicken's foot moved in the boy's hand. It was he who had shown him how to work the tendon. Magnus was better at it than the grocer, who had thick fingers. In those days Stella went from one shop to the next. She would be received personally in each. Attention was given to Magnus to gain Stella's approval, to initiate the flirtation. To this boy the ritual seemed to take forever, when really what these men wanted to do was tongue-kissing, which didn't require any of the talk. Aunt Charlotte would have gone straight at it were she bothered, Magnus was sure. It was a parade with eggs and onions and 'a lovely bit of steak'. Eventually, two string bags would be filled. One would go in the basket on the front. Magnus would have to hold the other between his chest and his mother's behind. That left just the one hand with which to hold on.

Magnus was drawn out of his little tortured reverie by a groan from Stella. He couldn't tell whether or not it was a genuine expression of physical discomfort.

'Why did they shoot you?' Magnus asked. He wanted to give her the benefit of the doubt. He wanted to move on.

'It was a mistake,' she replied without hesitation.

'A mistake? I see.' He had hoped they were past this nonsense.

'They thought I was somebody else,' she explained.

'Right.' Magnus could feel the bile build in himself.

'They might try again,' she said. 'They might make the same mistake.'

Magnus had to admit this was all very present of her and well reasoned, given her chemical craziness. 'I suppose they might,' he replied in a most considered tone.

'Now,' he said with a sudden and grand air of finality,' I'm off.'

CHAPTER 11

Magnus with His Father in the Family Home

Edwin went to the window and gazed up into the night sky. He did it in such a way as to invite Magnus to come and stand with him. He had something to say, his posture was signalling.

'A clear night,' Magnus said, approaching. 'Plenty of stars . . . ' he added, just to move it along.

'Bloody cold . . . '

'No cloud cover.'

'It's us really, isn't it?'

'What?' Magnus asked.

'*We* give it all a meaning. All one hundred billion of us over the past fifty thousand years or so. The thinking ones, at any rate.'

'Where did you get that statistic?'

'WWW.'

'Ah.'

'Something called the Population Reference Bureau.'

'Yes. You're right, I expect. It could only be us.' He craned his neck, put his face closer to the windowpane, let his eyes track upwards to their full extent. 'Or . . . other creatures.'

Edwin scoffed.

Magnus needed to be more specific. 'Other creatures like us.'

This was an unusually sentimental remark for Magnus, and it rang hollow, and now Edwin scoffed again, this time with intemperate scorn. 'Like *us*?'

'You're right, I'm sure.' Magnus was happy to concede without much of a fight. He was standing in his coat. His grip-bag was by the hall door.

'Of course I'm right,' his father echoed. 'Look at me, then look at bloody Noel. Look at the difference.' He was referring to his best friend and former colleague. He liked to make out there was an enormous difference between them. 'What chance of your other creatures comparing? None.'

'You've been reading about the universe?'

'I've been studying Noel and his habits. And his indifference to his surroundings. It's a bloody disgrace for a retired architect.'

'And he's still your friend,' Magnus observed, looking to poke a little fun. It would be an easy note on which to leave.

'It's too late for anything else,' his father replied.

Already, Magnus was stumped. He slid his hands into his pockets and waited.

'I'm going hunting fossils tomorrow,' Edwin said presently. 'You could have come, had you stayed.'

What did this mean, Magnus wondered. Fossils? Since when was the old man interested in fossils? Was this the dawning of some kind of mental deterioration? He needed to spend more time with the father. 'I would have liked that,' he said.

Edwin looked at his watch. 'Right then.'

'I'll get my bag.'

CHAPTER 12

Magnus, That Boy on the Beach

Edwin drove Magnus to the airport. Companions again. Magnus was assailed by memories of one family holiday, and the day that made him special. He remembered men gathering around his father, to take in his mother. He watches these men dance with her on a shiny floor. Watches his father get embarrassed at the number of drinks offered. That is what happens in hotels on family holidays. Here, in Donegal, or anywhere else. To this boy's eyes, it is curious that his mother seems more than lenient in her judging of her male admirers, and her lovers. She readily accepts baldness, flabby stomachs, even bad dress sense as part of the male condition. There is no such allowance made for women. At the same time, she is ever conscious and proud of her husband's appearance; expects that he will always be well turned out in well-cut tailored suits, and even on the beach wears stylish trunks, his one pair of expensive sunglasses, the right amount of hair oil, whether or not she is present.

Magnus confuses his mother's ability to accept compliments with her being patient. Being patient, he has learnt as a good Protestant boy, deserves reward. He is intrigued by her general ease, which he sees as a proper kind of laziness. These traits are attractive and reassuring to men, but evidently not for Magnus' father; and not for him. How is that?

It has to do with being respectively husband and son, though that, in itself, is no explanation.

His father's flirting, by comparison, is pathetic, and he is told as much by Stella. But then, she is apt to declare any exchange witnessed between Edwin and another woman as flirtatious. Magnus has noticed that she encourages his father in this, and Magnus likes to observe her challenge him. It is the only public display of intimacy between his parents. On occasion Magnus will join in – 'You liked her, dad, because of her bloomers' – but he knows to make no comparison with his mother's cooing at other men.

Magnus isn't interested in the children of his parents' new-found friends. Instead, he vacillates over narrow-head Mary, a hotel waitress. She's a local girl. Magnus believes that however shy, whatever their size, Donegal girls are wild and physically strong. Mary, he thinks, is particularly strong, despite her slight frame. She wears no makeup, has pale skin and clear eyes that shoot light and promise the instant before she smiles. But when she smiles, she runs away. Magnus, virgin boy that he is, can find no way to present himself that stops her from running.

He observes her coming and going in the dining hall. Absorbs her body in motion. He has also seen her sitting on the low wall at the back of the hotel, drinking mugs of coffee and smoking her sister's cigarettes. He starts his long solitary walks on the beach with a detour that takes him by Mary's recreation wall.

The beach he goes to is usually deserted, being unsafe for swimmers and less accessible than Marble Strand. Magnus comes out from behind the hotel, crosses the road, the peat ditch, the puny wire fence, and strikes a straight line over the scrag-end of the golf course. The route takes him into rocky bog land. He changes course and heads down the near peninsula to the World War II pillbox that is well camouflaged as a craig. The three slit windows are still nicely intact. Magnus likes to come here because the fixture once had brute purpose. Now, it might be a place for sex. Mary's narrow head would fit nicely in the machine-gun slits if she turned it sideways. She might do it to make them both laugh, before they kissed, if ever she would come here with him.

He lingers here a while, then makes his way down onto the beach. On this special day there is a haze created by a miniature sand storm. Particles sting his face even before he gets out on the flat. The sun is shining temporarily and the white airborne sand softens the azure water and the deep greens of the distant headland. Magnus takes to the compacted sand and makes a march of it. He tries to get his thoughts in line with his thumping feet. He's trying to conjure a vision of Mary naked when, in the distance, he sees a crumpled form near the water's edge. A dark heap that can only be a human being. For some reason, young Magnus doesn't break into a run, but approaches in what he thinks is a grown-up manner.

It is a middle-aged man in a heavy coat. He seems to have thrown himself up the strand. One arm is stretched fully above his head, the other looks like it is sent to retrieve the first. His face is three-quarters turned into the sand. Magnus rolls him onto his back. The mouth is open and the teeth visible. The way they are set doesn't appear to be right, even for a dead man whose lips and earlobes have turned blue.

Magnus puts his fingertips to the side of the man's neck to feel for a pulse: his hand knows better than he does where to go. This man is stone cold. Stone dead. He is dry. The sea hasn't washed him up. There are footprints clearly visible. They stretch back down the beach and curve towards the cut in the dunes, beyond which there is a car park of sorts. This man has walked out onto the strand, turned along by the water, advanced a few hundred yards, and dropped dead.

The tide is coming in. Magnus looks about urgently, but there is nobody in sight. No one to call on and no place to go to get help without a substantial hike. Dragging him doesn't seem right, so, with great difficulty, he lifts the dead man to his feet and gets in a weight-dance with him. Magnus is overwhelmed by his lack of cooperation. A frontal bear-hug means that he had arms draped up over his shoulders in the manner of a drunk signalling for help. Trapped air is expelled from the lungs. It comes out as part gurgle, part groan. Magnus falters. A shudder travels through his frame. I'm only a boy, he wants to cry out, but he does not cry out. He is not only a boy. Nor does he let go. He accidentally stands on a foot and almost falls over.

'Sorry,' he says quickly. 'Sorry.' He treats the body with a positive roughness, thinking this man might still be in the world, and could come alive again if provoked. Furthermore, Magnus is fearful he might topple under the weight and have his ribs broken. He might get a dead man's knee in the groin and be destroyed.

There is a sweet-and-sour smell to the flesh. Pickles and talcum powder. There is the smell of spent tobacco. How long has he been lying there? Magnus cannot credit his own actions, but he seems to know what he is doing. He waltzes the body up onto the loose, dry sand and falls down with it. Fortunately, both land on their sides.

He lies with it for a moment, looking into the glassy eyes. This is a terrible intimacy. Some kind of test for his life ahead. Evidently, he has a strong nerve and can do such things.

He sits up slowly, draws his knees up to his chest, gazes at the tracks they have made from the water's edge, sees they have lost a shoe on the way. He looks again at the dead man's face. An introduction is pointless. He doesn't want to root through pockets. 'Sorry for this trouble,' Magnus says, tentatively putting a hand on the stranger's chest. When he does so, something comes over him. He feels honoured. 'I'll think what to do now,' he says.

He does not want to leave the corpse. He just sits with it, trying to think. He makes no conversation with the body. Sooner or later, somebody will come. He retrieves the shoe, puts it back on, ties the laces, sits again with arms around his knees, and waits.

There is no disaffection here. This father-son-brother-man hasn't died on Magnus. He has died on somebody else. For now, Magnus alone occupies the space beyond the moment of this man's demise, and he is in charge.

Eventually, people come. An elderly French couple with their two grown-up children. Given the configuration, it is not surprising that initially, there is confusion. The family doesn't grasp that boy and man are strangers.

Magnus hears himself let out a strange little laugh.

The elderly Frenchman is a doctor, which seems to Magnus right and proper, but this makes him laugh again. 'Sorry,' he says.

These people are very kind. They take care of Magnus first.

Afterwards, Magnus' parents tell him that he had stayed with the body because he was in a state of shock. His mother pets his hair: three firm strokes. His father is tearful when he pats his son on the shoulder. He nods repeatedly. He gives him extra pocket money.

But there is something more. Something significant. Edwin tells Magnus that this makes him a special boy, and not in a ghostly or spooky way. A boy marked out for engaging skilfully and empathetically with the living. Magnus wonders vaguely where his father gets his insight.

That same day in the hotel, Mary comes to see Magnus, says she has heard what has happened, says it is a fantastic thing he has done, staying with the body. She wants to know what it felt like. Like nothing, he tells her, and her eyes widen. She leads him to her staff quarters, kisses his red cheeks and easily puts an end to his virginity.

He waits there on her bed, too, until she sneaks him out. Still fiery and flushed, she borrows his steel comb and combs out her auburn hair as they descend the back stairs. She is ten minutes late for the dinner roster.

The following day Magnus and Mary go to the beach. He cannot precisely locate where he had sat with the body, but feels he should point to one specific spot. The dead man's car is still beyond the dunes. It is there by itself. A Morris Oxford with red leather seats. The driver's door is unlocked. The couple sit in, but leave the doors open.

'Weird, isn't it?' Mary says. Magnus doesn't think so, but she is shooting and smiling and he doesn't want her to run off, so he nods and changes up and down the gears. Sand comes in and blows around their ankles.

Mary asks if he thinks things will never again be the same in his life now that he has found a dead body – now that he has done what he has done with her, he thinks she really means.

'Yes, never,' he replies simply.

Mary is more than satisfied with this answer. She takes his hand and squeezes it.

'I can drive this,' he says, with a nod of his head towards the dashboard.

'So could I,' she replies.

He likes her saying that, and her saying it in a way that isn't boastful. He is going to reach across and kiss her, but just then a tow-truck with an A-frame winch on the back turns into the space. Mary knows the driver, who looks as though he has driven all the way from America. This man knows all about the dead man, and tells them – a widower from the neighbouring townland. Mary knows the family.

The keys to the Oxford are missing. When the mechanic has hitched the car to his truck and is ready to leave for the Garda station, he comes to Mary, takes her narrow head in his hands and kisses her. He then backs away with a fantastic grin.

Mary lets out a little joyful laugh and begins to run. Magnus runs after her. She is late again for her shift. That afternoon Magnus' formal statement is written down in the Garda station. He can see the Oxford in the yard through the sergeant's window.

The holiday is nearly over. He spends his last night in the quiet lounge, where old men smoke and read newspapers. He stays there by himself until it is time to go to bed.

Mary comes out of the hotel to wave him off. Magnus' parents revel in their son's embarrassment.

His steal comb is gone forever and Magnus is forever the boy who found the body on the beach.

CHAPTER 13

Magnus Tells His Wife, Florence, of His Father Abandoned as an Infant

When Magnus got home to London he was full of talk, not about his mother to begin with, but his father. In particular, the journey to America. He needed to think more about these events in his childhood, he told his wife, Florence. He wanted to tell her again about his aunts.

'And your mother . . . ' Florence said.

'Yes,' Magnus replied. 'Of course. About the three of them.' He told her again about the three Dooley sisters, Charlotte, Maureen and Stella.

It is an autumn Sunday evening. A soft breeze rubs gently on the corners of the Dooley house outside the village of Laragh, in County Wicklow. Three little girls – Charlotte, Maureen and Stella – are waiting for their father. They have soaked the crisp fallen leaves in the dog's water bowl, getting them ready for their dad to stick them back on the branches when he comes home from Wicklow town. He has glue. They don't know where, otherwise they'd have it out on the windowsill. But he is late and their mother won't hear of any glueing. So they are in their parents' bedroom. Stella and Maureen pretend to be their mother and father asleep on the bed. Charlotte, the eldest, has her lips pressed to a windowpane. Through the nineteenth-century glass she watches a single-engine aeroplane move slowly from the top of the broad, clear sky. The machine smudges, liquefies and re-forms in a wavy flaw in the glass, before it shrinks to nothing. It is some time after, that its boom-throttle drone becomes inaudible. Charlotte is thinking about the Reverend Tuttle's sermon, which concerned a shipwrecked Moorish sailor. The story has made her cry, it is so beautiful. It is the story of a Moorish fisherman whose body was washed up on a remote beach in the west. There were no reports of a loss at sea and no identification possible, so the people from the nearest village took it on themselves to give him his funeral. But the local priest wouldn't allow the body to be buried in the Christian churchyard. He insisted the Moor be buried the other side of the boundary wall. So the unknown fisherman was buried according to the priest's instructions. Some days later, people from the village came and dismantled the graveyard wall and rebuilt it so that the Moor was inside the boundary wall.

One day she will retell this story to a boy who tells her about finding a body on a beach. But that is a long time off. That boy's father has just been born. He is being carried to the Sparlings' house a few hundred yards away, as she stares out the window at the pink and yellow sky.

Some day that boy will want to know what his father thinks about his finding the body on the beach, for his silence makes the boy feel he has slighted his father in a way he does not understand. Doesn't his father want to ask questions? Or is it to be the same management that applies to the patients approaching in the asylums. Oh aye. The same averted acknowledgment, the same parrying of unwanted communication?

'You did a good thing, Magnus,' his father will say in time. He will churn the change in his pocket as speaks with what he hopes is a reassuring tone. 'The poor man.'

'Yes,' Magnus will say, 'but what do you think about finding a body?'

Edwin will stop the coin churning. He will straighten himself and incline his head to show humility. 'You were brave to sit there with that poor man,' he will tell his son.

'Not really. I felt like it.'

'You must have been upset.' *Upset* is a word his father seldom utters.

'Nah.' Magnus cannot find a way to explain what it is he feels. He hopes his father can guess.

But his father can think of nothing more to say that might soothe his son, and so he pats him lightly on the shoulder. There are no pertinent questions forthcoming. Magnus thinks that had his father been with him when he found the body he would have put a hand on his shoulder and led him away. They would have left the dead man alone and he would have forfeited forever the great privilege: that profound affirmation that is still working itself out. They would have gone to the golf hut to ring the Guards. There would have been Mars bars at the golf hut. Sugar for the shock.

The boy will tell his father the Reverend Tuttle's story about the Moorish fisherman and the village people rebuilding the churchyard wall. His father will revel in this small humane act, he is sure. He will appreciate the sound structural solution. His father might take a cue and turn his experience into a satisfactory parable.

But that is all in the future. His father has just been born and is being delivered to the Sparlings' doorstep. Aunt Charlotte and her sisters are little girls in the neigbouring house, and are oblivious.

It is a long way on foot from the gate to the Sparling house. There is the spicy smell of burning autumn leaves all the way up the gravel drive. The woman, Irene, carries the swaddled newborn to the doorstep of this Protestant gentleman farmer and his wife. The Ned man offers to do it, but she will not let him. She prays silently as they walk. She has the baby in an expensive, pale yellow blanket. It is the first item they have bought for the infant, and the last.

She rocks the sleeping baby when she pauses at the gate. Swings him gently as they walk the long lane. Rocks him again when they pause to take in the windows at the front of the house.

All through their teenage years, Charlotte will speculate endlessly with her sisters what the birth mother and father said as parting words, as they lay baby Edwin on the granite doorstep. They are sure the couple watched over him from the bushes, until the door was opened.

The collie barks in the barn, but the door is kept closed. The couple knows the dog is locked in with the Sparlings' Ford. It barks a lot, this old collie, making it a poor watch. Good with sheep, but useless otherwise.

They are away quickly, across the gravel and into the trees, where they wait and watch. The bloody old cockerel has been crowing for an age. Something has it addled. Wood pigeons flutter in the beech trees that line the lane. Cows moo on the adjacent farm, their sound carrying easily over the rise on the damp evening air.

A cat sniffs at the baby's rose milk cheeks. The baby flexes his tiny toes, squirms, and begins to cry, because he is hungry. He has soiled his soft blanket. That little spurt of parental nurturing is spent. The porch light is switched on. Its globe has a small reservoir of rainwater, which refracts on the infant's face, temporarily mesmerising him, though it is far beyond the field of sharp focus for a newborn. The hall door is finally opened. Mrs Sparling bends slowly to scoop up the child.

Take in this sight, Irene and Ned. It is the last you will see of your boy until God delivers him.

It-is-for-the-best. For-the-best. They stagger away in the dusk. They whinny as they go, sure that they are damned. She is ripped and bleeding again now that they shamble across the fields into soft darkness.

'And Edwin?' Florence said, apparently indifferent to the couple's trauma. Said it as though somehow the abandoned baby is not Magnus' father.

Magnus continued with his story. He skipped ahead to a time when Edwin was a boy.

There is a large field on the slope behind the Sparlings' house that adjoins the Dooley property. To the eight-year-old Edwin, this field is everything. It seems vast. It spreads up to the sky. It has one deep fold, and one dimple. Beyond the fold it appears to rise like a distant mountain, though it is elevated not more than fifty feet above the chimney of the Sparling house below. Meadow greens, browns in winter, and a bluish hue beyond the fold, depending on the season and the light. On the crest there is a hedge, which is staked to the hillside with a few hawthorn trees. In one corner, the highest point of the field, there is a break for a five-bar gate. Beyond the gate there are clouds, blue skies sometimes. The gate is the boy's marker. His undeclared goal. He can run for the gate but the field will beat him. The fold is so much deeper and wider than it appears on approach. It is deep enough to make a channel of fog when there is nothing more than a light powder mist spread across the rest of the field. A person is required to walk like a farmer, or trot like a dog. The young Edwin often sits on that gate facing east or west. Or he makes a tightrope walk of it, north, turnabout, south.

It is too big to call it his field. He just calls it the field. He is there, or he is not there. That is the shape of his world.

Five summers later, on a cool and breezy evening, Charlotte Dooley will lead him to the dimple to get naked with him. The ground is damp and the hollow in shadow, but that adds to their excitement. Charlotte's sister, Stella, is skilful at sneaking up on them. For a time she watches as they wrestle and tumble, then she startles them with her false alarm. They are being watched, she whispers harshly. The Sparlings are watching. Charlotte slides down into the hollow. She takes both their hands and leads them in a crouch through the long grass of the fold, to the boundary hedge, the adjacent field beyond, and on into the Dooley kitchen, where Charlotte makes sweet tea to aid her recovery from their reckoning.

'And your mother?' Florence said, more distant than before. Magnus ceased with his drama. His wife wasn't really listening. She was unreachable.

CHAPTER 14

Magnus, Florence and Their Baby

And so to the birth of their own child. To that which now required all their strength.

A winter yellow sun rises behind the fluted windowpanes, but their newborn baby doesn't open her eyes. No. The placenta has come away during labour.

It isn't all for nothing. It has been for this little thing, which Florence holds in her arms for a short time when they bring her back, tightly swaddled, from behind the sliding door.

Magnus takes a photograph of them together to mark all the love their daughter might take from the world. He wants to show her the world so that she might not be so utterly alone, but the glass is fluted. Though the baby has been washed, Florence wants to do it herself, which she does. And dresses her and swaddles her again. They give her her name, kiss her and let her go.

There is just the two of them again. The consultant will let Florence out soon, Magnus hopes. The professor will put her in a private room now. Yes. And Magnus will get on the bed and cradle Florence. That is as far as he can predict, as he studies the little flecks of Florence's blood on his shoes.

Edwin and Stella between them cradle the few facts of this tragedy. Magnus doesn't go into the medical details; doesn't repeat his account of the pre-birth prognosis. Rather, he speaks about the pre-labour ward, tells them he has woken with a waffle pattern imprinted on his forehead from sleeping on a hard chair, with his head on Florence's hospital blanket. A man isn't allowed to sleep full-stretched beside his wife. It is a health-and-safety issue. Events in Magnus' head are temporarily at odds with the schedule. There is a jump in the sequence. There are spurious reversals.

Magnus had kept Florence's parents informed with regular phone calls. They had been in to visit, of course. He had described the tramping of corridors, processions up and down the terrazzo stairs. Florence had liked the showers, but in the end the tramping had proved best. When Edwin and Stella arrive from Dublin, Florence is already having her first contractions.

Now that the baby is gone, Magnus takes the stairs. He stops at the chapel door. He has gone there several times during the long wait, gone there for the open window. Though it is winter, the air in the hospital is oppressive. The chapel is one of the few places in the hospital with a window a third party is at liberty to open. It is usually deserted, but twice Magnus has encountered the same man, a smoker who is there too, for the open window. His child is listed in the ledger of infant mortalities that lies open on a small, plain table at the top of the chapel. He likes to come here sometimes and sit a while.

Magnus is here to listen for the faintest echo, the sound a little one might make in passing. He has not seen the smoker look to the ledger, and neither does he now, but instead, closes his eyes and feels the cold air pricking his face. What he hears is the traffic in the street below, and he smells the fumes rising to the wide world.

Florence's parents are up with her now. In the lobby, Stella puts an arm around her son's waist. Edwin rests a pasty old hand on his shoulder. In Dublin, they had been getting ready to be better grandparents than parents. Magnus wants to continue with his useless reporting. He confirms that Stella was right to worry about the Sparling head, the bigness of it, but the midwife has been excellent at her work.

Last time Magnus had stood in the lobby, he had been anxious about when he had parked his car. This same man behind the reception desk had read his behaviour and made a dismissive gesture towards the street. He assured Magnus his car was safe from the clampers, provided he didn't park in the ambulance bay, or the spot provided for disabled drivers. He would not look at Magnus now. He did not want to intrude.

With a few lumbering strides, Magnus was out in the open air with his parents.

If they were living in London, he would have taken the pram and the newborn goods to his parents' house before Florence came home to the flat. He had the base for the car seat already. Had anchored it on the back seat as an act of faith. He had the car seat itself in the boot, together with baby blankets. The rest was in the grip-bag in a locker in the hospital. He'd get that later. He went back to the flat and gathered all the baby stuff.

Florence's parents lived in Cumbria. He couldn't see himself packing the baby stuff into their car boot. When Edwin and Stella went to their hotel, Magnus took it all to a friend's house in Holland Park. He couldn't bear to stay longer than a few minutes. They seemed to understand, though they were reluctant to let him go. 'I've to make arrangements,' he told them. He remembered he should go back to the hospital and collect that going-home bag that was in the storage locker behind the nurses' station.

'These things happen,' was as much as his father could say.

Magnus nodded bleakly. That was as much of an answer as he could give.

They went walking by the Thames. There was an unusually cold and misty breeze that created shivery turbulence in their ears. For a short time the sun turned into a white-hot moon in a ball of mist.

The two men walked in silence until they saw the smoky silhouettes of three boys playing on a clutter of barges in the distance. They were dare-walking the gunwales. Magnus and Edwin stopped to watch as they stretched their arms and proceeded in a strangely responsible and grown-up manner.

'Look at that,' Edwin said, putting both hands out in front of him. 'Stupid bloody kids.'

'Look at them,' Magnus echoed.

'Get down off that,' Edwin gave out in a strangled shout.

Magnus was already walking on. 'Let's finish this,' he said over his shoulder, meaning their damp little walk along the edge of oblivion. 'We'll need to get back.'

'We will,' said Edwin. 'I'm with you, son.'

Though the distance between them was considerable, the boys on the barges froze, with their arms outstretched, to watch the strangers pass.

'Hey you!' Magnus offered, in a sudden and aggressive shout.

'Don't distract,' his father warned.

'Yes, *you*! Get down. Get off those boats, or I'll call the police.'

The boys remained perfectly still. Magnus couldn't bear their attentiveness. He moved on, breaking into a shambling jog that he would not fully arrest until he lay down to sleep.

Part 2

CHAPTER 15

Magnus and Florence: Their Chance Meeting

Magnus first meets Florence on a foggy autumn morning in Battersea Park. He has smoked a joint, a rare indulgence for him now. He is busy revelling in the self-awareness the conditions have brought. He is floating on the long soundwaves the low barometric pressure produces. He looks over the wall at the river. He can make out wooden seagulls below. They nod at him with stiff necks. He nods and moves on. He likes the fog thickening behind him. Likes being acutely aware of the motor function of his body and amplified sensitivity of his skin as the damp air moves over his face and hands. What he feels is hope as he lets his mind run where it will, lets his thoughts out into the soft troposphere, where they can do no harm. He is drifting in his Chinese scroll when a couple appears out of the brume. The man he recognises as a neighbour. The woman on his arm he has not seen before.

At the time, Magnus is living by himself in a narrow house in a street of narrow houses across the river in Chelsea. Many of his neighbours are solicitors, barristers and bank managers. The younger ones work in the city. This man, of indeterminate age, is altogether in another category. He lives in a basement in the adjacent street with his rescue dog. His solitary loping on the pavements, his stoical expression and steadily shifting gaze give the false impression he has been specially stationed in his flat. Magnus makes a point of greeting him when their paths cross. He likes him, though he knows little about him, and it seems absurd that a man with a rescue dog is living in a basement flat in Chelsea. He talks to him when the opportunity arises, but little is ever exchanged. This is a man of integrity, Magnus supposes. A solitary fellow who goes to work in a luminous waistcoat and on occasion saves lives. Magnus is curious, not least because he speculates that there is a complicated personal history riven by great hurt. He wants to test his theory. He hasn't seen him for a while, and now he is approaching with a woman on his arm. He can't see any dog.

'Hello,' the rescue man calls. It is Magnus who, until now, has always opened the greeting.

'Hello,' Magnus replies. 'Thick, isn't it?'

'Can't see your hand in front of your face crossing the bridge.' The neighbour introduces the woman as Florence. Magnus shakes her hand. She says nothing, but smiles timidly.

'No dog?' Magnus says, expecting that it might still appear out of the mist.

What is the arrangement, anyway? Is there another occupation? Is he on a retainer? Magnus can find out through channels, but he wants to hear directly. Wants to engage because he feels he has an affinity. And what about Florence? 'It's getting thicker all round, wouldn't you say?'

'Yes,' she replies. 'Isn't it eerie?'

'Where's your dog?' Magnus asks his neighbour. For some reason, he needs to know about the dog. The need is probably to do with smoking the joint.

'In quarantine.' The man has been abroad on a mission. An earthquake in Gujarat, southern India.

'I've read about it. Terrible business.'

Evidently, his neighbour doesn't want to speak on the matter. He wears the same stoical expression Magnus normally associates with him. He practices the same wandering gaze, even in this fog. Magnus can't tell what he feels about being without his dog – or, for that matter, being with this woman.

'Well done,' Magnus hears himself mutter stupidly.

The rescue man nods in a friendly if formal manner, to indicate that this is the end of their exchange, but waits politely, in case Magnus has more to say.

'Let's hope we can find our way home,' Magnus says. Definitely the joint talking.

There is another tentative nod. Rupert, that's his name, isn't it? Rupert, and now there is Florence. Magnus gives his broadest smile, which he fears might be too broad, but why worry?

They go on their way. The couple doesn't seem to float as well as he does. Perhaps because they are tethered to each other. He watches them until they disappear, which doesn't take long.

One month to the day, he meets Florence under the entrance arch to Victoria Station. 'What kept you?' she asks, as though there is a train for them to catch to some lovers' destination. This simple question carries all the promise of the future. He kisses her cold, beautiful lips. The affair with Rupert is finished.

Magnus is her lover. She has gone to great lengths to seduce him. Though she doesn't need to, she persists. He is high on their passion, baffled by contentment. Hers *and* his. In Magnus' experience, passion and contentment don't come together.

Magnus is late for that first date because the Cabinet Secretary had called him in to his office to tell him he was to be promoted.

He married her, they were happy together, they had that baby, and now, on his return from Dublin, he found Florence wandering in the street where they lived. She hadn't been to her work at the British Library. She was going in, she said.

'In where, my darling?'

'An open clinic. They can help. Maybe you'll come.'

And so the visits began. Florence to the clinic, Magnus to see Florence. The periods she stayed at the clinic grew longer.

'I'm in control here,' she said to reassure him after her first overnight. 'They follow,' she added. He understood from the slightest flick of her head that she was referring to the doctors. She spoke not in rage, but with humility.

Her musky smell and the smell of her perfume came to him on radio waves, the short stitched through the long. 'Yes,' he said. 'You've told me.'

'Have I?' She seemed surprised.

He noticed that there were two grey dust-marks on the cheeks of her behind. She sat with her arms wrapped tightly around her legs, and rocked gently. She was making her plans in the smallest crater on the moon.

He saw she had dust in her hair, too. Where had she been? Under the bed? In some cupboard? Had she found an alternative place to sleep?

'What are you looking at?' she asked, stopping her rocking motion.

'I was just thinking – '

'How lovely my hair is,' she said, interrupting. 'Liar,' she added.

'Dust,' he said. Now that he was provoked, he quickly moved to brush his hand through the blonde tufts. He flicked his fingers across her scalp before she fully realised what he was doing. Though she moved her head to one side, she offered no further protest. Instead, she repeated his action, only more vigorously, and looked for particles of dust in the air.

'There,' she said. 'Done. That's better, isn't it?'

'Much,' he said.

She had sunk to the bottom of her being. The light in her, Magnus believed, was not extinct, but locked away. She was not mad. A person was mad if they could not work and they could not love, and Florence was capable, but Magnus faltered in the face of the unbreachable silence that lay behind her utterances.

She released her legs now and moved onto the side of one thigh to be closer to him in that low easy chair with wooden arm-rests that she had come to see as his chair.

'Listen to me,' she said, 'or we'll both die. We should be like small animals.'

Magnus looked at her, nodded forlornly, and took her hand to squeeze it. She leaned towards him dutifully, in anticipation of a kiss. She would send him on his way with a kiss. There would be no promise in it. Just the sensation of her pressing her cold lips briefly on his.

She saw this was not enough for the man she loved, so she kissed his arms and his cheeks, pressing the words of love into the fatty layer of his skin, so that they might be there for all his living life. She believed this kind of kissing would keep her sane. Florence was neither dreamy nor dopy. Rather, she was vulnerable and impulsively brave. Attractive-dangerous to other impulsive beings. Magnus didn't fit the bill, though he recognised the condition, and so wanted to respond in kind. No, what might look like impulsive behaviour in Magnus was most often the product of long-term desire and quick reasoning. Furthermore, Florence was convinced that madness, if it was coming, would manifest through her mouth – which explained something of why she responded to Magnus' forceful kisses with utter conviction.

'You should go now,' she said brightly when she was done.

Though he had been with her only a few minutes, he got up and left. It was the thing to do. Before he had left the room, she took up her position at the window, from where she would wave to him. Though it was chilly outside, she kept her window open.

Once he was out in the car park, Magnus turned to wave. He knew to look for her at the open window. She had told him that the wind in the trees whispered her name, and that if she continued to listen, she would in time decipher how she should reconstitute her life. Her melancholy glide brooked an overwhelming desire to hook onto some wider reason or logic. Magnus had told her about the sounds he had heard as a stupid boy in the Mojave Desert. She had listened intently. This was the result.

CHAPTER 16

Magnus at His Desk in Whitehall

Magnus Sparling, Under Secretary, stood behind his desk, staring out of the window. His back was rigid, his shoulders squared, his hands limp at his sides. Such stillness was a way of grieving for the small life that had been stopped, he found. Today, however, he was unsettled in his standing. It had to do with his telling Florence about his father being abandoned as an infant and his mumbling over the story of his Irish aunts. This regaling had been at the expense of their own loss, he was sure, though there was nothing new he could speak to on that; no additional comfort forthcoming from a man with expertise in maintaining the smooth running of democracy. The effective dissemination of reliable information counted for nothing in this private matter.

The financial analysis Magnus had conducted department-wide had been commended by the Minister and cited at the monthly Civil Service Steering Board confab as a model forensic audit. There were mixed feelings, of course – nobody liked to be accused of waste – but there was no doubt that Magnus' star was rising. However, the business of the working day that was about to begin had already become too much for Magnus. But that was his secret. Freddie Proctor, diligent and loyal Assistant Secretary, would be knocking on the door presently. Freddie was a man of confused expectations when it came to his rise in the service. He would be too preoccupied to read any anxiety in Magnus' face. Very soon, the door would open and Freddie Proctor's weak eyes, protected by bulletproof spectacles in black Italian frames, would appear, and Magnus would feel the nauseous thumping of a righteous pig galloping on his chest, its heavy body lending a terrible force to the small, stabbing trotters.

Freddie would begin their working day with one of his intimate gestures designed to signal that this day, like all other working days, would require daring; that what he was about to say was in strict confidence, ran contrary to protocol – not to say acceptable practice – and certainly wasn't part of any brief he might slide across Magnus' desk. There would be a few carefully understated facts delivered with a sickening humility, then a reworking of the lips to indicate that he had already hatched a plan. There were those in the service who, like spiders in car wing-mirrors, apparently lived their lives oblivious to the dynamic forces about them, the benefits and the dangers indistinguishable, one from the other. For all his scheming and his tactical ruthlessness, Proctor was one such individual. In this moment of weakness, as he saw it, Magnus had a strong urge to abandon his post and walk the damp pavements, to stop arbitrarily, to stand in other places.

In the event, it wasn't Proctor who first knocked. It was his boss, the Permanent Secretary. He called to say that his meeting with the PM was postponed until 11.30. He had come in person so that he might ask after Magnus' ailing mother. He was curiously deferential, even embarrassed. His manner heartened Magnus, though he could not think why. The Permanent Secretary then withdrew, as though conscious of reinstating a cloistered silence.

There was time for a brief visit to Florence in the day clinic. Magnus would show up unannounced, as he had done several times before. She had liked that. She liked standing with him by the window.

Florence inhaled deeply the smell from his skin at the nap of Magnus' neck and in his ears. It appeared to be a kind of animal probing, but really, it was to retrieve something utterly familiar. She blinked incessantly. Magnus knew she was trying to hold on to him, trying to fix him with each successive image that registered between each rapid eyelid movement. He signalled to her with a squeeze of his hand. She rubbed her palm across his chest. Magnus had learnt that she got upset if he wasn't wearing the same clothes when he visited. It was only now that he saw that Florence was in her bare feet. Her troubles had never before reached as far as her beautiful bony feet, and yet incongruously, her little movements promised that *she* was going to save *him* from madness.

His eyes narrowed. He leant away with a rigid back, like a pianist leaning out of his gentle, melodious notes. For just one brief moment he was in rapture. Then he leaned into her again, lest he lose the run of himself.

'What are you doing?' she asked. She wanted to know why he was breathing into her hair.

He had no answer, so he held his breath until she gave out with a little laugh. But whatever he was doing, it wasn't enough. 'Did you buy me something?'

He hadn't bought her anything, he told her.

'Good,' she said.

Then he spoilt it by asking if there was something she would like.

Florence had become preoccupied with her body, which appeared strange to her. It possessed power she did not control. She touched it as though she expected to be disgusted by its elasticity, but for some reason was unable to comprehend its form.

'You're looking at my face,' she said, touching her cheek.

Magnus reached to touch the same cheek, but she moved away. She spun on the balls of her bare feet. Magnus had learnt that if she wanted to dance for their dead baby, he had better let her do it. Get out of the room, if necessary. Let her flail and weave, bob and grind. She'd come looking for him when she was finished. There were songs that were a trigger, but she didn't need music playing. She could run it in her head. The first time she did it, Magnus stayed: he didn't know that that was what he was doing, of course: staying. He went along with her for a time. He danced. But she left him behind, so he stood and watched.

What was the tune in her head? She wouldn't say, and he couldn't guess. He could see that it brought her pleasure. The kind of pleasure sometimes got from courting danger.

So what was this? He really did want to be part of it.

She was rising, she said.

Rising?

Rising on expectations of a better life.

That first time she finished abruptly and left him in the room. However, she did call from the end of the corridor. She wanted to walk in the garden.

Her dancing was mad, but it was sensual, it was sexual and all-embracing. Anybody who saw would know. That was the danger, Magnus decided, and he wanted more. He wanted to be in the room with her, and she wanted fractious love-making. Wanted to aggressively squeeze her pleasure out of him. This would be an end in itself. If he got something out of it, well and good, but that was incidental.

Magnus signalled with a glance at the bed that he was willing. For both of them this urgent intimacy had become irresistible. It was their lifeline.

'We're little animals,' she said afterwards. Already, she seemed worn out.

'We are,' Magnus agreed.

'We are just passing the time,' she said.

'We are,' he replied.

'We haven't talked about your mother. We haven't talked about her being sick. You should tell me about her. About your trip to Ireland.'

There was a terrible helplessness to her sudden insistence. 'Well,' Magnus said with a heavy sigh, 'it was – '

She interrupted: 'Involved, yes?'

She wanted to know, but was already signalling with a tilted head that this was beyond her meagre patience.

'Yes,' he replied. 'I'll tell you another time.'

'No need,' she said with a click of the tongue, to indicate that she would be very much more cruel the next time they indulged in small talk. Was there something the matter? Something that wasn't quite right wasn't entirely wrong. The position was still tenable. Adjustments could be made.

Only now did Florence start to dance.

CHAPTER 17

The Call

Thirty percent of the Permanent Secretary's lower-jaw movement seemed to be entirely independent of the upper. When not operating in the seventy-percent mode, it would suddenly slide to one side or the other, like a typewriter bar with worn ratchet teeth. Apparently, this was unpreventable. He had become adept at sliding it back with an uncanny mirror action. This he could do without breaking the rhythm of his speech, but his words would get squashed as they emerged from the throat and were tossed sideways in the mouth before coming out into the world with a pronounced Bloomsbury curve.

Magnus noted that among his English colleagues, this had a curious effect. Many appeared to check a strong desire to respond in kind. He could see them lock their teeth and move their necks in their collars. In contrast, it just made Magnus draw back his chin and raise his brows. This, he had recognised, was an inappropriate response. Our friend would slowly slide his jaw back to neutral to register the hurt. This was mesmerising, and emptied the head of rhyme and reason. That was why Magnus looked away at regular intervals. Which, of course, was also a mistake.

The meeting with the PM had been difficult, with unpalatable but accurate information tendered clearly and concisely. Entering the security cylinder with the Permanent Secretary in the tunnel that links the Home Office with 10 Downing Street, Magnus was thinking that he didn't care about this stuff any more. As they left the tunnel, Magnus switched on his mobile. It rang almost immediately. He thought it might be a doctor in the day clinic ringing about Florence. But no. It was the Guards ringing from Dublin. His mother had given them his private number. She was too distraught to telephone herself. Furthermore, this news needed to come from the police.

Her husband had tried to poison her.

'Thank you for the information,' Magnus said. 'Can you give me a number? I will call back shortly.'

'Everything all right, Magnus?' the Permanent Secretary asked. He saw the change of pallor in the face.

'Yes. Thank you.'

'Your mother, is it? Not in hospital again, I hope?'

'My mother, yes. I have to ring back.'

The Permanent Secretary, scarcely breaking his stride, put a hand lightly on his shoulder. 'You follow on.'

When Magnus rang the number he had been given, he spoke to a detective in the serious-crime squad. The detective confirmed that the allegation had been formally registered. Mrs Stella Sparling, née Dooley, had come down to the station in person to make her allegation and to give her statement. An investigation was under way as to whether, indeed, there was a case to answer. The detective asked if he might speak to Magnus in person. Magnus agreed.

This, of course, didn't answer whether or not his mother had maliciously invented a story involving paraquat. It didn't immediately tell him whether or not she was dangerously deluded, or whether, indeed, the old man had tried to kill her.

What if it were true? The idea inspired by the sight of Stella lying in the hospital bed – really dying, for once, but then not dying. After all, hadn't he himself speculated about this, even willed it in a moment of rage? Hadn't he thought it would be a blessed release?

'Yes, of course,' he told the detective. He would do all he could to help establish the facts.

'It's an inquiry, you understand, Mr Sparling. Nothing more as yet.' He said this to ease the shock, to show that he was discreet, and, no doubt, in deference to Magnus' high rank in the British Civil Service – a fact Stella would have made clear, however great her distress.

The detective's tone was no help at all.

CHAPTER 18

Tell Me Straight

Magnus travelled to the airport hunched in a corner of a taxi, then sat lumpenly on the plane to Dublin without speculating. He did not allow his mind to race, but rather reclined with his dead man on the beach.

The dead man on the beach visits regularly, or rather, Magnus visits him. It is not like a flashback in a film. There are no high-angle shots, no floating around him. There is only the intimacy he has experienced. It is, as his father predicted, neither ghostly nor spooky. The eyes do not spring open. There is no talking. The stranger lies precisely as Magnus discovered him, and Magnus relives precisely the small actions he has taken with only the sound of the sea and the wind. The journey to retrieve the shoe – that is the only variable, the distance being imprecise, and therefore the time it takes never the same.

Others go to spas, to church, to doctors, to religious retreats, to their supplier, so that they might rest a while and learn to be patient. Magnus returns to his dead man on the beach. To his long picket. It is his measure against all the world.

'I've to give you change,' the Dublin taxi driver said deviously.

'Yes please,' Magnus replied. A hefty pile of coins were passed over the driver's seat.

What his father saw was a man get out of a taxi and stand with his toecaps over the edge of the curb-stone, spilling coins into his trouser pocket. At this distance, he didn't recognise him.

What Magnus saw was an old man with a dog. This was, indeed, his father, the man now accused of attempting to poison his wife, also known as Magnus's mother. He was struck by how much more stiff his father had become in the short time since his last visit. Had the stiffness anything to do with being wrongly accused, or with guilt? The dog, too, was stiff. Did the dog know something?

Edwin was further up the street, and about to cross to the far side. He had one foot on the road. Looking left, then right, then left again, he turned from the hips. He was determined to make immediate progress.

This dog's moan was more expressive than its bark. It was used to being ignored and was no less glum, no less ill-tempered, than its master. It waited at his heels with its head down. For both, it seemed, happiness came and went unexpectedly, and always in small packages. Neither man nor dog could any longer show affection, each to the other. The dog actually belonged to Jack and Marie, Edwin's neighbours. This wretched dog was indentured without hope of reprieve. It was a token go-between that did not go between, a rank and indifferent peacemaker that would be further neglected and only stink more in this time of crisis.

Magnus thought better of calling out. Man and dog hurried stiffly into the middle of the road, separate but together. The dog peeled off as it picked up a scent that took it along the broken white line. Edwin paid no heed; made no call as he cranked left, right and left again on his hips. Now that he was in the middle of the road and in real danger, he was doing a little shuffle that suggested mean-spirited pleading. I'm a good timekeeper, it seemed to be saying. I'm good at turning up. Let me on my way, you bastards.

It was only when a pizza-delivery motorcyclist let out with a prolonged blast of his Honda 50 horn that Magnus' father took note of the dog's position. It had moved into the path of the oncoming motorbike, barking its ancient bark. Its front paws lifted off the ground with each *groak*. Its chin was close to the tarmac as it made ready to go at the wheels. The pizza youth swerved, lashed out with a foot, shouted something obscene through his toughened plastic visor. There was a great sense of release in the profanities that came from Edwin's mouth. A great passion in the hoisting of two stiff fingers in the wake of the pizza youth on his motorbike. Once up in the air, he could not easily take them down. He made no representation to the dog. There was a glance of relief; no reassurance; no calling to heel. There was just shared indignation. Man and dog stiffly crossed from the centre of the road to the far pavement.

Magnus scarcely recognised his father in this behaviour, which made him think that his father was guilty as charged. 'Hello, dad,' he shouted.

Edwin turned. Suddenly he seemed baffled, even lost. 'Oh,' he whispered sweetly, and smiled. 'It's you.' There was no animosity in the voice. No disappointment. Though the smile was familiar, it registered with Magnus as entirely inappropriate, even downright deceitful.

The dog kept moving. It was reworking its gait, making ready to carry one rear leg spare while it looked to pick up the scent it had lost.

Magnus fell in beside his father. The dog fell in behind both men, its nails scratching on the pavement. The rhythm was at once pathetic and menacing. Magnus felt the pale daylight moon burning the back of his neck. A thin church bell rang. He couldn't think which steeple let out with so light a sound. The smell of damp earth came from the adjacent gardens and rubbed over the parked cars. It came out through the gates rather than over the hedges, in thick, blousy wafts. Magnus never remembered these gardens giving out like this.

'You want to get straight to it?'

No. Edwin didn't. The few words he put out as a reply deadened the space between himself and his son like a mattress. It wasn't a good start. No matter. Magnus was sure he'd have an early breakthrough.

Edwin noted that his son had packed a light bag, and assumed from this that he wouldn't be staying long. 'Did you have a good flight?'

'Yes.'

Magnus never had much time to spend at home. That was understood. Walking together was usually a treat.

'Did you do it?'

No reply.

'Did you, dad?'

No response. The scratching dog-nails got closer.

'Did you do what they're saying you did?'

Nothing.

Magnus had an exaggerated sense of order. It had something to do with his having had a bedroom that overlooked the park when he was a boy. It made Magnus both x-ray clerk and sonar operator, able to hum the straight melody of another's life while he probed. To Magnus' childhood eyes, people were civilised, whether they strolled or jogged or even staggered their way through life; reasonable even when they shook a drunkard's fist and gave chase. Trees and shrubs knew their place and were content. Birds in the park were on holiday. They would fly away if disturbed, but they would always come back. Magnus and his father tramped the park in silence until they saw the park-keeper come out of his lodge with his bunch of keys to do his rounds of the gates.

'Evening,' Edwin called formally.

'Evening,' replied the park-keeper.

Magnus caught himself shaking his head in disbelief. He'd have to break this absurd pretence of normality. 'I'm going to the station in the morning,' Magnus said, using his formal civil-service voice.

'To see that detective?'

'Yes, to see the detective.'

'You're going to explain me away,' Edwin said boldly.

'If I can.'

'Go on, then.' Edwin seemed to lose all the tension in his muscles. His body appeared to fold in on itself.

'You think this will all blow over if nobody talks?'

'You've talked with the detective on the phone already, I take it?'

'Yes. Briefly.'

'Well, then . . . '

'What do you mean?'

'You'll know.'

'Know what?'

'You'll know you haven't a chance. You'll know that they've made up their minds about me.' His father was so sorry for himself. Magnus took this as a further indicator of guilt.

'We'll see,' Magnus said. He managed to make his reply sound tempered and wise.

The two men went home via the back lane. The old gate shuddered on its hinges.

'There's a lot more clover in the grass,' said Magnus.

'The bees like it.'

Magnus stopped to take in the back of the house. 'The window frames could do with a lick of paint.'

'I don't mind,' said Edwin. 'I've to paint your Aunt Charlotte's.'

'What? The whole house?'

'The hall door. That will do. Then he mumbled: 'I might get her one of those canvas covers with the deckchair stripes instead.'

The spurious air of normality prevailed. Behind them the evening sun rolled along the top of the back garden wall. It made the sound of a marble in a pipe. It dropped into a bucket of rainwater with a fizz, as it had done countless times before.

CHAPTER 19

Magnus Begins His Interrogation

The restaurant was busy. This seemed to add to the tension.
'You come here with Noel?' Magnus asked.

'I do like to come here,' was the approximate answer. 'It's cheap.' Edwin got an instant kick out of pretending to be extra tight with his money. 'Cops and bin men come here,' he added for effect. Proof of a thrifty menu, if proof were needed.

'We used to know the chef.' His words were laced with irony.

The hope of an early breakthrough was already receding. There was need of some soothing talk. Magnus thought it would be useful to pursue his father's long-standing friendship with Noel. 'This town you go to . . . '

'Yes . . . ' Edwin was easy with this line of questioning, though his answers had a gentle weariness to them.

'You go with Noel?'

'I do. I go with Noel.'

'Isn't that the place you used to go to with Stella?'

'With your mother, yes.'

'That was a long time ago, I know . . . '

'A long time.'

'And now you go with your pal, Noel, for the sun?'

'September was the last visit.'

'And what do you do down there? Just drink wine?' Magnus made his question appreciative.

'And we have coffees in the square.'

'You get a tan on the beach?'

'You take a tram to the beach. A twenty-minute ride. We'd go to the beach once in a while. Sit on the promenade under an umbrella. Have a glass of wine and a coffee.'

'Lovely.'

'We'd have dinner, of course. But much later in the evening.'

'A holiday with your best mate. It doesn't get much better, does it?'

'We'd argue, mostly. But the days stretch. Any heat we generate has gone by dinnertime – which is a bloody shame, wouldn't you say?'

Magnus left a silence – which, under the circumstances, was a mistake. 'You tell Noel everything?'

Edwin knew immediately where this was going. He held up a finger.

Their food arrived. Edwin ate heartily and without ceremony. Magnus picked judiciously.

'Can't you see?'

'See what, son?'

'I'm looking out for you. Give me the facts. Together, we'll get everybody to see it as you see it.'

Edwin nodded, but said nothing.

'There's lot I know about how Stella has treated you, and about your fury.'

'Fury? What's this fury?'

'Is that the wrong word? Tell me.'

'You're a credit to me and to the civil service. I mean it.'

'I can give you good counsel. But I need to hear from you what has actually occurred.'

Again, Edwin nodded and said nothing. 'Tell me about your suffering.' Using the word *suffering* released adrenalin in Magnus and made him red-faced.

'I'm looking after myself,' Edwin replied, further adrift. 'It's difficulties more than suffering.' His words expired before they were fully airborne.

It was Magnus' turn to nod.

'There's a small junction in the town . . . ' Edwin said from a distant shore, 'not the main square. There's a drinking fountain in the middle, four mature trees: London planes, four benches. Every day, in the late afternoon, there are old fellas who come to sit there and talk. The local restaurant sends them out coffees on a tray. These old fellas don't pay. And they don't expect to pay. They're shown respect. They have their conversation and their companionship. That's why they live long lives.'

'You and Noel sit down with them?'

'We do, sometimes.'

'And they talk to you?'

'It's difficult with the language, but there is an attempt.'

'They imagine you have your own bench and your own drinking fountain at home, I expect.'

'We don't get the coffees.'

'No . . . ?'

'You'd be there a long time before you'd get the coffee.'

'Fair enough.'

'Then you'd refuse it out of politeness, wouldn't you?'

'What . . . you and Noel?'

'Then, eventually, you'd accept.'

'You just have to show up regularly.'

'You'd need to be regular, and you'd need to learn Spanish properly.' Edwin seemed to be floating on a warm autumnal breeze that would send the fallen leaves of his four plane trees scratching around the fountain. He was thinking of going back there soon, with Noel, if Noel would go again. 'Short fellas,' he said softly. 'The coffees,' he added for clarification, lest Magnus think he was talking about the old men. 'No milk. In a little glass on a saucer.'

Magnus left a silence to show humility. Then he spoke again. 'I should talk to Noel about this business?' he asked in the voice he reserved for asserting his authority.

'About this?' Edwin repeated, coming up to meet him. 'What is *this*?'

'About you,' Magnus continued calmly.

'If you've finished talking to your mother, and you want to talk to somebody else about me, you talk to Noel.'

Was his father mocking? Magnus couldn't judge.

'His brother died, but he's all right. It's his birthday next Monday. I'm taking him out for his dinner. At Christmas we'll go to the carols at Saint Patrick's Cathedral.'

'That's all good. I'll talk to Noel.'

'He always fancied your mother.' There was no resentment in his voice. Just the same maddening, pragmatic tone.

'Really?' Magnus declared with sham surprise.

'There's something wrong with his back now,' Edwin put in as a rider. 'He can't bend over. Otherwise, he's all right.'

'He has back trouble, too . . . ?'

'He can bend down,' Edwin said, amending his statement, 'but he can't get back up.' This, he felt, was more convincing.

'So, he doesn't do much bending. But he can talk.'

Edwin settled back in his chair, then leaned forwards a little. 'When I told Noel I was the accused, he shook my hand with great forbearance. Have you ever noticed his hands? Big hands. He has a powerful grip still.'

'What did you tell him about the situation?'

'I told him she was accusing me. I told him she had gone to the Guards. I told him this before I was called in for the interview.' Edwin paused here. Being required to attend a police station still had him reeling. The interview itself must have traumatised him, Magnus was thinking. 'You remember when his wife died? You remember the funeral?

Magnus said that he did.

'You remember my shaking Noel's hand when they sent her through the curtains? You remember that?' He took hold of Magnus' forearm, clasped his hand on his son's wrist, made Magnus do the same to his. 'It was like this.' Edwin's jaw became stiff with emotion. 'Do you understand?' he asked.

Magnus understood from this sailor's grip of life that his father could not express in words the strength of the bond. 'Yes,' he replied. 'I do.'

'Like this,' Edwin repeated, making the hold ever stronger.

Out of respect, Magnus said nothing more until his father let go. He had never had such a handshake before.

'What were you asking about Noel?' Edwin said, as though he had suddenly lost his way.

'You gave him details . . . .'

'What details?' It didn't seem to matter to him any more where this conversation was going.

'An account of Stella's accusation. The type of poison. The cup on the armrest. Circumstances . . . .' Self-loathing was rising in Magnus, but he had to persevere.

'He didn't want details,' his father said flatly. 'He didn't want anything from me.' Edwin leaned back in his chair and looked away, full of resentment.

Magnus looked down into his own lap and found that he was gripping one hand tightly with the other. He brightly jolted himself out of this little stupor. 'Last time I was over, you told me you and Noel went to Amsterdam . . . .'

Edwin responded with an equal and sudden flash of brightness. 'Did I tell you about that trip?'

'You went to learn how to behave as old men. You gave me some guff like that.'

'Four nights in Amsterdam. It was a good hotel. Noel picked it out.'

'You went to see the Rembrandts: his self-portraits in particular.'

'We went for the art. Of course we did. It's never too late to study the masters. The mistake we make is thinking they're no longer relevant.'

'And what did you learn?'

'You don't know what you'll get looking at a painting. You let it do its work.'

'The self-portraits are extraordinary, I know,' Magnus acknowledged, trying to gain ground. 'You have him look at you with his unblinking eyes . . . .' Already he was struggling, but Edwin cut in.

'Whichever portrait, whatever his age, he appears not to be in a downward spiral, but steady in himself.'

'Nothing disguised,' Magnus ventured lamely.

'No distractions. In charge. Officially and entirely himself.'

Magnus looked hard at his father.

'Noel says he's going to grow a beard.' Edwin was still travelling across the aged Rembrandt's dark eyes, his yellow cheeks and facial extremities rendered in *sfumato*. 'But he won't, of course . . . .'

Magnus had already spoken to Noel on the phone without telling his father. He had gone straight at it: 'He's told you about his situation?'

Noel Ffrench, with two 'f's, had made little breathy noises to indicate that he knew what Magnus was referring to. 'I asked him how he was. "I'm good," he said. "Very good." I knew there was something up when he added "Very good".'

Noel wouldn't say on the telephone what Edwin had told him. As far as he was concerned, it wasn't something to be talked out as reported speech. He took it that Magnus had been told what *he* had been told. 'He's shaken to the core, of course. As I am.'

'You think Stella's making it up, Noel? Just to get at him.'

'That is my opinion, for what it's worth.'

'Why won't he deny it?'

'We could ask, but he wouldn't tell us,' Noel had said appreciatively. 'He's playing smart, your dad. I wish sometimes I was that enlightened.'

'Why does he need to play smart, Noel?'

'He doesn't want her dealt with, whatever she's at. You know she's been in with the Guards?'

'They both have.'

'That's the form.'

'Edwin's a right Charlie, at the same time.'

'You think?'

'He should be out on his own. Better for the both of them. Push on, push out, is what I say.'

Noel had wanted to ask Magnus if he, too, thought his mother had been inventing, but that was something to be volunteered, not extracted.

'It'll all work out,' Magnus declared after an alarming silence. 'Can we meet? Just you and me. You can help me clear this up.'

Noel readily agreed.

CHAPTER 20

Aunt Charlotte, Aunt Maureen

It was late when Magnus talked to Aunt Charlotte on the phone, but she was expecting his call. She was her usual home-baked self. Magnus felt he could rely on a concise debriefing. How had his father received his mother's accusation? Magnus asked his aunt. Was he confused? Did he have wet eyes? Was there a little shriek of joy?

She wouldn't talk about it. If she had witnessed any significant reaction, she wasn't declaring it. She would only say that he was inscrutable.

'There was no guffaw?' he said, trying to goad her.

She scoffed. 'The Guards interviewed him. And they'll go at him again.'

'Never mind the Guards: *I* have to know. You must tell me.'

'What can I tell you?'

'No reaction you could measure?' Magnus persisted. The implication being that there had to have been a significant reaction, and that Charlotte was in denial. There was no indication of any kind?

'Magnus . . . I would tell you.'

'Nothing at all: think again.'

'Don't you want to ask about your mother?'

'I'm coming to her.'

'She's all right. I have her grounded.'

'Is she drinking?'

'I keep her topped up, poor thing. Short measures.'

'We must get to the bottom of this quickly.'

'If you ask me, it's an affectation.'

'You're telling me Stella has concocted a story?'

'I wouldn't put it past her. What do *you* think?'

'The Guards have interviewed you?'

'I've had a visit, yes. They think it's an affectation, too.'

'I know they didn't say that, Aunt Charlotte.'

'Well of course they didn't. But I could tell by how nice they were to me.'

'I see. Is Stella going to stay with you?'

'She's talking about going to Maureen's. Thinks she'd be safer in Scotland. Will I put her on?'

'No. I'm coming over.'

'I'll get some biscuits in.'

It was later still when Magnus rang Maureen. Aunt Maureen was an earnest woman. The one most like their mother. Maureen had been the one most interested in keeping the family house in Wicklow, keeping the farm productive, though it had never in their lifetime been much of a commercial proposition. She wasn't a thwarted romantic, like Charlotte, or a mistress, like Stella. She was the cautious one. She wanted to know the makes and the brands of everything. She kept receipts, applied hand-cream all year round, was afraid of infectious diseases, to which she believed she was unreasonably susceptible. She was afraid of sunstroke and alcohol. She didn't talk about sex, but craved it more than her two sisters with a kind of simple urgency. They knew it, and teased her mercilessly. She was the aunt most concerned about the effect on Magnus of finding the body on the beach. She was suspicious of her nephew's supposed maturity for his age. Boys were not as robust as their fathers liked to think. They were pushy little savages who needed strict guidance and cake, preferably from Fullers bakery. Aunt Maureen was the only one to advocate counselling for Magnus after the discovery in Donegal. Maureen was loyal, but she was the first to take flight. To abandon the beloved house in Wicklow when both parents had died. To get married and have children. To leave Ireland, where, she said, she had always been happy. She could be trusted in an emergency. Of that, there was no doubt. She could be relied upon to come back, or, as in this case, provide sanctuary. She would, in any shared difficulties, stand to in her best clothes and worry. Magnus knew she would be climbing the walls.

'Maureen, you leave this all to me,' he told her. 'I'm looking into it, and I'm going to set it right. I'll tell you what has happened and what it is we're doing, when it's clear to me. Till then, I need you to be patient and to be skeptical about what you hear.'

'I will, Magnus,' she promised gravely.

'Make no assumptions.'

'I won't make assumptions.'

'Draw no conclusions.'

'What can I do? There must be something.'

'I might ask you to take in Stella for a time, or I might need you to come and stay with your sisters in Laragh.'

'I'll come now. I *was* coming, only Charlotte said not to just yet. But I'll come now, Magnus.'

'No. Charlotte is right.'

'We must all be patient, Maureen. I'll find an explanation.'

Early next morning, Magnus drove south out of the city, taking the road that followed the coast, then cut inland and climbed into the mountains towards Laragh.

What would have prompted Edwin to try to poison Stella? Magnus speculated that the old man was out on one of his solitary drives in his precious Daimler. He might have slowed to take in one of the roadside memorials that were familiar to him, but to which he usually gave no attention. One of those half-sized crosses or plaques with cut flowers that acted as a grief conductor for the living, and GPS for the dead lest the information be needed. There was also the drive-safely message. Passing one of these would not normally have made Edwin slow down, but this time he was thinking about Stella.

Magnus sped along the narrow roads without looking at the speedometer, windows down, his face taking a blustery battering. He stretched his mouth in a manic fashion, so that when he talked to his father again, his father might feel compelled to make his mouth bigger, too, and thereby less discreet.

'Tell me, old man,' Magnus shouted, trying to make his mouth match the size of the windscreen. 'Tell me what you've done.' He didn't recognise his own voice.

CHAPTER 21

Magnus Confronts His Mother

Magnus went close to Stella, squatted beside her chair, took one of her hands. He could see she was still in shock, still making a brave effort to remain composed. 'Stella, I came as quickly as I could. How are you?'

'Magnus, can you credit this?'

'Last time I was here, you'd been shot.' Magnus ignored Charlotte waving at him to avoid any such taunt.

'What are you saying?' Stella said. 'What are you talking about?'

'Your time in the hospital, your telling everybody you'd been shot: that has to be taken into account.'

She withdrew her hand from his.' You're talking nonsense.'

'Well, you've survived,' Magnus said, rising to his full height with a sigh. 'That's the main thing, isn't it?'

'Good God. You're in league with him.'

Magnus turned to leave.

'Don't go,' his mother pleaded. 'Please. I didn't mean that. Of course you're not. Of course.'

'He didn't do it, did he?' Magnus said, with a little nod of encouragement. 'The whole thing is invented. You've invented it.'

'There was paraquat in that glass.'

'I'm sure there was,' Magnus replied – but not cockily, as Charlotte might have feared. Not in a judgemental manner. He needed to investigate with all the devious insight of a blackmailer. '*He* didn't put it there, though, did he?'

His mother's eyes began to well up. He felt that if he pressed hard he might get an early result.

'I understand, Stella.'

'Understand!' she scoffed. 'You don't understand anything here.'

'Ah, I do.'

'It's all changed. Everything has changed.'

Did she mean changed from a distant time when she and his father thought they belonged together; were lovers?

'Yes, well, there's no disputing that. Look, he's getting old, and – '

She cut across him. 'He's dangerous. He's deranged. Thank God I'm here to tell you.'

Magnus nodded heavily, looked to Charlotte, who gazed back with unreserved admiration for him, in spite of his rough tactics. 'Tea,' she said with a start. 'I almost forgot.'

'Do you want to know how he is?' Magnus asked. Inverting the ratio of concern counted as small talk, and small talk was needed.

'How is he?' Stella enquired with magnificent boldness. 'Apart from being deranged.'

'He's getting a brace for his back.'

'He's been lifting. He doesn't know how to lift.'

'I asked. He says he hasn't lifted anything heavy.'

'You would think an architect would know better about lifting. There's something fractured?'

'Nothing has shown up on the x-ray. They say it's muscular.'

'He's torn something with his lifting.'

'Anyway, he's getting this brace.'

'Men heal faster,' Stella declared, pinching the flesh of her forearm several times in quick succession. She said it as if she was saying they could grow mustaches. 'He's wearing a brace, you tell me, and he's deranged.'

Charlotte returned with tea things on a tin tray, and threw open the French windows onto the back garden. It was a little chilly to be sitting outdoors, but she seemed to think her sister needed an abundance of fresh air. She got them outside. She settled a car rug on Stella's shoulders. 'There now, dear.' Stella appeared not to fathom her comforting words, nor feel the weight or warmth of the rug. The rug, Magnus observed, must have come with her, as he recognised it as the rug from the back-window shelf of his father's car.

Stella saw her son taking in the rug. 'Did he give you a lift here?' she asked with sudden alarm. 'Is he out there in his precious car?'

'No.'

'You didn't tell him I was here, did you?'

'Of course not.'

'He drives around aimlessly. He's a danger to everybody.'

Charlotte interposed herself, turning her back to her sister. 'When you were a baby, Magnus, and you wouldn't sleep, Edwin used to put you on the back seat of his car and drive you about the district until you fell asleep.'

'Huh,' said Stella.

'No baby seat then?' said Magnus, just to encourage his aunt.

'No safety belts either.'

'I remember him getting the seatbelts.'

'He was always a danger,' continued Stella determinedly. 'You wouldn't think it to look at him.'

'He liked to drive his boy around,' Charlotte said proudly.

'Did he sing to me?'

'There was no lullaby,' Stella bleated.

'I didn't think so,' said Magnus. 'Neither of you can sing.'

'He talked to you, though,' Charlotte insisted.

'Yes? How do you know?'

'He brought you round to me sometimes.'

'Really? You got in the car?'

'Not often,' Charlotte said uncomfortably.

'You never came on these nursery drives, Stella?' Magnus asked.

'Oh, she did, sometimes,' Charlotte answered for her sister, 'didn't you, Stella? It became a ritual, you could say.'

'You liked to keep your little fists clenched in the air,' his mother declared, smiling suddenly and directly at Magnus. This was sentiment that surprised even her. There was a little pause to make allowances.

'Then, I take it, I began to sleep when it was time to sleep?'

'You did, darling.'

Magnus thought about his father driving them around the back streets of Bakersfield for want of a lullaby. Then he went at his mother again.

'You've made this up, haven't you?' His tone was the essence of patience and understanding.

'Hah.' Nothing Magnus could say would shock Stella. He admired this trait in her, though it was maddening.

'You invented this story.'

'You're very smart, aren't you?' This time Stella was responding to her son's tone. She wasn't about to be chamois-leathered into any flimflam take on events.

'You've no idea what you've done.' He managed to say this without a change in key.

'It's been done to me. I'm the victim.' Stella was being equally restrained. Competing with her son provided for a predictable rhythm, even with the brakes on.

'You're the victim. You're the victim.' Magnus repeated the phrase as though he were looking for a clue. 'Have you any idea what you've unleashed? Are you trying to destroy everybody?'

'He's trying to poison me, and you take his side?'

'He'll try again, you think? Might try with an axe next time?'

'You're a cruel son.'

'Don't play the mad one with me. You're taking full responsibility for this.'

'I'm lucky to be alive, you beast.'

'You're my mother. I'm here to help.'

'Hah.'

'We are where we are.'

'A beast.'

'I can manage the situation.'

'We'll see your father in prison.'

'You didn't drink it.'

'I saved myself from his filthy act. I – I – I –'

'You're a remarkable woman.'

'How could a man do such a thing?'

'You acted in desperation. We can start there.'

'How can anybody . . . ?'

'The Guards are on to you, Stella.'

'You're a cold, cold beast.'

'You're the one breaking hearts. Who have you talked to about this?'

'Charlotte is distraught about the whole affair. I'm playing it down, of course. And Maureen is in the dark.'

'You're a fantasist. A dangerous fantasist.'

'Am I? Am I, now?'

It struck Magnus that Stella expected him to conduct a rigorous interrogation, and that she accepted it was natural that she be held under suspicion. 'Tell me the truth. I can fix this.'

'Your father tried to kill me.' She began to sob.

The sobbing was genuine. Magnus hadn't expected it. 'Dear God,' he said. Then he turned to one side and ran the palm of one hand up his forehead.

'Yes,' his mother intoned, 'dear God.'

Magnus began to pace. The steps were precisely measured. 'God almighty,' he said, dropping his voice to a thoughtful murmur. He crossed in front of her, then behind her.

'Have a drink,' Stella said, determined to show her naked mettle.

'I don't want a drink. You have a drink.'

'I will.'

'You'll have to ask Charlotte.'

'No, I won't. I know where it is.'

'Out of common courtesy.'

'She'll have one with me. We're all in this. We're all rocking on our heels. Except you, of course. The unshockable Whitehall man.'

Short exchanges, Magnus was thinking. Challenge her. Get her rattled, then soften her with drink. She seemed prepared to cooperate with such a regime.

No drinks were got. It was too early. Drinks couldn't be substituted for tea. He'd get her drinking later, and see.

'You did – you invented this piece of theatre,' Magnus said, going at it again. Aunt Charlotte was giving them time alone. She was sitting in the kitchen with a tea-cosy over the teapot. 'The Guards are on to you.'

'You're lying about the Guards. I had a long talk with the detective, I'll have you know.'

'Richie. Yes. You liked him, did you?'

'He knows what's what. You needn't worry.'

'I can go to Richie and make a case. You were under stress. I can settle this. There'll be no serious consequences.'

'The case is made – no thanks to you.'

'I can be very convincing. I know how men like Richie work.'

'I'm making plans. I have a new life ahead of me.'

'Fair enough.'

'I'll not be stopped.'

'That's the spirit. Let's clear the decks.'

'Your father is for the asylum.'

'I'll get you the best therapist. We'll write it up. We'll show it to Richie, and he'll let it all go.'

'Mr Richie says I'm under protection.'

'Does he? That's nice. It just goes to show how much he likes you. We get you written up, and he'll see you right.'

'Listen to yourself. You've turned bitter. What's happened to you?'

'I'm here to fix this situation. I'll fix it, then you can have your new life. The old man, too.'

'But you want the plain truth?'

'Yes. I do.' Magnus noticed for the first time that his mother had made a bad job of her makeup. There was too much of it.

'Your father tried to poison me. There. You have it.' She appeared to be imagining the paraquat rapidly spreading through her, her body cells shutting down by the millions. 'I'm so terrible alone, Magnus,' she said.

'You have Charlotte looking after you.'

'She doesn't believe he did it. I know she doesn't, though she won't say.'

'*I* don't believe it.'

'You're only saying that. This could kill me yet, Magnus.'

'Just tell me what you did,' he said, 'and you'll be fine.'

They watched their tea go cold.

'If he did it, he has the Guards fooled,' Magnus said quietly.

'Your father is a clever man.' There was steely pride in Stella's answer. It just slipped out. Belatedly, she added a bitter squint.

'We all hold our breath.'

'He's going to get away with it.'

'There isn't the evidence, you see.'

'I gave them the mug.'

'A mug with paraquat in it. That's evidence of what? No.'

'I might have put it in there myself.'

'Detective Richie will be thinking that is a possibility. Yes.'

'Stop it, Magnus.'

'What did you do? Did you ring the Guards and get them over, or did you bring the mug with the paraquat down to the station?'

'I rang. They came and collected me. They took away the mug in a plastic bag.'

'An extraordinary moment, any way you look at it.'

'Nothing I can say will make you see.'

'There's no evidence either way, when it comes to it. *You* put the paraquat in the mug; *he* put the paraquat in the mug. Whatever.'

'What a life.'

'In effect, the case is closed. I'm to organise help.'

'Help?'

'Yes. Help. Psychiatric help. That's what I'm being advised by the authorities.'

'Which authorities?'

'Your friend, Richie. He has advisors, of course. Of course he has advisors. Legal and medical. They can call on such people in these cases.' Magnus was going dark. His mother began to bawl: for herself, he thought. He got up and walked around the garden. 'Let's have a drink,' he shouted encouragingly. 'You and me. To celebrate.'

Stella studied his every move with her big waterlogged eyes, grateful for something, though she didn't know what. He took off into the dining room. He lurched about, putting together the measures. He searched high and low for the baby cans of soda water. Stella came in after him to watch. She was grateful for any kind of connecting, she wanted to say. For making this exchange normal, when really, it was absurd. He was his father's son, after all, and more than clever.

Later, while Charlotte and Stella held hands in the kitchen, Magnus moped in the garden. He lifted his eyes to the wider countryside, but they kept returning to the familiar garage, which opened onto the side lane. He wandered in that direction. Once inside, he took stock of what was on the shelves. There were bottles of paint stripper, ancient linseed oil and such. There were jam and Marmite jars with screw-top lids. These held a jumble of nails and screws and rusted wing-nuts and small coils of copper wire and lamp flex. Underneath the shelving on one wall was a plywood panel that housed a collection of hand tools crooked on nails. Magnus' father had organised this for Charlotte, who was quite capable of using these tools. She appreciated his good work and squirted 3-in-1 oil on moving parts once a year to show her appreciation.

Magnus stood on a wooden box to inspect a gap on an otherwise cluttered shelf that ran the length of the garage, close to the ceiling. At one end there was a cluster of bottles containing paint that had been transferred from half-used tins; bottles that, no doubt, were unopenable. Other bottles containing solvents and cleaning spirits. Then, there was the gap. Magnus inspected the gap. He saw rings in the thick, oily dust that coated the shelf, where yet other bottles had stood. It was the smart thing to do, of course: discard several bottles, not just the one bottle of paraquat.

When he came out of the garage, he found his aunt standing in the garden, waiting patiently for him, it seemed.

'How is he, Charlotte?' Magnus asked with a heavy heart. 'His general disposition? You see him more than I do. Has he gone strange?'

'Strange . . .' she reflected on the word itself, rather than the man. 'No.'

Charlotte wasn't the nursing kind, but she was compassionate. She went to Edwin and Stella's house regularly now. She had made herself a companion without Edwin realising it. Mostly, she just hung around and talked about articles in the newspaper, and about she and him being sensible. She had put a rug on his easy chair, which he had removed, but left folded over the arm-rest. Twice she got takeaways because he wanted to. She ate all her takeaway, though she would never order such a thing herself. The other evenings she spent with him she did the kind of plain cooking Edwin did.

Magnus saw that she had taken on some of Edwin's traits. His quiet, imprecise walk. His pattern of moping. Charlotte had been to the massage chair in the shopping centre, put in her four euro for her ten minutes. She knew Edwin did this, because she had followed him there. She told Magnus about these trips.

'He just sits in the vibrating chair?' Magnus asked.

'That's what anybody does, dear, if they pay for that kind of thing.'

'You watched him put his money in, then he just stared into space?'

'Sometimes he has a second go.'

'It's not like him, is it, Charlotte?'

'You couldn't tell, just by looking at him.'

'You came around the corner in the shopping centre and there he was, vibrating in the chair?'

'I followed him.'

'You followed . . . ?'

'Yes. I was on my way to visit when he came out through the gate. I called him but he didn't hear. I think he's going a little deaf. Anyway, he seemed to be on urgent business, so I followed.'

'That's not right.'

'I was never right, Magnus,' she said mischievously. There was no hint of embarrassment or regret. 'He didn't see me, if that's what you're worried about.'

'Come on, Charlotte, it's a little bizarre, you have to admit. Him doing that, and you spying.'

'It's not a kiddie's ride.'

'I know, but . . . '

'I had a go myself, after he had gone.'

Magnus shrugged, shook his head, struggled for something useful to say.

'I'd hate to think he was lonely,' his aunt said matter-of-factly, 'that nobody was interested.' Then she asked, 'You want to come to the service today?' This was no normal question. It had to do with showing resilience in a crisis. Magnus understood this, and went with her to the church.

Charlotte hadn't said much about her sister's supposed brush with death, and neither had their sister, Maureen. Charlotte sat close beside Edwin in the pew. She had her hymnbook open at the right place for each hymn, and each psalm, well in advance of the opening organ prompt. She recited the page number to Edwin. She was in awe, Magnus speculated, because of his attempt on her sister's life. So it appeared. How bizarre was that?

There was tea, cake and scones in the school hall after the service. Charlotte went ahead of the Sparlings because she was helping out behind one of the trestle tables. She had a little pixie girl with long silky hair and round glasses next to her to pour milk. Using both hands, she also poured orange juice from a very large jug. Charlotte's table was in front of the piano because she played that piano for the junior infants. These events relied on individuals taking responsibility and sticking with whatever loose logic could be bent to tradition.

People stood comfortably in their coats with tea and cake, conversed in small, polite groups. The heating in the hall wasn't turned on. People kept their coats on, thus saving on the church's heating bill. The young man who had played the trumpet in the church was sent by the reverend from one group to another to be lauded. He was ignored only by the elderly widows, who were busy making their selection of cake they intended to take home. There were squares of tinfoil ready for parishioners for this purpose. Widows and spinsters dictated what was surplus to the day's requirements and could be taken home. This they determined as soon as they were admitted to the hall, and they knew who baked best.

Magnus observed Charlotte serving his father in front of one of the widows. She pretended he was a stranger and flirted with him politely.

'There you are, Mr Sparling. Wasn't the service beautiful? Just a dash of milk, Gillian, for Mr Sparling. Good girl.' She had the girl come out from behind the table and shake his hand.

It suddenly struck Magnus that his aunt was in love with his father. For how many years, he wondered. How had he missed this simple truth?

CHAPTER 22

I'm Your Son

Edwin found Magnus standing in the doorway between living room and hall, taking in air outside his breathing quota.

'What's the matter?' he asked.

'Just . . . the smell . . . '

'What smell? Dog?'

'Not dog. Not pure dog, at any rate. Dirty old vacuum cleaner.'

'That passes for the smell of living in these parts,' his father declared. The attitude seemed wistful, almost sentimental, before he waved Magnus out of the way.

Magnus went to the kitchen and made the tea. He brought it into the living room on a tray and put it out on the table as a butler would. He was conscious that his mundane actions seemed extraordinarily deliberate, even sinister in his father's presence, but for now, all his actions would be part of a ritual. That was a component in getting the truth out of a person, wasn't it? Coppers, schoolteachers and spymasters did it to worm out information. The motor-neuron function of the brain seemed to know what was required. The clock on the mantelpiece ticked above its weight, adding to an artificial sense of calm.

'Go ahead,' Magnus said carefully.

There was no reaction. Not so much as a twitch.

If it had been a brainstorm, a fit that had led Edwin to put poison in Stella's cup, the consequences must be clear to him now, Magnus was thinking. If it were so, then his father wasn't mad, and the attempted poisoning would constitute a crime of passion. In either case, Magnus decided, he would encourage the temptation to confess. 'So . . . ' he said. He left this little hooked word hanging in midair. It was perfectly pitched. The tone suggested that clarity had already been achieved and now all that remained was for humanity to be served. It was the kind of modest beginning at which Magnus normally excelled.

Edwin shook his head. 'Now you're getting angry, and I'm sorry for that.'

'*My father* is accused of . . .' Magnus opened his arms wide, in utter disbelief, 'of attempted murder. I'm asking him whether or not it is true.'

Edwin looked into space. Said nothing.

'You were so enraged, you forgot there was a human being drinking down that paraquat.'

'You're referring to your mother?' Edwin added for absolute clarity.

Magnus returned with a harsh laugh. His father laughed, too. His laugh lasted much longer. Magnus had to intervene because there was pain in it. 'You reached a breaking point,' he said. These general terms had to be used to winkle out the dirt.

'Not me, son.'

'A person can only take so much.'

'You think? All right.'

Magnus smarted with frustration. He looked at his father and saw that he was afraid. Saw an old man who didn't feel loved. Didn't expect to be loved. He was entitled to be afraid. Magnus abruptly rose to his feet and made restless animal movements.

Edwin sat as he was, eyes glistening. Was this a display of weakness or strength? Magnus couldn't tell. 'It's nearly six o'clock,' he said, gesturing to the television set. 'You'll want to watch the news.'

'How did you get to be so . . . so . . . ' Edwin couldn't find the word. 'So like you are.' Then, the word came. 'So controlled.'

'Controlled . . . ' Magnus repeated. That didn't hurt. It just pointed to limitations.

'And controlling,' his father added. 'That job of yours . . . .' The words had gone again.

'I thought you approved. You do. You approve.'

'You're good at it. You don't have to tell me.'

'Very good,' Magnus corrected, in an uncharacteristic burst of self-regard.

'But, you let it in too much,' Edwin said, tucking his fists under his ribs. 'Into your personal life.'

'Personal life – ah yes, well . . . ' Magnus was trying to sound deeply ironic. After all, pouring a glass of poison for one's wife must be deemed to be a controlling act, but now *he* was tongue-tied.

'How are you coping?' Edwin asked after a long silence. To Magnus this seemed like a lunatic attempt at role-reversal.

'You mean, how is Florence?'

'Yes.'

'She's making progress. We're moving on.'

'Good. I'm so glad. Your mother and I think about you constantly. You're coping?'

'Yes. I'm coping.' Magnus was resentful. His father's words sounded wildly insincere, and that was unbearable. 'I'm not here to talk about Florence and me.'

'No . . . .'

'But thank you anyway.'

Magnus squirmed. He jabbed at the 'on' button of the television set. He couldn't let the broadcast run beyond the opening summary of news headlines. He lowered the volume on the set, left the picture as distraction. 'You got the idea when you saw her lying in the hospital bed, didn't you?'

Silence.

'You're only sorry she didn't drink it down, the poor bitch.'

Edwin let out a bitter and involuntary guffaw.

Magnus didn't flinch. 'We need to make a start.'

'There is no case against me.'

'Speak it out.'

'I speak it out and you won't be shocked, is that what you're saying?'

'You *know* I won't.'

Silence.

Both men were angry now. Edwin went to the window where he stood and watched his neighbour, Jack, tidy up after the bin men. Jack liked to push the Sparlings' wheelie-bin back into their drive after it had been emptied. He did it for Stella. This wasn't about neighbourliness. Stella saw it for what it was: an act of evangelical flirtation.

Edwin was on to him, too. He wanted to say: *Listen, Jackie boy, you have no idea how far behind you are in the field.* But Jack was a pathetic old bags and would be content with that. Better to play long-arm fetch with Jack's dog and leave the man to his watery daydream.

'You really want to help me?' Edwin demanded, turning sharply to face Magnus.

'Yes, I want to help you. I'm your son. It's the rules.'

It was a flat statement that was curiously disarming. It took the heat out of their exchange and made Edwin come and sit down on the couch beside his son.

'Yes, yes, it is . . . ' he said, looking at the pattern in the faded Persian rug. He waited for Magnus to say something else, but nothing came because he, too, was waiting.

'Are you getting any sleep?' Magnus asked.

'I sleep.'

'I'm thinking about your back . . . '

'It's hard getting up. I can bend *and* I can come back up. Noel can't come back up without help. I can come back up.'

'I'm sorry you have pain.'

'That's enough about backs.'

'You won't let me help?'

'You're helping. You are.'

'How can I believe you know what you're doing? You tried to poison her, you didn't try to poison her – either way you don't present as a man who knows what he's doing. Put me right, dad.'

Magnus observed his father looking about the room. 'Stella and I were going to re-decorate,' Edwin said wanly, then he turned again to his son. 'If I said I did it, would you tell?' he asked in a deceptively light voice.

'I'd make a judgement. If something needed to be said, I'd find a way.'

'You'd tell?'

'I'd advocate – if anything needed to be clarified, put in context . . . . '

'If I told you I did what she's claiming, and I asked you not to speak out . . . ?'

'I'd make a judgement. I'd advocate.'

'You'd talk me into a confession?'

'I'd talk you through it.'

'And if I didn't want to confess, would you lie, once you knew?'

'I can lie.'

'You'd advocate, as you call it, before there was any speaking out?'

'I'd persuade you of the best course. Trust me, I will know the best course.'

'You'd tell her, I expect. You'd tell Stella I'd confessed?'

Magnus tilted his head to one side, then straightened it again. If telling was the order of the day, telling her would be part of routine procedure.

'That would warm her up,' his father said with some relish. He rubbed the bristles on his chin. 'I've got to work things out, haven't I? I've got to think clearly. Be straight with myself about what's being said. That's what you're saying, isn't it? I've got to think about the future. That way nobody can find fault – with the way I'm thinking, I mean. Can they?' There was a pause, then Edwin added: 'I forgot to get our groceries.'

CHAPTER 23

Rendering Normal

A hand slid over the nape of Magnus' neck and squeezed, with something just short of kindness. It was his own hand he discovered. He worked his head to make a partnership of it. The gravelly squelch was still there. As before, it came with rotation, but now also when he tilted his head or rocked it from side to side.

The nameless dog – the dog on which a name would not stick – was whimpering in its sleep. It was the small hours, but he went at it again with his father. 'Are you sick?' Magnus asked, tapping the side of his father's head.

This intimacy made Edwin flinch. 'I'm full of shit, these days, son. I want to give myself a good thump. I do. It's a good thing you're here.' He lumbered to the window, planted his feet apart, leant forwards so that he could rest his hands on the cold radiator. 'I was warned,' he said. '*She* warned me – your mother.'

'Warned you about what?'

'About leaving. She was going to leave. I told her that was the thing to do. We should separate.'

'It's the obvious solution. It's been that for years.' Magnus was skeptical. 'What's the timeframe on this announcement of hers?'

'She told me, then she got sick.'

'You had nothing to do with that bout of sickness, we know.'

This barb made Edwin lift his hands off the radiator and straighten his aching back. 'She's been leaving for years, now.' He made this a statement of fact.

'And what about *you* leaving? It's for the best, you say, and you go.'

'Are you going to see your mother, son?' Edwin asked. He had turned from the bay window and now shuffled closer for the answer.

'Oh, I am.'

'That's only proper.' He patted Magnus lightly on the shoulder. 'Just remember, 'he said in a fair voice, 'your mother is committed to tormenting others.'

He began rubbing the small of his back. 'When we first met I was around her like a hula-hoop.' Edwin was so amused by his own innocence that he scoffed. 'There was a time when we fought and both of us got something out of it.'

'It wasn't hell?' Magnus asked.

'No. She's a discerning scrapper, your mother. She can be kind, of course. When she talks about me to others. You really think I'd kill her off?' Edwin asked. The question came smartly and in a crisp voice. He had stopped rubbing the back, and his hands were ideally placed to offer dramatic effect.

It was an interesting choice of phrase, Magnus thought. His father had willed his face blank in preparation. It had taken real effort.

'You sound like her, now,' Magnus replied. He could sense the distress in his father, but he couldn't see it. 'You saw her lying in the hospital that first time, you heard her rant for days, and you thought . . . '

'I've thought about her not being here, yes,' his father admitted.

'You've fantasised?'

'No.'

In a spontaneous gesture that might usefully distract, Magnus told the old man about his fantasy. A magnanimous roller-coaster ride that took him back through his ex-girlfriends. One glorious connection with each, whatever the intimacy or the rancour there had been in the relationship. He loved them all, even the duds, and they, of course, loved him, and showed him as much in that fabulous moment. That way, he was sure it was a true fantasy.

Edwin gazed uncomprehendingly at his grown son. It was the crushing look Magnus remembered from boyhood, the look his father had given him when he was plucked out of the Mojave Desert. The old man had let out a little laugh of incredulity then, and he did it again now.

Suddenly, Edwin wanted to make a clarification: 'Are you asking about what might have been? Don't grasp at that, son.'

'One thing gets you thinking about another. Then, naturally, you begin to speculate.'

'You fill all that bloody space you're on about.'

'Something like that.' Magnus could see that the abstraction was making his father addled. He pressed ahead. 'Irene and Ned, look at the space they left.'

There was no look of incomprehension. 'It was a long time ago.'

'I'm sorry. I don't want to upset you. I just want to know if this stuff strikes you the way it strikes me.' What *is there* in that space? *That's* my question.'

Edwin's eyes came down from the ceiling and rested on the view up the hall. 'Nothing comes to mind,' he said carefully.

'What did you get from that visit to Bakersfield all those years ago? Tell me.'

His father shrugged. It was such a painful shrug that Magnus wanted to retract his words, but instead, pressed on. '*I* got something. I got to be with you for something special.'

'That was good, wasn't it? Even if you did take off on me, you little brat.'

'Going into that house was lousy. I hated it. Hated you for being weak. For using me.'

'As you say, it was a long time ago,' Edwin repeated in a more remote voice.

'There's not a day goes by that I don't think about you and me out there together. How big is that?'

His father didn't know how big it was. Magnus saw a space that could be filled here and now. 'You've done plenty for me. If you trust me . . . if we could get that close again . . . you could use me now and I'd be glad. I swear.'

'Sorry if I used you,' Edwin said.

'You've fantasised about Stella being dead?'

There was a philosophical point that needed to be raised here. 'You want to be able to find people, don't you?' Edwin asserted. Your ex-lovers. Even your enemies. You always want to keep track, don't you, son? If your mother was dead, I'd never be able to find her. Now that, I can't imagine.'

Was the old man play-acting? Magnus found himself suffering a kind of temporary amnesia. He stared at a piece of mangled plastic in the corner. Edwin's crisis had brought about a shift in his commitment vis-à-vis the dog. The dog belonged to his neighbour, Jack, but Edwin had bought one of those clutch-ball-and-throw sticks with which he could engage the animal without having to bend repeatedly, and thus save his back. He had done this to strengthen the bond, but the dog wasn't up to the retrieving. Edwin let it chew the stick. It was this that had Magnus transfixed. His amnesia lasted only seconds in real time, but completely derailed him. But then, Magnus had special knowledge of his father's ability to render normal the extraordinary, and to take the hurt.

'This will soon be over,' Edwin declared.

'Oh?'

'It will be finished with.'

'Well that's good news, isn't it? You're not thinking of trying again, I take it?'

There was no reply. Rather, a continuation. 'If they question me again, they will just ask the same questions.'

'You put the paraquat there on the arm of the chair, didn't you?'

There was an understandable pause. Magnus shaded his face, making a cave with his fingers, keeping his eyes locked on his father. He rubbed his temples with his thumbs.

'There's no case for me to answer,' Edwin said presently to the little animal in the cave. 'You should see that, Magnus, and accept it.'

'Tell me you didn't do it. That it's all in her imagination.'

'I didn't do it.'

Magnus slowly took his hands away from his head. It was the first outright denial.

'It's her malicious invention . . . ' Magnus said, fishing for absolute confirmation.

Edwin wouldn't say. Almost nodded, but stopped short.

Edwin found himself standing in the garage looking vacantly at objects. His memory was not some box out of which he arbitrarily pulled scraps of his past to paw and throw back. He was still vitally connected. Still committed to having the largest and most concise manifestation of his life he could assemble in his head. He liked to think he was using this to stay alive. That he could bar intrusions. Useless thoughts got flushed through. He revelled in birdsong in the garden: he was listening to it now. Later, he would hear the humming of that engine under the bonnet of his car. These sounds were good flushing agents.

He resolved to see his son's probing in the same light. Let Magnus probe. Let him expunge the superfluous and be enlightened.

'That old bike,' he said with a jerk of the head. 'You should use it.'

It was an old man's present, and an old man's way of giving: you can have that; take it away with you. This irked Magnus. 'I don't want a bike.'

'Use it to get around.'

Where did the old man think he'd be going? Did he think he'd be doing circles in the park? 'I won't be staying long.'

'She won't be using it,' Edwin said, jerking his head in the opposite direction, referring to Stella. 'Hasn't been up on it in years. She'd want you to use it.'

Magnus hated that bike for still being in the garage. 'Man, you have to fight your way in there.'

'Yeah?'

'Yeah. All that clutter. All that junk. You can barely get the car in. It's a disgrace.'

'You've been in there, have you?'

'Yes. I've been in there.'

'Snooping around.'

'Yes. Snooping around.'

'Well, you don't have to worry.'

'It's a fire hazard.'

'There's things in there . . . ' He didn't finish. Didn't go at it again.

'Things . . . ' Magnus echoed dismissively. Then, as suddenly as the tension had surfaced, it subsided. Snooping was acceptable under the circumstances – that seemed to be the message. 'The bike is there if I need it,' Magnus acknowledged.

'I wouldn't trust the brakes,' his father said presently. 'Not entirely.'

Magnus looked at him hard, expecting to find a subversive grin, but what he got was the old man sucking his teeth. 'What?'

'The brakes . . . '

'The brakes don't work, but you want me to use it?'

'I'm just warning you,' he said, mildly indignant. 'I don't want you breaking your neck.'

Out of the blue, Edwin said: 'Do you want some books? You can take any of my books.'

Edwin's books were precious to him. In his voice, Magnus heard despondency cut with a wistfulness. He had encountered this combination in politicians and senior public servants – a person being marvellously defeatist, sometimes to acknowledge culpability, but with mitigating circumstances. Or it was an assertion that they had been beaten a little early by forces to which we all eventually succumbed.

'No, dad. I don't want your books. What are you thinking?'

'They're no use to me.' He didn't mean it. Magnus knew that, but had to follow through because the offer was genuine, and that was touching.

'You don't believe that. Even if you never opened another book, they're there. That matters enormously, doesn't it? You can look at those shelves and wonder. You can pull down any one of them. No no, you're just pretending. Shame on you.'

The old man was gratified. 'I want you to take something you'd like,' he persisted. 'You appreciate books.'

Magnus felt that his father might take something down from a shelf and force it into his hands. What was going on? 'You should hold on to what you have,' he heard himself say. 'Don't be giving things away.'

'You'll be getting this house,' he announced bluntly. ' But you're mother won't want to sell it if she survives me.'

If she survives me had an unfortunate ring to it. 'Look,' said Magnus, putting his hands out and spreading his fingers, 'whatever makes sense. All in good time. I didn't come here to talk about inheritance.'

'You should have it before either of us goes. Better hurry up, says you, eh? Ha. Insofar as I communicate with your mother, I'm talking to her about the house. She'll do it, I'm sure.'

There was more of that marvellous defeatism in the wan smile that came with these remarks. Magnus was set gently rocking on his heels. Edwin put a hand on his shoulder. 'You choose some books, son,' he said. 'I can give you a canvas bag.'

Magnus had his father marked as a man who would want to reread all his favourite books in old age. It was disturbing to him that Edwin was prepared to part with them willy-nilly. It wasn't right.

When Edwin left him alone in the room, Magnus found himself looking along the spines of the novels, the biographies, the books on art and architecture, and poetry. There were more upstairs, and on shelves on the landing and in the bedrooms. In the corner where he was looking now, there was a substantial collection of popular romance hardbacks by authors he had never heard of, that had been on the shelves since he was a child. Unlike the others, they were dressed in. A long time ago they must have thought it was something they should have. Maybe they kept them for their lush covers and their titles.

Magnus stood at his bedroom window scanning the park across the street. He was watching for a fox his father said made regular visits, stepping out through the railings and pausing a long while before making its way along the pavement and across into Jack's front garden, never theirs. The waiting at the window and the watching eased him into a trance. It had him running a memory stream, had him in a lonely rapture from teenage years. He shook himself out of it. He needed to be properly orientated towards the here and now – which, of late, presented as remarkably illusive.

The patience and endurance Magnus showed interrogating his father wasn't entirely matched by physical fortitude. He was tired. His legs were giving out underneath him. He had been standing at the bedroom window too long, and now he desperately needed to lie down. Which he did, and went to sleep directly. In his sleep he was perfectly orientated. The back of his head seemed to provide for this on the basis that there would only be confusion when he woke.

CHAPTER 24

Detective Richie

Magnus put on his coat and checked himself in the hall mirror to make sure he was ready to be interviewed by Detective Garda Richie. He made a formal entrance to the kitchen, where he found his father shelling and eating nuts over the stainless-steel bin. Edwin had already been drinking, and was fully aware of his drunkenness.

'Want some?' he asked, holding out the bag of pistachios, giving a little giggle for encouragement.

'No thanks, dad.'

He went on eating without a break until the bag was finished. Magnus thought it best to sit it out. If he could read anything in his father's expression, it was only that the pleasure derived from this packet of nuts met precisely some need in him. For Magnus, it was an opportunity to demonstrate that there would be, for a short time longer, a perfect tension between his patience and determination.

'There's another bag,' his father said, cleaning his teeth of nut fragments with his tongue. 'Don't know where it's gone to.' He knew about Magnus' appointment. Knew they would question him. 'You don't want to be late,' he said, waving limply at the hall door.

Edwin had taken to looking for fossils in the stonework of buildings across the city. He had brought the dog with him. It didn't like these corners to piss on. It didn't know where to stand when the old man was inspecting the walls. It got under his feet. It got pushed out of the way. Edwin poured over the rough and the smooth, moving the tips of his fingers across the surfaces, seeking out the stone imprints. Edwin was not a religious seeker. These little nuggets incidentally revealed the profound pleasure of the natural world. This ancient architect could appreciate the abundance of fossils in the city's fabric. A man could be hollowed out, and still he would wonder, if he cared to look.

He was thinking he would go on one of his fossil-hunting trips while Magnus was with the detective. He might do it without the dog. Metropolitan fossils were a good distraction for a man accused of attempting to kill his wife.

On the way to the Garda station, Magnus imagined committing the crime himself – imagined attempting to poison his mother. He needed something to happen in his imagination to clear this impasse. That was where the important action would take place right now. He needed to throw his weight around in his head to see what might give, so he thought about poisoning Stella.

He assumed the motive and set aside the moral argument. Proceeded on the basis that the action was essential. It was an exercise, after all. It didn't take much imaginative muscle, which was good, because it was a relatively short journey to the Garda station, and the traffic was moving smoothly.

The act of poisoning was easy enough if a person kept to a simple plan, was meticulous, and maintained their nerve. Getting the lethal liquid was not difficult. Many such liquids were available for a range of ordinary purposes. The action hinged on whether or not it was credible that Stella had knowingly or inadvertently consumed the stuff herself. Never mind circumstantial evidence to the contrary. A court would have to prove that in this instance he, Magnus, had deliberately administered the paraquat.

It wasn't difficult to imagine at all. He walked it through in his head, made it happen in real time, and allowed for a pause on the stairs, in the bedroom, in the kitchen, in the hall, as he thought a murderer might. In the projected living room, he stared at the chair she liked to sit in. The fat arms of it. The side table. She'd been in hospital, right? Hallucinating. Deluded. Bitter and twisted for years, and now very depressed after her hospitalisation.

The problem was, of course, getting her to drink it. Some of it, at any rate. A little would do. He could force her. Grizzly, but effective. A little down the red lane would be enough. And a little more, to be sure. He would have to be careful that there was no bruising.

In this fantasy there was something about her meeting her end via the mouth that was vaguely satisfying. Satisfaction that was enhanced by the prospect of mourners eating Aunt Charlotte's thick, well-filled sandwiches after the funeral. It had to do with primal nurturing, or the lack of it, Magnus was thinking.

This was an exercise that permitted no moral judgement, he reminded himself. Was it credible? That was the question.

Yes, he decided.

Could he see his father, Edwin Sparling, do it?

Magnus was seized by a debilitating numbness of the head. A sudden, if temporary, paralysis in his powers of reason. When this lifted as the taxi slowed by the rank of double-parked Garda cars, Magnus could only conclude that Edwin might have done the deed.

The visitor's seat was more comfortable than he had expected. Magnus sat across from the interviewing detective with his eyes wide and unblinking. It was a worldly and wily stare. There was no resentment evident. Both men were looking for a way to show patience and equanimity, and to begin their formal exchange with a simple challenge.

It was Magnus who seized the initiative. 'He told you nothing?'

'Oh, we had a long talk,' Detective Garda Richie replied. His confident tone suggested that he thought Edwin would come squarely to the matter in good time.

'Nothing useful. You couldn't get inside his head. Is that what you're telling me? Well, it doesn't surprise me. He's a quiet man.'

'He is. I like him.'

'Are you allowed to say that?'

'No. I'm not.' He followed on directly. 'If your father didn't do this thing, we'll establish that.'

'And if he did . . . ?'

'It will be evident. We're both here to establish the facts.'

'Yes.' Magnus was used to clever, slippery chaps. Knew how they probed to ascertain the breadth and the depth of a person's knowledge, and their confidence. 'I feel I can talk to you.'

'You can.'

Magnus knew that sometimes, these people used an inappropriate or ambiguous phrase, or a contrary tone, to maintain their own smokescreen.

'There are few facts to examine.'

'It's difficult. I can see that.'

'And I'm required to speculate, to begin with.'

'I understand.'

'To begin with, I'm saying.'

'Yes. I hear.'

'You might do it with me.'

'If you're asking for background . . . '

'To begin with.'

'You want to hear about the family?' Detective Richie winced, which surprised Magnus. 'Well, what is it you want?'

'You don't know yourself what he's done.'

'If he's done anything.'

'There now – you have it . . . to begin with.'

'Can I see the cup?' Magnus asked. He didn't want the tone of this simple question to be too casual, nor the words too weighty. He failed on both counts.

Detective Richie studied Magnus closely. He seemed to be waiting for an echo. Why would a man want to see such a thing? Did he doubt that the cup belonged to the household?

No. Magnus just wanted to gaze upon the object. It might help him contemplate the proposition. 'You do have it here,' Magnus continued, 'in one of your plastic bags?'

For all his composure, Magnus was incredulous. Shock, the detective knew, could cause a person to fixate on a particular object. He'd seen a man kiss a hammer in that same chair. Shock could make strange with a pair of hands. 'We do,' he replied presently, 'we have the cup. One of a set from your parents' kitchen.'

'With the blue stripes?' It sounded like a trick question. That was not the intention. 'Those awful thick blue-striped cups,' Magnus added, 'from the sixties.'

'I remember them myself,' the detective said formally. Magnus wanted to see that particular cup, but he wasn't going to be let just now. 'What do you suppose happened?' the detective asked, changing his tone expertly, but affecting a clumsy shift to a more comfortable position in his chair.

'Nothing,' Magnus replied flatly. 'Nothing happened.'

'You fully understand the accusation?'

'I do.'

Detective Richie seemed to think it wise, in the interim, not to repeat the phrase 'attempted murder', lest it lose some of its potency. Best to keep it all in what he saw as civil-service mode. 'Drama, you think?' he said with perfectly pitched understatement. 'I understand,' he added, without waiting for a response.

'You do?'

'I do, of course. People with high emotions . . . ' He didn't finish. Didn't take that line anywhere for now. Instead, he invited Magnus to make his observations with a sudden quizzical freezing of facial muscles. Magnus blanked this with a wistful swivelling of the eyes. He picked out objects in the detective's office: propelling pencil, shop-bought sandwich in plastic, grubby computer keyboard, filing cabinet with key in lock. He named each item in his head as he took it in. Detective Richie was a smart man. He'd know he was being stonewalled, and would change tack.

But by way of encouragement, Detective Richie gave out with a series of slight, sharply canted nods. It was like watching somebody with a tic. There was the urge to imitate. To try it out in case it brought some perverse comfort.

Magnus could resist. He was a master at ignoring tics. The civil service had taught him that. Only the Permanent Secretary defeated him.

'Tell me about the investigation,' Magnus said, knowing that the file was piteously thin.

'What is it you want to know?' Detective Richie asked, knowing that Magnus was a smart fellow in public service and would be comfortable with his tightness.

'My mother dialed 999,' Magnus said, to lead him in directly.

'She did.'

'And then?'

'We responded.'

'Oh, come on.'

'She made her accusation.'

'You know she's been in hospital?'

'She told us. St Vincent's. Cardiac trouble.'

'She went off the rails.'

'Are you saying there is a history of mental illness?'

'She went completely off the rails. The doctors and nurses will confirm that.'

'March of last year, wasn't it?'

'Yes.'

'She made a full recovery, as I understand it.'

'She was deluded. She told me she had been shot. She said the Guards were in to interview her.'

'It's not unusual to be disorientated, wouldn't you say, given the drugs administered.'

'You'll not have that particular interview on file.'

'It's very upsetting, this whole business, I know.'

Magnus didn't appear upset. He was clear focused. Intent. The detective was gratified by the sharpness of the exchange.

'There were the DTs, of course, as well as the drugs they gave her,' Magnus added.

'We had the doctor examine her, though she drank none of the liquid.'

'And the doctor said she was as strong as a horse.'

Richie smiled. 'She's in good health.'

'Physically.'

'You're suggesting there should be an assessment of your mother's mental health?'

'I would have thought that was essential in these cases.'

'We are investigating whether or not there is a case to answer. Are you suggesting your mother's mental health is in question?'

'Well, we could say that her nerves have been at her,' Magnus declared with heavy irony.

'And what does your mother think of her son, Mr Sparling?'

'Of *me*? Magnus readily grasped that this was the cunning, oblique, slippery stuff for which cops were noted.

'Yes.'

'Why do you ask?'

'She seems to think you have the answers.'

'What answers?'

'That you know what's been going on. Has she reasonable expectations, Mr Sparling?'

Magnus took a moment to consider what his mother thought of him. Magnus was special from that day on the beach. That was him taken care of. What a discovery: Magnus was mature for his age as a boy. At the age of fourteen, didn't he do the sensible thing when he got lost in the desert and find Indians to take him to a petrol station. He was gifted with wisdom beyond his years. Well balanced. Good mannered. Intelligent without being boastful. He couldn't hide any of it, and that made him a decent fellow who never deviated from a decent course in life. It was no surprise at all that he was now a top-ranking Whitehall civil servant. Leave it to Magnus Sparling.

'Say what you will, Magnus, you'll not be bad to your mother' – he could hear her say it in his head – 'I know what you're made of. Your father does, too. You know him. Didn't he take you everywhere with him?'

'She has high expectations of others,' Magnus told the detective.

'Is easily disappointed in people, is that what you're telling me?'

'Easily disappointed. Yes.'

'She's given to exaggeration, perhaps?'

'Look. I haven't seen much of my parents for quite some time . . . '

'You were saying her nerves have been at her . . . .' He began to write on a cheap narrow-rule A4 pad. 'You don't mind?' he said, belatedly holding up his pen, then stabbing the paper. 'I need to hold a clear picture.'

Magnus indicated that he had no objection. He, too, was comfortable with the exchange, despite the slippery cop stuff. Conforming was, after all, central to his existence.

'I will, of course, be asking the same of your father,' the detective continued. 'About his mental state, I mean.'

'He's a rock.'

The detective wrote down the phrase. Now this, Magnus found a little annoying. Then, Detective Richie clumsily changed gear. He rose to his feet, took a few steps in his shiny flannels. His caramel-coloured shoes had thick leather soles. Obviously he didn't get to run after villains in the streets, Magnus noted.

'It's a continuum, isn't it?' Richie said, pretending to gaze out the window. The windows were grimy. They hadn't been cleaned for a year or more. Cutbacks.

'What is?' Magnus enquired.

'Mental health. There isn't a dividing line between those of us who are mentally ill and those who are not.'

He was testing Magnus. Seeing if he would follow wherever he was led. Seeing how readily this public servant would offer an opinion. He hadn't offered much thus far, but that didn't throw our interrogator.

'It's a continuum,' Magnus echoed mildly.

'So the experts tell us, Mr Sparling,' Richie added, quick to match that mildness. He turned on his thick leather heels for effect.

In short, mental was better than legal for Magnus. Mental didn't frighten him. He felt he was still connected. He knew a lot about the mental continuum, but he didn't need to tell the cop. The old man had quietly gone mad – yes. Magnus had to admit that was how to make sense of such a poor show of judgement. Same for his mother.

Clearly, there wasn't any hard evidence of a crime having been committed. Unless something new came to light, this investigation would be a ritual acted out in the name of thoroughness. Magnus knew how this detective was operating and, to be fair, the detective had quickly grasped that fact. They both would play on regardless.

'It's a difficult business,' Richie said, and left a considerable gap before adding, 'wouldn't you say?'

These flaccid general observations were dangerous. They could break concentration. They could make a man feel patronised and get drawn into his resentment. Magnus Sparling was well acquainted with this primitive technique. 'It is,' he replied.

'You must be distraught in yourself. I meant to acknowledge that properly the first time we spoke on the phone. I'm sorry.'

He had acknowledged it. 'I'm sure you come across this kind of situation on a regular basis,' Magnus said.

'No,' came the reply.

'This kind of *difficulty*,' Magnus added with renewed emphasis.

'This kind of difficulty . . . yes. Where we have an accusation – a very strong accusation – and an equally strong denial . . . ' he didn't finish.

'And nothing much to go on.' The moment these words left his lips, Magnus knew that his concentration had been broken.

Detective Richie cultivated another silence. Then, he said, 'We can ask for a psychiatric assessment, you understand?'

'You can insist?'

'We can. Under certain circumstances. Of course, a voluntary assessment might be the way to go.'

'Yes. I see.'

'I knew you would, Mr Sparling. And I'm sorry for the trouble.'

Magnus had recovered from his lapse of concentration. This would help close it down, the detective was saying. The definitive report could be written and signed off.

'Are you suggesting both of them?' Magnus asked calmly.

'We'd take an interest in both, yes.'

A state-appointed psychologist was not mentioned. They could be drafted in later if it was established that there was a legal case to answer. There was no need to burden the exchequer.

Suddenly, the matter was in Magnus' lap. The whole sorry mess. When Detective Richie walked him to the lift, there seemed to be no criminal investigation in the offing. Detectives, however, were all cunning fellows, and some more so than others.

Two plain-clothes cops in the lift greeted Magnus as though he were a colleague from another department. Magnus left the building shaking his head. Recently, he had been hearing a gravelly squelch when he turned his head to the left or right. He couldn't tell whether the sound travelled the normal route in through the ear, or was picked up by the hearing apparatus inside his head. He was hearing that gravelly squelch now when he shook his head. Tilting didn't have the same effect. Not yet, at any rate. This was an age thing, perhaps. He hadn't yet reached the age when this sound would also come with tilting. This was a new caveat for Magnus, though he felt he had it coming.

Everywhere, it seemed, he was seeing magpies in pairs. Dirty, oil-smeared, decrepit specimens hop-hobbling in his path, calling at him with their bad-tempered rattle. They were in the trees outside the Garda station in Harcourt Street; they were strutting on the pavements; they were congregating in the park opposite his father's house. What class of jaundiced luck was this, he wondered. He had an urge now to raise two fingers to the lot of them, but these pairs didn't look his way. They were expert at merely presenting themselves.

CHAPTER 25

Noel Will Have the Truth

Magnus went directly to meet with Noel. Noel Ffrench, with two 'f's, was Edwin's oldest living friend. It would be accurate to say they were as brothers. The older they got, the more they resembled siblings.

'Noel and I don't much like each other any more,' Edwin had told his son, without conviction.

'And why is that?' Magnus had asked.

'You got me there.'

Noel had spruced himself up for the outing. He had oiled his thinning hair. Had tied a good knot in a clean tie. Had brushed his stained suede shoes. Had put a hanky in the breast pocket of his sports jacket. By turns, he smelt of Old Spice aftershave and sleeping dog. His walrus moustache was thicker than Magnus remembered. It still held its colour. His glasses were very much larger than previous models. The lenses were thicker and made the man's eyes appear ridiculously sincere. His distended stomach had become a defining feature: it had blown out that very day, it seemed, if one judged by the way he walked to the pub nearby.

'How's your mother holding up?' he asked Magnus.

'Have you seen her since this episode?'

'No.'

'Edwin's been acting strange, you have to admit.'

'Strange? What's strange? He has a sore back, if that's what you mean. How's his back?'

'He says *you* have a bad back.'

'No I don't. Is that strange, or what?' he added without interest.

'He's confused, you think?'

'Confused, telling lies, making mischief . . . who knows?'

'And that doesn't bother you?'

'I tell you what bothers me: my hearing isn't what it used to be. I can miss some of what's said if you're not talking directly to me. Women's voices in particular, if they're being reproachful or they're confiding. It's like they're talking to me in a dream.'

'That's nice sometimes, I expect.'

'No. It's just confusing. I have to be careful. Get them front-on. If I don't get them front-on I still get the gist, but the words . . . '

'They float off.'

'No. They're too soft.'

They went into the pub, found a quiet corner, ordered coffee. 'Look at that,' scoffed Noel, 'feckin' tubes of sugar. That's new for in here. I'm not sleeping, Magnus. I'm worrying about Edwin's situation.'

'Edwin's and Stella's.'

'And Stella's. Of course. Stella and her sisters, and you in the thick of it.'

Tactically, Magnus thought it best to give Noel a little time to come out with whatever had been agreed with Edwin as a patch-up job. He got him talking about the trip to Holland to view Rembrandt paintings.

'Old men looking at each other, and no nonsense,' Noel observed dryly, and made a great snuffling noise.

This gave Magnus mental hiccups. It made sense, of course. He held his mental breath and continued to nod. 'The two of you just flew to Amsterdam . . . '

'It was your dad's idea to go. We were complaining too much. We needed a project. We went to see the paintings. We couldn't get enough.'

'Like a couple of old queens, if you ask me.'

Noel let out a great burst of savage laughter. 'Wait till I tell Edwin.'

'He's always looking to go somewhere, isn't he?'

'Yes. He is.'

'It's not restlessness. He's hunting. Don't ask me for what. Edwin is a secret hunter.'

'He's looking for contentment, I expect.'

'He's done good work, Magnus. He's a fine architect. Retirement doesn't suit him.'

'I know.' There was a pause. Magnus could see that Noel wanted to disassociate himself from the concept.

When Magnus asked about the accusation laid against Edwin, Noel's eyes brightened. He leaned in and whispered like criminal, 'I forgive him.'

'You forgive him?' Magnus repeated with a steely burr.

'And you should forgive him, too.' Noel's bright eyes were no longer darting furtively left and right. They were searching Magnus' face for the pragmatism and the forbearance he was sure was there.

'He confessed to you?'

Noel waved these words away into thin air. He wasn't going to speak on such terms.

'You'd forgive him had he succeeded?' Magnus asked.

There was no poisoning, Noel said, his bony hand now adjusting the glasses on his face.

'This is incredible,' Magnus declared. 'You think Stella is safe now?'

'Yes. She's safe. It's some kind of bloody theatre.'

Magnus went at it afresh, as he thought. 'You meet Edwin and you talk . . . ?'

'Yes, we meet and we talk. Why wouldn't we talk?'

'You've talked about him trying to poison Stella?'

Noel widened his eyes, made them bulge with reproof. Then, he changed tack. 'Your mother likes me. Always has done. I'm a good influence on Edwin, she'll tell you. She likes Edwin and me talking.'

Magnus didn't know where this approach was leading. 'She's a smart woman, my mother,' he said.

'She is,' Noel replied positively.

'Noel, you sound just like my father.'

Noel didn't like that. Impersonating a friend wasn't how friendship worked. He drew a shallow breath through his teeth. 'You think your mother invented the story?' he asked.

'Do *you*?'

Noel gave the slightest of shrugs.

Magnus said, 'The cops aren't sure either way. You must tell me if you think she's lying.'

Noel held his steady gaze for a moment longer, then let his eyes roll off Magnus. 'We must be thankful,' he said carefully.

Magnus straightened his spine. 'I'm talking to myself here. I am, amn't I?' There was no direct reply. Noel clicked his tongue several times, then told Magnus that Edwin had been getting quietly drunk and weeping. 'That's been going on a while now.'

'Since before – '

'Yes,' Noel cut in. He was now intent on probing. He carefully peeled off his big glasses and held them at arm's length, his elbow resting on the back of the adjacent chair. 'There's something you're not telling me,' he declared in his plain, dry-throat voice. His big eyes were no longer roaming. 'Are you going to rat him out? You can talk to me. I'm not squeamish. You don't get embarrassed at my age.'

'You sound a lot like him, Noel. That's a fact.'

'I'll be talking to your dad again. He's not hiding from me.'

'There's nothing you can tell me now . . . ?'

'You could visit him more often.'

Magnus nodded despondently.

'I'll call him when we're finished,' Noel repeated once again. 'You happy now?'

Magnus was convinced that Edwin had, indeed, confided in Noel. Had fully confided. Magnus was sickened that the same was not afforded, father to son, and that he had not known about his father getting drunk and weeping until Noel Ffrench had told him.

CHAPTER 26

My Father, a Man of Action

'I've talked to Noel. Magnus lowered his chin and raised his eyebrows to encourage a confession on the basis that Edwin's friend had let something slip.

'So, he asked about my back?'

'He did. He was concerned about you.'

'Was he complaining about his feet?'

'Not to me.'

'He saw socks he liked, going cheap. He bought six pairs. He complains they burn his feet.'

'Where is she now, dad?' Magnus said heavily. 'Where is Stella right this minute? Do you know?'

'Gone,' Edwin replied pleasantly. He knew it was a test. 'Like smoke through a keyhole.'

Magnus didn't like the tone. Didn't like his father's forced wistfulness, didn't like his own bitterness. 'You *know* where she's gone.'

'To her sister. You know that. Stop trying to catch me out. It's hard to get used to this new regime, isn't it?'

Magnus looked at his father incredulously, but the fizz had already gone out of the old man's words. Magnus could see he was tormented.

It was Magnus' turn at the bay window. 'Do you remember Taaffe?' he asked.

'Taaffe? No. Who is Taaffe?'

'Primary-school toughie.'

'The name doesn't ring a bell. Should I remember? Taaffe . . . ?'

'I tried to kept away from him. When you heard that Taaffe was bullying me . . . . You're sure you don't remember?'

'Remind me.'

'I came into the classroom one day and you were sitting in the desk beside Taaffe. All the kids were looking on in astonishment – except the teacher and Taaffe. The teacher began the lessons and you stayed there all morning. You must remember.'

'Oh yes,' his father said mildly. Whether or not he did remember couldn't be judged.

'Miss Lavery, the teacher, pretended you weren't there.'

'I must have arranged it with her.'

'Of course you did. I saw you lean in towards Taaffe and just stare at him. It gave me goosebumps.'

'Did I talk to him?'

'No.'

'Good. He never gave you any more trouble, did he?'

'Never.'

'I'm sure it was your mother's idea.'

'That was a red-letter day. I saw that my dad would take action.'

Edwin pretended not to see the significance. Later, Magnus found his father in the garage, sitting behind the wheel of his Daimler. He got in beside him.

'I'm thinking about Stella being dead again, the old man said, keeping his eyes on the imaginary road ahead.

'Are you? Well that's helpful.'

'I'm thinking the deceased partner comes to meet the survivor halfway. They want to harmonise. Even Stella.

Magnus noted that his father had cast himself in the role of survivor. 'There's a coming together, is that what you're saying?'

'There is. With obvious limitations.'

'All the acrimony is – redundant?'

'A lot of it falls away.'

So, this was a picture of Edwin, the wife-killer, in mourning. It was intriguing. 'You could look forward to that,' Magnus said deviously.

'There's no planning for it,' he father insisted.

'It's a comforting thought.'

'There's no meeting up with them after,' Edwin added, as a sinker.

'No?'

'No. You want to make your peace across the divide.'

'I understand.'

'Nature helps. Out in the garden is a good spot.'

Magnus was finding it difficult to keep up. 'In the quiet . . . that's where you commune . . . .'

'Or in the park.'

'The park. Our park? Yes . . . '

'I'm sorry for the anger I've caused.'

'Let's walk.'

'I've to get the groceries. Have you change?' Edwin asked in the car on the way to the shopping centre. 'I need two two-euro coins, or four one-euro coins, or eight fifty-cent coins. Or any combination that doesn't include brown coins that adds up to four.'

Magnus was able to make up the required amount. He did not ask what the change was for. He just handed it over.

Edwin parked in an underground space reserved for parent-with-child shoppers. They ascended on the moving slope behind the kiddie rides. There was something in Edwin's gait as they made their way along the concourse that spoke of his longing for the right kind of separation, the fixed proximity, the forgiveness and the peace that came with it. Loneliness was not an issue. Any tears Magnus would shed for his dead mother would only help in the process of realignment. A son could be properly separated, too, and the whole sorry business be well represented.

Edwin shuffled quietly along to the spot where there were internet consoles and a massage chair. He'd never seen anybody sit here, though he assumed all kinds might use a machine like this. Nurses, murderers, retired policemen. He sat down, put his coins into the slot, and pressed the start button. 'Good idea,' Magnus declared unconvincingly when he saw what his father was doing, and stepped into a newsagents. 'Just getting the headlines.'

A big-stride hippie accompanied by his petit flower-child woman passed the massage chair at close quarters. He made a scrubbing bear-paw sound with each step in his enormous old boots. She made no sound at all. They both acknowledged Edwin and he readily responded. The greeting had something to do with the chair, or common humanity; he didn't know which. Why hadn't Magnus become a hippie, he wondered idly when the couple had gone and the meter had run out on the massage. It certainly wasn't anything he or Stella had said to put him off.

Magnus was too much like his father, he decided.

CHAPTER 27

Sailor's Grip

Magnus's job made him patient, even wise, in the face of unfinished business, but he was leaving for London feeling defeated. He was convinced of his father's guilt, but had no certain knowledge of it. He was getting himself ready in the hall when his father approached with a smile of dismay and bursting with emotion. They had invested their recent exchanges with a curious and powerful flatness. Edwin wanted to embrace his son. Show his strength that way.

'Your mother says I tried to poison her,' he said, taking hold with a gentle clumsiness. 'I did not.'

'I hear you,' said Magnus.

Edwin pushed himself off. The slowness of the movement blighted Magnus' efforts at meaningful engagement. His father peeled away, like a fish into the dark. How callous he himself had become, Magnus was thinking. How curiously disconnected from his mother and father, whatever their states of mind.

Magnus took a walk around inside his head, imagined Edwin in Charlotte's garage reaching down the paraquat from the high shelf, stared into the living room at the spot where Stella's body might have come to rest. He drew an imaginary jack-knife chalk outline. Or did they use duct-tape on carpet? Magnus could summon the image without difficulty. In his mind he could advance on her blank, staring eyes without getting involved. Take in the no-breathing aspect. The deadness of her.

'Have a lie down,' Edwin said breathlessly from behind him. 'Catch a later flight. You're very tired. I can tell.' Edwin had already taken the car out of the cluttered garage. It was sitting in the drive ready to take them to the airport. Magnus struggled with the hall door, forgetting for a moment that Edwin now locked it from the inside.

'Sorry. Sorry, son,' Edwin said, fumbling for his keys. Magnus steadied his father with a strange and vigorous handshake that he changed to a sailor's grip.

In the car on the way to the airport, Magnus wondered if he had contributed to Edwin's murderous inclination. He recalled standing at the ward window staring down into the hospital car park at a lamp made fuzzy by soft rain, recalled letting his eyes drift across to Stella in her bed, imagined her leathery little heart boxing her brittle ribs, and in that moment had found himself willing a sudden stoppage. An all-embracing, deadly seizure that produced the final cardiac uppercut. He had imagined hearing the beady swish of the curtain being pulled around the bed, had imagined hearing the light tread of the reverend's feet down the corridor, had imagined seeing the undertaker wiping off her makeup so that he could start from scratch.

A man under pressure sometimes comes to regard his trials as being connected to each other with an uncanny synchronicity. On the plane back to Heathrow, Magnus cautioned himself against such thinking. Instead, he recalled lying down again on the beach next to his blood-talisman, but the body kept moving away. Magnus was strapped in his seat and was sitting bolt upright, and still that righteous pig, that pig of panic he had come to fear, was able to get up on his chest. It started with a modest tattoo, and built from there. He thought about the baby, and Florence in her moon crater. Whispered their names. 'Just remember,' Magnus' friend in Holland Park had said when he broke the news of Florence's pregnancy, 'that when your wife looks at your child, she sees the best of you. And *you* are what's left.' His good friend who had later taken in the baby gear for indefinite storage.

Part 3

CHAPTER 28

The Boy Saved from the Desert

'Did you dream you'd be out here?' the Mojave asks Magnus. It seems like a perfectly sensible question. Magnus likes the bigness of it. He shakes his head to indicate that he had not, but this is a chance to talk big.

'I found a body once,' he says. He needs to make this story his own again. These people, he thinks, will be interested.

'You did?'

'Yes . . . .' Now what does he say? They don't seem interested, at all. 'It was on a beach.'

'You called to cops?'

'No. I stayed with him until somebody came.' Their not being interested didn't feel bad.

'Like you stay with this car without gas?'

'It was special,' Magnus declares, without knowing quite what the old man means.

The old man nods. Magnus doesn't know what kind of a nod it is. He wants to say that this is another special day, this one gone bad for his father, and turning good for him, but he takes his lead from his rescuers. He keeps it flat.

'This one died of old age on the beach?'

'I think so.'

'You did good to stay.' The statement is bereft of drama, so ordinary, so uncomplicated. Magnus is overcome with a fit of nodding, which is greeted with indifference.

At the gas station, the old Mojave takes a Coke from the cold box, gives it to Magnus and puts him sitting in the shade of the porch. The wind is up again but the air is dry and hot. Magnus feels that his cheeks will blister. He hasn't felt that

149

until now. The old man stands in the doorway to speak to the station owner, a wiry fellow of indeterminate age, with silky black hair and glasses. These men know each other. Magnus hears the owner call the Indian, Pete. Hears Pete say: 'John, I found that boy in the desert. He's been kicked in the head by the sun.'

'Needs attention?' John asks, stepping out from behind his glass-tomb counter in his cracked shoes, which somehow go with his broken front teeth. The tops of these teeth have been snapped off along a clean diagonal line.

'I guess. Somebody needs to talk to him. Find out where he belongs.' His finder doesn't mind Magnus hearing their conversation. In fact, that seems to be the purpose of holding open the door with the edge of his boot. The teenager stays in the truck. The other one sits down on the porch bench beside Magnus and rests his feet on their heels.

'How far did he go?' John asks, looking out the window at the back of the boy's head.

'Well off the road. About ten miles out. Lost near the cut.'

'He weren't walking?'

'No. In a Buick. No gas. No one else around.'

John goes to the window for a closer look. Takes in the boy with his jaw slack. 'You think he stole it?'

'Maybe.'

'He speak to you?'

'No. Just his name. Magnus.'

'Magnus . . . ? Magnus what?'

'Don't know.'

'How old, would you say?'

'Fourteen. Fifteen.'

John sidled back beside Pete. 'He don't look American in them clothes.'

'No. He don't.'

John guffaws. When they bring Magnus inside, the wind blows into the shop. The ring-pull on the blind taps on the glass. On the porch the one called Judd lulls his head in the boy's direction, looking askance through the dusty window.

Magnus acts a little strangely. He rests his chin on the display counter over the sweets and stationery, cigarette lighters and Indian beads. But he's not looking at these goods. He's taking in the glass surface that has been dulled by a mesh of tiny scratches. He hasn't yet determined whether or not this is a terrible predicament. The warmth from such a display cabinet would normally be pleasing to his hands, but his skin is burning and the sweet, oily musk smell of the place mixing with body odour is making him weak at the knees.

'You see something you like?' the owner asks in a loud, upbeat voice.

'No,' Magnus replies in a whisper. He is finding it difficult to think straight.

'Too bad, too bad,' says the owner with a crooked grin. 'I could give you a knockdown price.'

'Thank you,' says Magnus. He ceases his whispering because the old Mojave is squinting with annoyance at his puny utterances. He wants him to speak out so that he and his sons can forget him and go about their business.

A gaunt but attractive middle-aged women comes from the back to stand and watch. She strikes an angular pose to give notice that she isn't about to say anything but is keen to listen to the news. When Magnus brings his head up, he nearly falls over. Somebody gets a chair for him. America is gentler than he has imagined. Even the hunter in the woods by the shopping mall trod softly. It is his own actions and those of his father that have made their passage difficult. It seems to Magnus that these are actory people not easily shocked, and good at coping. A man like this gas-station owner will continue to wear his glasses in heaven. They won't bother giving this man the tops of his teeth.

Meeting the bloods was bad. Being on the road is the thing. Magnus prefers the company of the Mojave to the gas-station man, but this is part of being on the road. They have brought him here, so he will do as he is told.

'You steal that car?' the owner asks, with a little private encouragement.

Magnus shakes his head.

'Your daddy's car?'

Magnus shakes his head.

'Your momma's car?'

Magnus shakes his head.

'You rented that car?'

Magnus shakes his head because *he* didn't rent it.

The Indian stamps his foot. It sends up a little cloud of dust. 'Magnus . . . you got burned up. You speak to John, here.'

Magnus nods.

'What do you say you tell me who your mom and dad are, and I'll give them a call?' John says, looking at close quarters. The burning isn't too bad, he determines.

Magnus offers no reply. Instead, he looks out the window to young Judd. Looks at his cactus ink tattoos. The gas-station owner prods Magnus' arm with a knuckle. 'What do you say?'

Magnus has a flash of Walt, the dead man in his casket at the beauty spot in the mountains. Was his gas station anything like this one? A man could die easily before his time in a place like this. Magnus takes a deep swig from his Coke, and this makes him choke.

'I got things I got to do,' Pete says.

'You need gas,' John asks.

'No.'

John gives the boy another light poke. This one is accompanied by a sudden bad-breath smile. 'These folks are leaving now. You and me – we'll make a call.'

Edwin's blood-mother doesn't appear to be the same person. Seems older, more dithery. As for Edwin's father – he holds back in the kitchen. He is three-parts ghost. Edwin can see they are more afraid than before. This second visit confirms he has come to disturb their lives. It is true.

Edwin puts out his hand to shake the hand of his stranger mother, even as she is dancing her nervous dance in the hallway. She cannot make sense of her son's immediate predicament. Neither of them can grasp what Edwin wants. They are fearful that there is some awful price that they must now pay.

The boy has gone missing – it is a primal alarm sounding, but they can't understand what might have happened and how the path leads to their door. They need to know urgently what it is Edwin wants. They see the tightness in his chest. His shallow breathing. They see he is trembling. When Edwin spells it out, they offer to get in their car and come looking.

At the same time, they invite him in. This adds to the confusion. They are glad to see him again, she says.

It is obvious now that he should go to the police.

The cop comes in his cop car, before the Mojave can leave Magnus in the gas station.

Magnus waves to the Indians from the front passenger window as the squad car turns. He continues to wave out the rear window as it pulls away. The Mojaves don't wave back. They are showing their collective disapproval of a boy going out into the desert without knowledge, without dreaming the dream of a tortoise that can find water, without sufficient gas in the tank.

Magnus waves furiously, but they do not wave back. They just stand and watch the squad car drive into the distance. The gaunt woman keeps her arms folded, but she is smiling triumphantly. What's this to her, Magnus wonders. He will never know. The gas-station owner does wave, or rather, raises a hand in the air and leaves it there for a time. His glasses catch the sun and produce a blinding glint, which prompts Magnus to give up and turn to face forwards in the seat.

'You heard John Peatree telling me you don't talk?' Hunter Dobbs, the cop, says. He waits patiently for a nod. 'That's all right. I wouldn't want you talking to them. You ain't scared, are you?'

Magnus shakes his head.

'I knew you weren't. I'm just making conversation.' He looks over the boy again. 'You're not too burned up, but we'll let the doctor see you, then we'll decide what to do. You lose your hat?'

Magnus shakes his head cautiously. This is going somewhere.

'You don't have a hat?'

Magnus shakes his head.

'But you have a car?'

Magnus hesitates before he nods, even more cautiously than before.

'Don't you worry,' says Hunter Dobbs, speaking the words slowly, 'I'll see you get your car back. I know those guys. They can take me to the spot. You want your car back, don't you?'

Treating a boy as though he is an adult – that is an old trick, even if it is the way to go. Magnus offers no response this time. Hunter Dobbs continues regardless.

'What's these guys names? I forget. The Mojave – they tell you their names?'

No response, but Magnus is thinking that Americans are good at getting together to do stuff. Good also at cheering and clapping.

'It looks real bad if I go asking them to take me to your car and they say, "Hey there, Hunter Dobbs . . . " and I'm supposed to know their names – particularly the old guy...'

'Pete,' Magnus says. He's sure this cop knows the names of the Indians.

'Pete,' Hunter Dobbs shouts loudly, and thumps the steering wheel. 'That's him. That's the old guy. So, what do I call you, because it gets embarrassing for me if I can't introduce you to the doc.'

'Magnus.'

'Magnus? Now that's a name. I don't know anybody called Magnus. Not until this minute. And where are you from, Magnus?' Hunter Dobbs's voice is booming, the result of his success at getting the little burnt fella to talk.

But Magnus isn't going to say where he is from.

'You got any questions for me, Magnus?' It is that generous American voice that says I'm looking to share all the fun we can make together, little brother, starting right now. They are coasting down the road in this cop car that has everything a cop car should have. Magnus relaxes into the seat and puts his hands up over his head to stick the tops of his fingers through the heavy wire mesh that divides front from back.

'The old Indian – he isn't really called Pete, is he?' Magnus ventures.

'Yes, he is. It suits him, don't you think?'

Magnus shrugs. He can see Hunter Dobbs trying to place his accent. 'I'm not from America,' he says.

'Didn't think you were,' Hunter replied smoothly.

'You think I'm English . . . '

153

'I do not.'

Magnus likes the way he talks. Likes the playful exaggeration. 'Scottish, you think . . . ' he goes on.

'Where you're from is your business,' Hunter says cheerily. 'You'll tell me if you want to, when you want to.'

Magnus doesn't know what to make of this, so he just looks out the window, but he thinks he should finish. 'The other Indians . . . their names are Judd and . . . and . . . '

'I don't know the boy's name, either,' Hunter chips in. 'Now, that Judd, *he* has a temper. But, that kid's name . . . nope, it isn't coming back to me.' He laughs.

'That's their real names, you swear?'

'That's their names. I swear. And I don't swear much.'

The radio squawks into life. Headquarters wants to know is the boy being brought in, because the doctor had arrived at the station. Magnus takes his fingers out of the grille. He is being talked about over American cop airwaves. Hunter Dobbs confirms. Has ID been established? Negative. Hunter Dobbs winks at Magnus. A little shudder runs down the boy's ribs. He asks if there is a weather forecast due on the radio. He wants to listen to the weather.

'Oh, you do?' says his new friend.

'For the sake of the car,' Magnus explains.

Hunter gives out with a snort of amusement. 'I'll get you the weather, Magnus,' he says. He is thinking he likes the boy's name.

Hunter Dobbs is the first person Magnus has encountered who properly fits the description: old before his time. The man is skinny and tough and battered, but this doesn't seem to bother him. Not any more, at any rate. This sort of aging happens quickly, Magnus assumes – which is funny for a man who can't be hurried. Hunter Dobbs is the perfect fit, he is thinking, because he is a good actor and can carry it. That makes him a good cop.

The muscles around Magnus' eyes are sore from squinting, but that isn't why he asks Hunter Dobbs if he can have a go of his gold-rimmed mirror sunglasses. This country cop knows about the wild, about cars, animals and guns, as well as local villains. At home, all the country cops posted in the city didn't know who the villains were and, fortunately for the rest, had no guns and no sunglasses. Magnus wants to see through American cop sunglasses.

Hunter lets him have a go, but just for a minute. Magus looks out at the expanse of desert with this exquisite filtration, but his body shudders. How can a desert be so cold at night? He had not known cold like it; a cold that makes you afraid. His muscles ache from contraction, from keeping his arms wrapped around himself through the stormy night. He had been brave all that day with his father, but not brave enough – which was why he's shuddering now, he thinks.

'I better have them back, Magnus,' Hunter Dobbs says, holding out his hand.

The sun is sinking fast. All kinds of desert-night creatures will be wetting their bellies or sticking their long tongues into the tiny streams that run unbroken under the fences of military installations, and across terrain worked for borax, silver and tungsten.

'What were you doing out there, Magnus?'

'Looking for coyotes,' Magnus lies.

'You see any?'

'Nah.'

'They're always watching.'

Somehow, this answer is satisfying for the boy.

Magnus tells Hunter Dobbs his father doesn't talk much. It has to do with concentrating. If his father loses concentration, they will lose their way, and then he will forget why they have come to America, and they will never get back home. That would be no bad thing, except what will happen to his mother? She will be lost, too. Nobody will die, but they will all be lost.

'You could remind your dad why you came to America,' Hunter says, trying not to sound cunning.

Magnus doesn't mind telling the cop why they've come here. Tells him about visiting his father's blood relative, his real mother. There is a danger his father might just leave him in a motel by accident. Fathers can do such things if they are in a trance, like his dad. Magnus says, he knew to keep his mouth shut on the way to the relative. Keep it shut unless he had questions about something he saw on the road, or about food, or music, or the evangelical ministers on the radio, or he was reporting a cop car or a truck with a gun rack, or a dead skunk. After they met the blood it was different, he explains.

'You see a dead skunk?' Dobbs asks. He just can't help being smart.

No, but Magnus' father has told him to watch out for them.

'And your dad knows how you two got here?'

Of course he knows. There's nothing wrong with his head. They had flown here in a plane from Ireland. They had hired the brown convertible car to come looking for the blood relative.

'Ireland?'

'Yes. Dublin.'

Can Magnus write down his address?

He can. He writes it on the blank side of a form Hunter has on a clipboard.

Is there a telephone number?

Magnus recites the telephone number. Hunter gets him to add that on paper. And who will answer the telephone if somebody calls?

His mother, of course.

And her name?

Stella.

That's a nice name.

That's what he calls her, Magnus adds. He doesn't call her mum.

And he calls his father by his Christian name, too?

Yes. Edwin.

And he likes that?

He does. Except he hadn't called him Edwin for days. Not since they arrived in America to visit the blood relative.

And who is this blood relative? What's their name?

Irene. He doesn't know the surname. He'll ask his father when he's out of his trance.

Does Edwin go into a trance because he has taken something? Pills? Or has been drinking?

No. He's been too busy concentrating.

Ah . . . And does Stella not want to come to America?

No. They'd had a row. She and Edwin will be splitting up when they can organise it.

And does Stella know about the trip to America? Did she come to the airport to wave goodbye?

She knows about the trip. And no, she didn't come to the airport. She shouted something awful from the window as the taxi pulled away from the house. But it will all work out now that they've found the blood-relative and she's not wanted either. It will work out unless his dad is in trouble now. Is he in trouble?

People are just concerned.

Does that mean trouble?

It can't be said for sure, but he's not to worry.

Cops can find out about the blood-relatives, can't they? Edwin should have gone to the cops first. Do cops stop to pick up dead skunks? Do they carry a shovel? Do they put them in the boot?

Where did he learn to drive?

An American car is easy to drive if you're not a shortie, and you've been paying attention. Magnus is no shortie, and has been watching his father driving, has been imitating him. He still won't be able to drive in Dublin.

He tells the cop about staying at the Silver Rails, and at the Providence.

Hunter Dobbs is a good skin, he decides. He asks for a go of the handcuffs. If he gets a go of the handcuffs, he'll ask to hold the cop's gun.

CHAPTER 29

Rain Dance

At the police station there are questions about the blood relative.
'She's a nice lady?' the desk sergeant asks.
Magnus shakes his head, indicating firmly he does not think so.
The sergeant tries again. 'She's difficult to like?'
Magnus nods. Difficult.
'She'd be your grandma . . . .' This has already been established, but the sergeant thinks confirmation might soften the boy's attitude.
Magnus nods. She is, unfortunately.
'So, you want to try to like her?'
Magnus shakes his head. He doesn't like the suggestion.
'That's too bad . . . .'
Some kind of concession is called for, he realises, so Magnus nods again.

'My grandma lived in Tucson,' the sergeant says. "She kept chickens and a whole heap of junk in her yard. Used to embarrass the hell out of me when I went to visit.' The sergeant sees that Magnus had become more attentive. 'Tell you what . . . I wish I'd spent more time with her.' He gives Magnus a long look. 'She's gone now,' he says, eyes blazing.

The doctor is overweight. His watch-strap is too tight. Somehow, that connects with him being patient. Even his sweating is the patient type. Little beads that don't form rivulets. He has a soft voice: he talks to himself and wants to be kind. This notwithstanding, his examination seems to Magnus to involve a disproportionate amount of gawking and psychological strategies to politely test for madness – which, in the end, is no bad thing, because evidently, Magnus is not mad. He had thrown up out of the window of Hunter Dobbs's cop car

157

just as they pulled into the station lot, but he is suffering from mild sunstroke, the doctor confirms. He might throw up again. Rehydration is essential. These cops know the drill. Something out of a sachet is dissolved in water and given to him. Medicated cream is applied to the skin that has been exposed. Magnus is to rest. A mild sedative is prescribed. A follow-up appointment is to be made with a doctor.

When the examination is complete, the doctor squeezes Magnus' head between his big doughy hands, and smiles. 'This boy . . .' – he breaks off to commune with Hunter Dobbs and the others, each in turn – 'this boy is lucky, and he knows it.' He takes his hands away, as though wanting to see if the head will remain on the shoulders. 'Don't you?'

Magnus nods. The head stays on. The doctor is pleased. 'He knows it,' he confirms to himself.

'We can get the car back,' Magnus says plaintively.

His father turns his head slowly and stares at him uncomprehendingly.

'It can be found,' Magnus assures him. 'It's not too far.'

The staring continues, then Edwin breaks the fluttering silence. 'You can find it out there in the desert?' His voice is small, patient, unsettling.

Magnus hesitates, feels his ribs contract, as they did when he threw up outside the house in Bakersfield. 'They can find it,' he says.

'Who?' his father asks, leaning his face in, making like he wants to scare his son with this one-word question. 'Your new friends?' he adds.

Edwin begins to shudder. This shuddering becomes a mock rain dance. It seems to Magnus that the sadness in his father has turned to a terrible meanness. He is mesmerised by his father's inhibited foot-lifting and his loose arms, which are extraordinarily strange and unfamiliar in their movement, but then, he has never seen his father do any kind of dance.

When he stops, Edwin sinks onto the bed, but sits bolt upright. His father needs comforting, Magnus realises, but does not know how he can comfort him. 'We can get the car back tomorrow, dad,' he says.

A boy knows all the lines on his father's face. Knows how they bunch together to form a smile or a frown. Can read their configuration the moment his father steps through the door from work. But Magnus has not seen this alignment before, this complex bunching. He has seen his father merry with drink, but never wretchedly drunk with worry. 'It just needs petrol,' Magnus adds. 'We don't need to fix the roof.'

Nor has he seen his father cry, and now he sees the man's angry eyes fill with tears. Magnus cannot fully connect this terrible reality with his taking the car into the desert and running out, but he knows he has brought it on. It has a lot to do with being loved, or not being loved. It makes him want to dance his father's dance and cry his own tears.

But he does not. Some unknown force determines that he should stand as he is and bear witness with his entire being. *This* is the end of boyhood as surely as his father's meeting with his blood parents marks his father's coming of age. Watching this dance, *not* the driving into the desert, is the end of boyhood. The bloods, he notes, did not perform for his dad.

They retrieve the car. This is not the companionship Magnus wants, but it is part of their journey. They fill the tank. John Peatree's mechanic fixes the roof, though it doesn't sit quite right.

All the way back to Los Angeles, they have the windows and the roof up, and the air-conditioning on. There are jets of warm air leaking in, and that is new. The car doesn't sound the same. It doesn't like where it has been, but that has to be ignored.

Before they return the car, Edwin drives them around Hollywood, but they don't feel like swanks. They stop to visit a department store, to buy the shirts they had promised themselves they would buy for the desert climate, shirts they will bring home now. They drive down part of Sunset Boulevard, but Magnus can identify no whores and doesn't dare ask his father to point them out.

Magnus feels he has cheated his father on the car, and he hopes this city tour will make up for that, but his father is tired and inattentive, and Magnus believes he has failed to be a good son.

They are both inured, not despondent. They are sleepy and dull-witted – which is how it should be for two people exhausted from their trials. Together, they have done this thing and already some great but ill-defined opportunity is passing.

Edwin continues their baggy tour, even when Magnus falls asleep. He runs low on fuel, and finally he has to make a dash for the airport, because he has miscalculated and they are running late.

'We're here, Magnus,' he calls out.

Magnus wakes, blunted and speechless, but the Sparlings are not yet at the airport. Not even close to it. It will be another twenty-five minutes before they reach the airport buildings.

CHAPTER 30

Home and Adrift

As the plane banks over Dublin bay, Magnus and Edwin can see the mist creeping in from the sea, up the River Liffey, with fingers pushing up the River Dodder, the Tolka, the Royal Canal and the Grand Canal.

The plane puts down on a wet runway with a jolt and a screech of rubber. There is a welcome in Irish, which reminds Magnus that he is still in school.

Damp, cold air seeps in from around the mouth of the gangway. The faces of the ground staff at the door are evidence that the cold and the damp is general and persistent. But the air is also fresh and familiar, and offers assurance of quick re-assimilation.

Stella is in the arrivals hall to meet them. To a stranger's eyes, she might appear to greet Edwin as though he were a sick relative coming for treatment, but Magnus can tell by the way his mother takes his father's arm that an important judgement has been made, and it is unforgiving. He can tell by the way his father lets her hands sit that this judgement has been anticipated.

Stella embraces Magnus. Kisses him and playfully rubs away the lipstick. Magnus can determine less from this than from her fixed linking with his dad, and there is much to determine, given that they have gone on this voyage of discovery without her, and without her blessing. She looks stunning, of course. That is to be expected. And today, she has made a special effort.

'Now,' she says, 'you both are very tired. I'm taking you home. We'll put hot-water bottles in the beds and you can sleep all day. Then, you can tell me all about it.'

Stella has come to the airport in a taxi. Edwin wishes he had driven to the airport in the Daimler, now that he must acknowledge that a new but ill-defined phase in their life together has taken hold.

Magnus wants to assert himself here. In the taxi home, he thinks of telling Stella everything, but decides he should tell her only that it has gone wrong. The journey hasn't worked. The blood-family is bad. God is to blame. But his father is silent, so he says nothing.

He could give her details about things that didn't matter. About the clothes. The food. The motel. Not about his father being drunk, or his own meeting with the Mojave. They were special. Deeply personal. He could never adequately explain.

Stella is the one doing the talking in the taxi. She knows about Magnus driving the hired car. Edwin had told her in a desperate phone-call. She pretends she approves. Magnus feels he should show false modesty. He finds it difficult to conceal the excitement he still feels at his dad taking his hands off the steering wheel, never mind his protest drive into the desert.

She would want to know that he had thrown up, but he doesn't tell her, because he wouldn't want to tell her why. It would put his dad in a bad light. It would make it look like she was right about it being a bad trip in the first place. He might tell her he was nearly shot by a hunter in the woods beside a shopping mall. He can do that because it isn't about bloods, or his father, or the quivering of his own heart. A heart that is sometimes there in his chest, sometimes not.

On their return to Dublin, Magnus finds there is feeling of disaffection between himself and his father. It is not acrimonious. Edwin simply has withdrawn, and this is a consequence of their trip. Magnus' father remains affable, but in a most vague manner. The reunion with his blood-parents has not given him the contentment he seeks.

Magnus is sure he has failed his father by being curious instead of obedient. Closeness has not been achieved. He had failed to reach the high standards that went with being a chosen companion. He had betrayed his father by stealing the car and driving into the desert. He had been easily seduced in the house of bloods. He had eaten the cake. He had been boy-stupid, and too much his fourteen years when more had been called for. He had been the boy who had found the body on the beach. Now, he was the boy who had run away.

Part of the punishment was that Stella would not talk to her son about the American venture, though she wanted him to give her information. It fell to Aunt Charlotte to show interest, and her interest was enormous. She collected Stella and Magnus, and brought them to her house. She laid on a big spread in the dining room, which was a most unusual act, as all meals, except Christmas dinner, were had in the kitchen.

Stella was not speaking to Edwin. Aunt Charlotte met him separately in Bewley's Café in Westmoreland Street after his work. With a little coaxing, she thought she might get a lot out of him, but he refused to talk about the reunion in Bakersfield, other than to give the barest facts. She didn't press him. Instead, she squeezed his hand, smiled across the marble-top table, and let her eyes water.

'You were captured by Indians?' Charlotte said. That much she had already gleaned from the boy.

'I was,' Magnus replied.

'You were not, you little liar,' she said, bursting with excitement and trepidation. 'Tell me everything.'

Magnus knew she wanted to hear about the bloods, so he told her. He passed on every detail he could recall. She listened patiently. She seemed to grasp every nuance. She made encouraging noises that Magnus knew were not forced. He liked her getting emotional.

'You were minding your daddy,' she repeated more than once, to reassure her nephew. 'You did such a good job.' Charlotte was fully aware of the trouble between Stella and Edwin, and that Magnus had been taken to America against her sister's wishes. 'That was a good thing to say,' she said, when Magnus told her about being sorry for throwing up on the bloods' lawn. What he wanted to tell his aunt was that he was sorry for having eaten their cake.

He told her about them being afraid. About visiting Sean and Angelica's rooms. Then, he jumped back. 'Dad and I were in town early,' he explained, 'so we hung out with some tramps.'

'Did you? And how did you like that?'

Magnus shrugged. It was all right. Then he said sheepishly, 'The Indians . . . I wasn't actually captured.'

'But it must have been scary,' Charlotte came in without hesitation. 'What kind of Indians were they? I'm very interested.'

'Mojave.'

'Mojave,' Charlotte repeated, as though the word triggered a magnificent vision.

'They don't say much,' Magnus went on. He pretended to play down his encounter, but really, he wanted to share absolutely everything.

'No?'

'But maybe when they're by themselves . . . '

'Oh yes. I'm sure.'

'They gave me a lift out of the desert.'

'That must have been wonderful.'

Magnus didn't quite know what kind of wonder she was referring to, but he was encouraged. She got him to describe the Mojave, physically. She asked about their clothes and their speech. Magnus gave a description, and also gave an account of the storm and reported on the pickup truck. Charlotte was very impressed.

He didn't like the gas-station owner with the broken slanty teeth, though he couldn't say why. Hunter Dobbs, the cop, and the doctor at the police station were good. He gave descriptions of them, too. Charlotte was enthralled, but asked again about his father's meeting with his blood relatives. Magnus gave physical descriptions of his grandmother and grandfather. He told her that only his blood grandmother had any time for him, that the grandfather, Ned, was a waster. He didn't like either of them.

'Oh, and did I tell you about meeting the hunter with his gun and his dog in the trees by a shopping mall . . . ?' He jumped here when he thought Aunt Charlotte was losing concentration.

After America, there were no more trips accompanying Edwin to the county hospitals or asylums. There was a bank strike, a heatwave, and the first motor show to be held in Dublin. It was two months before Edwin could reconvert the remainder of his dollars at the bank. Edwin did take Magnus to the motor show in the heat. They wore the light shirts they had bought in the US. The notion of trading in the Daimler on a new Ford Capri now seemed absurd.

Magnus' aunts pulled at him more than they ever had before. Pulled playfully at his ears, buffeted his cheeks, stroked his head, planted more lipstick kisses. His mother, too, seemed to fuss over him more than she had ever done, but she was also absent from the house more often. His father spoke to him in the same moderate voice that Magnus had taken for granted, but now his words had shadows.

Stella and Edwin still attended gala dinners in Dublin hotels. Stella went to the same hotels at quieter times with her lovers. There were, after all, up-to-the-minute establishments occupying the twilight place between public and private, where Stella and her partner would meet other clandestine couples in the bars and the lifts.

One school half-day Wednesday, an occasion when Stella's lover had cancelled, Magnus asked his mother why she was looking at him as though he was a stranger who smelled of something rotten. She told him his hair was too long – which was unreasonable, because she liked it long and he said as much. She wasn't prepared to listen. At fourteen, he was too old to be taken to the barbers, but Stella got him in there, and somehow made him feel she was accompanying him as a favour.

She had her way of descending the steep stair tunnel. She made a lot of noise with her high heels on the flecked linoleum steps that had metal trims. This ensured that when she arrived in the shop with Magnus lagging behind, the three barbers were waiting with broad, expectant smiles. Though it had been some time since she had been there, they recognised her heel-strikes, and she was more than welcome.

'Well, hello, Mrs Sparling. And how are you?'

'Hello, men,' she replied. Magnus liked to shout 'Hello, God' in empty churches. It was like that.

The men in the chairs knew it was a welcome return. They smiled, too. They knew it was humiliating to have your mother take you to the barber's at the age of fourteen. They seemed to grasp that that was the point of the visit.

'He's been with the Indians in America,' Stella announced.

'Has he?' Johnny, the oldest and oiliest barber, said. This one disgusted Magnus. Unluckily, he was the one closest to finishing with a customer. Magnus would get his chair. 'It *is* long, Mrs Sparling,' Oily John said, snivelling over her prudence, and giving the boy a patronising wink. Then, in a mock whisper, added, 'We'll not scalp you.'

But he did, of course. That was the punishment. Magnus shouldn't have gone with his father to America without expressly seeking her permission – which would have been denied. She had listened to his stories of their adventures, and this was the result.

'America,' said Oily to Stella, 'that must have been the trip of a lifetime.'

'I didn't go.'

'Oh, you didn't?' Oily declared, lost in admiration. 'And are you going anywhere nice for the summer?' He had kept the rhythm with his scissors. Had professionally adjusted the angle of his customer's head without any effort.

'We're going to Donegal,' she said in a neutral tone. 'Again.'

'Donegal. That's a lovely place. Never been there myself, but beautiful, I hear.'

'Magnus likes it. Don't you, dear?'

'No.'

Magnus was soon in the chair.

'There's a lot on here,' Johnny said. 'When did you last get it cut?'

'I don't remember.'

'Oh, you don't remember?' Johnny was glad to have the boy rise to the bait. 'Before you went away to America?'

'Obviously.'

'He wouldn't get it cut when he should have,' Stella said, glad that the game of humiliation was fully under way. She made it sound like she had pestered him up to the last before waving him off on the plane – which Magnus thought was devious.

'She didn't want me to go,' he snapped. Could he drive a wedge between them? No, he didn't think so, but he had to try. Heavy emphasis on the 'she' was good. Was he really at the centre of this? Magnus took a hard look at himself in the mirror.

'Ah well, you see,' the barber said, leaning back on one heel, 'that's your mother.'

'She hated me and dad going.'

Stella came in again, steering decisively. 'As regards the hair, Johnny,' she said, 'a sensible cut is what's needed.'

'There's a lot here.'

'He put on a spurt in America.'

'Is that what happens when a fella meets with Indians, ha?' Oily gave Magnus a dunt on the shoulder.

'Travelling long distances in jets, maybe,' Stella added.

'Maybe, Mrs Sparling.'

Stella gave the barber a terrible Caesar-like nod that allowed for a free hand. Magnus' hair began to fall onto his shoulders and slide off the nylon cape. Johnny was taking large lumps at a time. Magnus wanted to spring out of the chair and punch his tormentor. He couldn't bear his Mojaves being treated as a joke. He wanted to curse at his mother in front of these men. He resolved he would not talk to her in Donegal.

When he was a small boy sitting in this big chair, he used to glance at his mother in the mirror to make sure she was watching. 'Close your eyes,' she used to say when he was getting his fringe cut. Well, he wouldn't be closing his eyes today. He kept his eyes locked on himself. 'I want it layered,' he said through gritted teeth.

'Oh aye,' came the reply.

'No fringe.'

'A parting in the centre, is it?'

'No.'

'I'll see you right.' Then, instead of addressing Stella in the mirror, he turned to her directly. In Magnus' eyes, it was an insidious courtesy. 'There's a lot on here,' he repeated.

'I don't want much off,' Magnus snarled.

'I know,' Johnny said. Stella was smiling indulgently at the barber. This smiling went back as far as Magnus could remember. Why hadn't it been his father's job to take him to the barber's? This was sickening.

Johnny got quicker with his scissors.

'That's enough,' Magnus announced.

'I can't leave it like that, son. You can see I've only done one side. Leave it to me. You'll be the smartest boy in school.'

'I don't want to be smart,' he whinnied. He wished he was an adult and didn't have to whinny.

Stella was rooting in her handbag. She was enjoying her visit. She had acknowledged every man in the shop, each with a slightly different configuration of her lips. The three barbers liked her witnessing their skill with scissors and comb. Liked having her inhale their smell, and the smell of men's dressing spirits in the air. The men in the chairs puffed with their willingness to submit to a shearing.

'What part of America were you in?' Oily asked.

'I drove in the Mojave desert.'

'Did you?' The humiliation had been redoubled. A boy driving a big American car, but still needing his mammy to take him to the barber's.

Magnus glanced at his mother. She was smiling at him as she had smiled at all the men in the room. She lit a cigarette. All the men loved that. They weren't interested in the desert.

'How's Mr Sparling?' another of the barbers asked. The tall, bony one.

'Very well,' Stella replied without hesitation.

'He was in recently. As you know.'

'A nice job you did on him.'

'Thank you, Mrs Sparling.'

'He likes Donegal, too,' she reported.

'That's good,' replied Skinny, suddenly at odds.

Magnus pressed his feet hard onto the footplate. 'I'm finished,' he said.

'Not just yet,' said his tormentor. 'When I'm finished, will you want oil?' he asked. Then, in the mirror: 'Will he want oil?'

'Yes,' his mother replied.

'Fuck,' Magnus said – which was a shocking thing to say. Not once in America had he uttered that word where anybody could hear. It was offered here not merely as a specific rebuff, but as a general cry of discontentment.

In any case, that changed the atmosphere somewhat.

CHAPTER 31

The File

'Fuck,' Magnus declared in his civil-service whisper when he switched on his phone again at Heathrow. He had missed a call from Detective Richie. After he rang Richie, he would travel directly to visit Florence at the clinic. Where was his beloved Florence in all of this? Magnus had been keeping her out. Keeping her safe. He had been protecting her in her moonscape. He was greedy for time with her. He wanted to get her out of the day clinic. Yes, it was time to press her to come out, he was sure. Magnus needed her at his side, just as a father had once needed his son to draw the heat and the chill from bloods.

He rang Richie before descending to the Tube station.

'Detective Richie . . . '

'Mr Sparling. I spoke with your father again.'

'You're going to tell me you learnt nothing useful for your investigation?'

'He's quite the gentleman, your father.'

'You still like him?'

'Yes. I still like him.'

'And you're allowed to say as much?'

'No. I'm not.'

'I suppose we'll never know.'

'There is nothing more for us here. The allegation remains on file.'

'Well, that is the requirement. Thank you, Guard. Now, I must go.'

'Of course. You're a busy man. Goodbye, Mr Sparling.'

'You're not going to ask me about making any psychiatric referral?'

'I am not.'

'Thank you, Detective Richie.'

CHAPTER 32

What it is to be Ready

'This is for you,' Florence said, handing Magnus a folded dress.

'How is it for me?' he asked.

'It's for your birthday.'

She was right. It was his birthday. He was unsure about what he should say or do. She held the folded garment steadily in front of him.

'You like this dress. You said it was your favourite.'

'I did, didn't I? And it is.'

'Here. It's your birthday, and it's something you really like.'

'But what will I do with it? I can't wear it.'

'You can keep it.'

'I prefer to see it on you.'

'You won't see it on me. It's yours now.'

'You think I would wear it?' he said, trying to make light of the gesture.

'It would be yours,' she replied solemnly. She wanted him to get it clear in his head that the dress was more than just material with a nice print. It was the finest poplin, superbly cut. It wasn't that it would remind him of her. It was that she knew he liked it. 'Happy birthday,' she said.

She was not deterred by his reaction, but she moved her body self-consciously. 'I've nothing else,' she said. She saw that he was getting upset. She wanted to reassure him.

'It's a beautiful dress,' she said. She was still holding it out. 'It's been one of *my* favourites.'

'I know,' he replied.

'And you didn't give it to me. No one gave it to me. I bought it myself.'

It floated between them on her palm. It was meticulously folded, but flattened imperfectly, not ironed or pressed. Flattened overnight under a mattress, perhaps.

168

Maybe this was the way forward. So he took the dress from her. Buried his face in it. Inhaled her smell. Without removing the material from his face, Magnus let out a broken *screak*, which was an unfamiliar sound to both of them.

Florence was greatly heartened. 'There,' she said. 'That wasn't difficult.'

He followed her out of the room, drew level with her on the corridor, and was first out the door, into the gardens. They had their established walk past the rose-beds, through the trees, around by the wall that buffers the noise of heavy traffic on the far side.

'This place is getting you down,' he said cautiously.

'They're helping me here,' Florence replied, after a time.

'I know they are.'

'I haven't been able to think.'

'There's nothing to explain.' Magnus didn't want his own grief surfacing. 'I understand.'

'I'm looking after myself.'

'I know you are.'

'Magnus, I want you to know that I'm ready to leave.' She flushed with the desire to know again the glory of being alive. 'I'm going to make us our own dinner.' She looked at him as though a little asteroid had fallen from the sky into her freshly shelled colander of peas. 'Then, I need to get back to the library. There's a mountain of work.' When she said this, Magnus was looking at her auburn hair, which was not fully gathered, nor brushed, nor braided, but was going its own way. It provided a perfect asymmetry to the broad, fine-featured face he studied. She looked at him directly. Didn't pout. Didn't blink. She swept back a strand of hair with a hooked finger. 'I tell you what: you have no idea how much work I have to do at the library. I hope I still have a job.'

Magnus nodded with gusto, said nothing, swallowed lightly.

'We had a good wedding,' Florence said. 'We had a baby. We had the funeral. People love us for that.'

'They do?' Magnus replied in sudden confusion.

There was no conceit here. 'They do, Magnus,' she insisted.

Her readiness, Magnus saw, was a small miracle. An irresistible force. He was overcome with relief.

Florence made him tell her again about his boyhood visits to asylums accompanying his father.

'They weren't just asylums,' he reminded her.

'Whatever: Edwin's going to work, he brings you with him, you carry his rolls of architect's plans. Go on, tell me, Magnus . . . ' Before he had begun, she jumped in again: 'God, you must have loved it. Come on, we'll get a coffee.'

They left the centre and crossed the street to a nondescript café, where she pressed him again to retell the story. She wound her hair in her fingers, while Magnus told her again about childhood trips to the regional hospitals in Ireland; those aging structures that were being renovated, extended. Modernised.

'Edwin liked to take me on some of his professional visits,' he opened with. 'I took it to be part of my broader education in life and was happy to go. It was usually during school holidays, but sometimes on a Saturday; occasionally he took my out of school for the day. It was educational, but there was another aspect. I recognised that I performed a service for him. I was a decoy of sorts. An ice-breaker. A diffuser of unwanted attention. I knew he was a shy man, and that shyness brought pain and embarrassment. I gladly took to my role as little grinner. I always put out my hand for shaking. I could distinguish between the hospital administrator, consultant, site boss and general medical staff member.'

' "Hello doctor. Hello nurse." I shook their hands with a firm adult downward stroke. If we came upon the chapel on our sorties down corridors, I would pull open the doors and call out, "Hello, God." '

' "Stop it," Edwin would whisper harshly – loud enough for anyone who might hear us to catch his admonishing tone – but, really, he was always amused. I can see him now flush with embarrassment and boyish mischief – which was why I did it in the first place.

' "Never turn down a cup of tea," he'd tell me, so I didn't. There was a lot of tea and biscuits and wanting to pee. He knew, of course, that I would wander when I'd go for a pee. He warned me against upsetting patients and staff. "Patients will stare," he'd say, "but you shouldn't be alarmed."

' "Expect loony stares," I'd echo. "I'll not mind." '

' "They might follow you a while," he'd say.'

' "They can come after me," I'd say, "I don't care." '

'He wasn't saying these were all good people. Innocents abroad. He was careful not to categorise, but to signal that he himself was at ease with them when the encounter was casual. "They might speak to you. Just smile and say, *Oh aye*." '

' "Oh aye," I'd repeat.'

' "With these people you don't want to know what they're on about, but you want to be polite." '

' "Oh aye," I'd say again. This was grown-up stuff, and I was glad to be included. It made me believe that my father, though shy, was not afraid. I loved that kind of secret connecting with him. I saw then that he practised what he preached with a genuine kindness, whether the encounters were with the placid or the jerky, unpredictable ones. None of my friends were getting this experience, and I didn't blab to them about it. I fancied I was growing up ahead of schedule – which is true. I was destined to learn best by apprenticeship.'

Magnus always concluded the story with this remark. It was a story Florence knew well and dotted on.

'By apprenticeship,' she echoed now with approval. Desperate to reconnect her being with that of Magnus, she wanted to hear again about his trip with his father to America, to what he called the blood-relatives. She would understand better now the meaning of it, she was sure.

So, Magnus continued, but chose to tell her again about driving into the desert, and his meeting with the three Mojave men. He described to her for the first time their strange accepting manner and their beauty. He thought she might like to hear about Walt's picnic. He hadn't told her about that before. Then, he told her about skulking by the bloods' window, and about throwing up on their patch of lawn. It came to him that, together, they would ask Edwin to recount the meeting with the bloods.

Florence asked with a sudden urgency about the trouble in Dublin. 'I need to know, Magnus. You must share.'

Sooner than Magnus had dared hope, even sooner than she had planned, Florence would be leaving the day clinic. She would stay home in the day and prepare to return to work, though she could not think what that preparation involved. She was making herself ready by force of will. She was afraid to let go of her little bundle, but she was letting go. She would help Magnus with his mother and father. It was time, though she did not know why it was so.

CHAPTER 33

A Life More Mysterious

Charlotte was curiously formal around Stella, and Stella responded in kind. It was, in effect, a way of keeping the peace. Their younger sister, Maureen, they both treated as more junior than her years, and she played along accordingly and kept her plans to herself. It had come as a great surprise when she eloped with her lover, a pharmacist from Leith, and went to live with him in Edinburgh.

Charlotte was reserved, but she was no less strong-willed than Stella. She was the unrufflable one who liked being the naughty aunt, and jealously guarded her position as favourite in the eyes of her nephew. She had made herself a counterweight to Magnus' mother. She could do this because she had remained single. She had been the quiet party-goer, the naughty flirt. When Magnus was a teenager, she had confided in him about her adventures with men. It was a kind of flirtation in itself. This was what a boy should know as healthy and desirable interaction between men and women. Magnus wanted to hear about this behaviour, not his mother's.

'Every child born comes with a loaf of bread,' Charlotte had told Magnus when he expressed concern about the baby that was due. In spite of this, Magnus concluded his aunt never wanted children of her own. Or, she had not met the man who would persuade her. She lavished attention on Maureen's two boys when they visited, and sent them expensive presents on their respective birthdays – presents they didn't fully appreciate as children – and over-compensated with gushing politeness now that they were grown men. They pressed hot whiskeys on her, and sweet biscuits. They sent her knee blankets and shawls from Jenners department store. She didn't like being treated as an old lady, but she never complained. Magnus saw her trying to practise her favourite aunt skills with his cousins, but her heart wasn't in it. Magnus had been the chosen one. That was something else his cousins didn't fully appreciate.

Later, Charlotte was the one Florence would talk to on the phone, the one Florence said was his true mother. Charlotte had been talking to Florence on the phone in this current crisis. 'I'm just minding you, dear, while Magnus is over here minding everybody else.'

The back brace had improved Edwin's posture and relieved the pain. In his new limbo, he went to the massage chair in the shopping centre wearing his brace. This journey was not for pain relief but rather, in some primitive way, it soothed the man and restarted the day. There was never a queue. No explanation was needed. Nobody, he thought, paid any attention. It was good for a person with a transmission problem.

Two youths sat down on a bench nearby. Edwin listened to their conversation. They talked as though they were old men. They seemed to think Edwin couldn't hear them because of the chair machine.

'He has that for you,' one said.

'He has?' the other replied.

'Yes, he has,' the first confirmed. 'When do you want it?'

'Today,' the second said, 'if he really has it.'

There was a preparatory lull. It had something to do with asserting rank, and the discretion that came with it. 'He gave it to the other fella. Actually, *he* has it.'

The position of the word 'actually' was important. Had it ended one utterance instead of beginning the next, it would have suggested limited knowledge. Moderate status.

'That was quick,' the second one observed.

'I'll be in to him now.'

'If you want anything else.'

'I'll ask.'

'You just ask.'

'I will. I'll have a think.'

'He has it in there for you now. At least, the other fella has it.'

The two of them just sat there, as if they were being tested. Life was becoming increasingly mysterious. It made Edwin want to live longer. When the youths got up and left, one going one way, the other going another, he imagined a follow-up encounter, just to see out his massage. He fancied it was fraught with dangerous little traps set in heavy rhythm.

'Did you get that?'

'I did.'

'Fair enough.'

'The other fella had it.'

'Didn't I tell you – he gave it to the other fella to give to you.'

'I have it now, anyway.'

'You have it.'

'Said, if I wanted anything else.'

'Who? The other fella?'

'No.'

'Fair enough.'

'I have it now, anyway.'

'You do. Thanks to me.'

Nothing more came. Edwin's therapy continued much longer than he expected. Maybe there was still some value to be had.

When Magnus came to visit again the following weekend, he found his father in the shopping centre. It was late, and the place was closing. There were just a few vacant stragglers making their way to their cars in the underground car park. Magnus got a hard look from the security guard he passed in the concourse.

'We're closing now.'

'Yes. I know. On my way.'

He saw his father sitting in the massage chair. No doubt he, too, had been challenged by the security guard. He was sitting perfectly still, just gazing through the spaces created between the single shoes displayed in the window opposite. The chair was idle. Edwin had no more change to feed it.

'Here you are,' Magnus called, trying to make light of it. Edwin took his time rotating his head. He seemed reluctant to let go of whatever was playing out between the shoes.

'I'm going,' he said robustly, as though replying to the security guard for a third time.

'Come on, then.'

'I'm coming with you now.' Edwin sensed the weight in his son's craw. It affected his rising from the chair, making him unsteady, when really, his muscles were capable. Once on his feet, he struck the pose of an old man ready to march. 'Lead on.'

He didn't ask why Magnus had hunted him down, or how long he had been looking for him before coming to this place. Edwin hadn't wanted a search. He wasn't looking for attention. He was here for a spiritual lift.

The two men walk-marched the concourse towards the escalator that led to the car park beneath. They passed the security guard, who had doubled back to make sure the old man was out of the chair. Doubling back was central to the job, as was spotting troublemakers. He just knew these two belonged together.

'Good night,' Magnus said with an odd intensity.

'Good night,' the guard replied begrudgingly.

'Huh,' Edwin offered.

They were the only ones riding the escalator. The car park was virtually empty.

'Take your time,' Magnus ordered.

'I *am* taking my time. You hired a car?'

'I did. I'm over there,' he said, pointing to a section beside the ramp.

'It's a bloody disgrace what they're charging for the hire of a car. Why did you hire a car?'

'It makes sense. That's all.'

'I can find my own car.'

'Of course you can. There's only a choice of three left.'

'You can leave me here.'

'I'll just see you started.'

'It's over there, and my car always starts. You can follow me in your heap. I'll be out of here before you're behind the wheel.'

'It's been through the wash again, I see. Nice and shiny.'

Edwin stopped suddenly, peeled away, walked to a drain at the dead centre of the empty car park. He followed one of the shallow channels in the cement that took run-off water. Not dizzy, but clumsy in the head, he leaned over the drain, clasping his knees in his large soft hands.

'Are you all right?' Magnus asked, lurching to his side.

'Yes, I'm all right.'

'I know you didn't do what you've been accused of.' He hadn't intended to let this out just yet. He had wanted more time to justify his own behaviour to himself. In any case, there was no reply. Edwin seemed to be looking into the drain with purpose.

'You *know*.'

'I know. I'm sorry for doubting you. So very sorry.'

'You can tell me how you know?' Edwin was speaking into the drain. There was a reverberation from under the grille.

'It's become clear,' he blurted.

'Charlotte persuaded you?'

Magnus did not reply. He wanted his father to face him, but that couldn't happen in this moment.

Edwin approved of his son's silence. 'Good boy.'

'Are you sure you're all right?' Magnus wanted to put his hand on his father's stooped back, but Edwin wanted to show he still had moral and physical strength, and was independent.

'Yes,' Edwin answered. 'I'm sure. We'll not talk about this again.'

And again, Magnus nodded and was silent.

'Good man,' his father declared without looking at him. 'Now, get in your car and follow.'

'I will.'

Edwin stayed bent over the drain for a moment longer, then slowly rose to this new phase in his life, to something short of his full stature due to his bad back. The clumsiness had departed.

Charlotte had come from Wicklow to visit Edwin. She was there in the house with Magnus long after Edwin had gone to bed. Magnus asked her about his father being abandoned on the Sparling doorstep. Why had they chosen the Sparlings? Was there a connection? If anybody knew it would be Charlotte. Charlotte fixed on the space above Magnus' head. 'When you hear about a foundling,' she said, 'you think of a baby being left on a doorstep in a city or a town, not an isolated house down a long country lane.' Already, she needed to digress. She referred to the thick hedges on either side of that lane, with their sweet pea and fuchsia battling through in season, and the creeper climbing the trunks of the beeches behind, and sheets of clematis and great clumps of lavender where the lane opens to the house. Charlotte knew the names of birds, insects and flowers. She could identify building materials and rocks. In her account of the event it became clear to Magnus that she was obsessed with the physical manifestations of this act of abandonment. 'A lot must have been known about the Sparlings,' she said. They were a childless couple. They felt special to be picked out. That was why they adopted the baby. That, and a strong sense of duty.

Magnus knew Charlotte believed that duty fulfilled was the root of personal happiness. He did not know that the perpetual and intensely private pursuit of this fulfilment explained the inscrutable expression she encountered when she looked in the mirror – an expression which, at times, made her grieve. When she gave her quick smile, she would always get a positive and equally speedy response. She reminded herself of this most reliable of screens when she dared to test that smile at her dressing table.

The Sparlings were content to be well chosen, she told Magnus. They had the money, and the space in their hearts and in their house. Adoption was more straightforward in those days. There was no one they or anyone else in the district could think was the mother, and there were no clues.

Why the Sparlings? Why their house? Was it random? Charlotte was thorough in exploring the logic, though she still felt the need to concentrate her gaze above Magnus' head. It was not random, she asserted. There had to have been prior knowledge. Some referral.

In truth, Charlotte observed, the Sparlings weren't much interested in the advice of the Reverend Tuttle. To be fair, Tuttle and his counterpart in the chapel, Father Rooney, made no dogmatic stand, nor did he publicly denounce the birth-parents. Tuttle offered practical assistance in a discreet, competitive manner. Details were taken by the Guards, and records sent to Dublin. The prescribed course of action was undertaken to the letter, but it was widely believed that the best result had already been achieved. When Edwin was twelve, Charlotte said, the Sparlings told him candidly that he was adopted. There was no reference to his being abandoned. They did not use the phrase 'given up'. He was chosen, they insisted, not rescued. There would always be pyjamas under a pillow for this boy in the house at the edge of the world – which was where the Sparlings' house and the Dooleys' house were located.

One sunny afternoon, in winter in another time, the young Maureen met a distraught woman in the lane, where it divided between the Sparling house and theirs. Magnus' birth-mother had made a clandestine journey back to the Sparling house, only to find that it had burnt to the ground. She had no immediate way of knowing the fate of the occupants. In her distraught state, she was thinking she should go now to ask at the local Garda station.

Maureen took her in to the Dooley house, sat her in the parlour, and gave her sweet tea. Her two sisters were no less attentive, no less kind. The house smelt of rosewater and dust and cooking – which was lovely on a cold, sunny winter's day.

This woman seemed not to notice the packing cases, the tea chests in the hall, the cardboard boxes, the general chaos. Stella and Charlotte had come specially to help their sister make ready for her move.

It was Charlotte who questioned Irene and established her identity. She who got information that was forthcoming only because the woman was in shock.

It was Stella who later insisted they keep this information from Edwin. Though they knew that Edwin had been adopted by the Sparlings, these were unreliable murmurs from a disorientated stranger. Edwin was *her* husband. She would decide, and she had decided.

It was Charlotte who told Edwin about his birth-mother's ghost visit. Edwin was calm about it. Philosophical, you might say, until he discussed it with Stella.

'You don't want this,' she told him directly.

He couldn't fathom her harshness. He was making a mistake, she was telling him. Making the wrong choice to engage. Where had this certainty come from, he wondered. What kind of protection was it she was giving? She made him feel foolish standing before her to be judged unfit, with his ribbed green pullover draped over his shoulders, cuffs folded one into the other at the solar plexus.

Furthermore, he needn't look to Charlotte or Maureen. Their sympathy was genuine, but they had no special take on the matter. There was a warning being issued here, Edwin thought. The women in our family aren't healers, she was saying.

Though she did not dare ask to meet her child, Irene did go to the local Garda station. It was her act of atonement. She formally identified herself as the mother of the infant laid on the Sparlings' doorstep. This was her way of providing a path to her door if her son so desired to acknowledge her.

CHAPTER 34

Gödel, the Mathematician

Edwin wanted Magnus to get stuff down from the attic. Old electrical goods for the most part. A kettle, a fan heater, a battery shaver with trimmer in a box with a mirror on the inside of the lid – never used. A bedside lamp. Never mind that the fringe had rotted away.

'Are you on the beams?'

'Yes, I'm on the beams.'

'Stay on the beams.'

'Still no insulation, and you an architect. Should be ashamed of yourself.'

'Just mind where you go.'

'Bloody hell, it's a right clutter up here. What do you want with this gear, anyway?'

Edwin watched the torchlight play in the open hatch. 'I want to be able to get at it. God knows when you'll be back.'

'Tell me again what you want.'

When Magnus had finished his task, he drew the attic hatch closed and sat at the top of the stepladder while Edwin leaned heavily against the banister and surveyed the tackle that had come down. The display on the landing carpet seemed to put him at a loss.

'I've been talking to Charlotte again,' Magnus said. 'I'm convinced she knows exactly what's been going on. I think she's ready to tell me.'

Edwin peeled himself off the banister, clutched the stepladder with one hand, and scorned his son with a hard look. 'You know Gödel, the mathematician?'

'No,' Magnus growled.

'He died in 1976. Of starvation. Not out in the wilds, but at home, in the city. He had a thing about being poisoned, poor man. He was convinced, you see . . . but there was no foundation for it.'

'He went mad?'

'He only trusted his wife to test his food, and when she was taken into hospital he died of starvation.'

Sensing a weakening of resolve, Magnus came down the ladder to face his father full-square. 'You've been thinking a lot about this mathematician, have you?'

'Not really.'

'This is a way of telling me the poisoning is entirely a fantasy?'

'No. I'm not trying to tell you anything.'

'What, then?'

'The things that can happen . . . '

'Poor Mr Gödel. It that it?'

'There's trust. Even if it kills you.'

Magnus took this latest exchange as further evidence of his father withdrawing ever more deeply into a state of delusion. 'I'm going to grill Charlotte. She'll have got it out of Stella. She'll have got her to confess her lies.'

His father took a half-step backwards. 'I did it,' he said. 'I tried to poison your mother.'

'There now,' Magnus said soothingly. He put both hands on his father's shoulder. 'There now,' he said.

CHAPTER 35

The Simple Truth

Charlotte harvested the greengages with a speed and efficiency that betrayed the country girl in her. She was surprisingly agile, rising up on her toes and stretching. She wasn't doing it to impress her nephew, rather to reward any patience shown to her. She had him hold the basket.

'What are you going to do with these, Charlotte?'

'It's fruit, Magnus,' she said without a trace of cynicism. 'We eat fruit.'

'Yes, but they're unripe.'

'I'm not waiting any longer. I'll make tarts.'

'With plenty of sugar.'

'You like greengages,' she assured him.

'I do,' he confirmed.

'Blackcurrants and raspberries, too.'

'Yes. How many times have I picked fruit for you?'

'Not often enough.'

Magnus had loved her city garden as a child, just as he loved the Dooley's Wicklow garden now. There was nothing prissy about either of them. This one was always on the verge of being overgrown. Plum and apple trees fought shrubs and thickets for branch-space and were in parts intertwined. The weave was thick enough to provide shelter from rain. The garden appeared not to have changed much in thirty-odd years. Charlotte tended it as Maureen had done, and she as their parents had. There were plenty of berries in season, to eat, always birds in the bushes making sudden movements. There was good cover on all sides of the irregular patch of grass Charlotte called the meadow. It was a good garden for throwing stones at cats.

When the three aunts got together to sun themselves in Charlotte's city garden, there wasn't much space left for a boy to play in the open. That didn't bother Magnus. He was happier watching and listening from the bushes, with their permission. The women pegged their deckchairs low, wore big hats, sunglasses and brightly coloured swimsuits. Charlotte never wore much makeup, but the others did, and kept most of it on for the sunbathing. To Magnus' eyes, only Aunt Charlotte's head belonged on her body, as hers was the only one that vaguely matched. And she had the best swimsuit. Always polka dots.

Edwin liked to visit when the Dooley women assembled on a sunny day. He liked the attention he got from his sisters-in-law. Liked their mocking ways. He would take his suit jacket off and roll up his sleeves. Charlotte always commented favourably on the perfect turn-ups he made, which took the shirtsleeves just above the elbows. Charlotte liked to sent Magnus to get a chair for his dad from the kitchen, and a cushion from the living room. She had a hat for him, which she kept on a peg under the stairs. She worried his forehead might burn on account of his hair oil fusing with perspiration, and thereby magnifying the sun's effect.

These sunbathing sessions would invariably turn into picnics, even if the sun disappeared behind clouds. There would be tea and biscuits and sandwiches – often in that order. Then, there would be whiskeys, and Fanta for Magnus. If it got cold, the party would decamp to the dining room, where the adults would sit at the heavy wooden table. Stella and Maureen would wear cardigans on their shoulders, in the vain hope that the sun would return. Charlotte would leave for a short while, and return wearing her silk dressing gown, which she tied expertly at the waist. Magnus felt excluded from the picnics in the dining room. There was no place to lurk in there. He would sit on the step of the French window with his back to the adults, and drink more Fanta until he wanted to go for a pee in the bushes, or until he saw a cat. He would set the bottle down gently and rise to his feet slowly. He would always try for a magpie. He hated the power they held over chance.

There were magpies in the Wicklow garden now. Skulking in the bushes. Magnus had seen the flashes of white.

'He says he did it,' Magnus reported. He saw no point in keeping the news from Aunt Charlotte. 'He told me, as though he was describing a religious experience, as though he had some vision of the way forward.'

'I don't go in for visions,' his aunt said. 'None of us do,' she added. Visions were colourful rubbish, or they were religious. Roman Catholic. Not for the likes of her.

'None of us,' he echoed.

Then, in a slightly odd turn of phrase, she said: 'Speculation is quite the other thing.' She lifted up her chin and projected to a wider world, lest her assertion be confused with any failure of the imagination. 'You want to be curious, don't you?' Then, she turned it further than Magnus could ever have anticipated. 'Do you believe him?' she asked, settling herself carefully.

'No.'

'Good,' she replied, 'because it was me. I did it.'

This did not register with Magnus immediately. He was too absorbed in his own disclosure. Charlotte didn't add instantly to her statement. She followed his sliding gaze, made sure that she met it when his eyes drew level with hers.

Then, it hit him. '*You . . .* '

'I put the poison on the arm of the chair.'

'You tried to kill your sister?'

'I did.' Charlotte was calm, even self-effacing. 'It was me. I should have told you before now, but Edwin told me to say nothing. I'm sorry. You don't doubt me, I hope, Magnus?'

There it was – the simple truth tumbling out of Aunt Charlotte's mouth. Magnus listened to the echo it made. He felt his ears turn white. In the underground car park of the shopping centre, when Edwin sought confirmation that Charlotte had 'told him', he assumed this meant, told him that Edwin had put down the paraquat for Stella. This was a hell of a turn on that exchange. Should he say now that he didn't believe her – just to begin with? Make her out to be the silly old maid desperate for attention.

There was heat still in the evening sunlight, but the air was cool, and ripe for transmission. This was the truth, he was sure. It hadn't occurred to him as a possibility, but now the sound this drama made was as clear to Magnus as the sound his pattering feet made under the desk when he typed.

This could all be written up in a few stark sentences. Bluntness, that was the way to spin it, if it had to come out.

Magnus could see Charlotte's fantasy, now. One day soon, even at this late hour, there would be a change, Charlotte believed. Too late is better than never. That made it never too late. She would be recognised as the white-haired mistress – for that was what she was, she would say. She would properly become Edwin's lover, and Stella, having narrowly escaped being poisoned, would acquiesce. She would finally give him back. Everyone would see the rightness of it. There would be nothing to forgive. Stella would still have him. There would be a beautiful arrangement. Everyone would be able for it. A great stock of the lord's favour would finally be bestowed on Charlotte, and she would pass this on to her darling Edwin. There was no more powerful force on earth than the turning of the worm. Save one outrageous act, Charlotte was a good and loyal sister. Had she succeeded, it would have been a sentimental poisoning, but they had all been saved, thank the Lord.

'Magnus, dear, you tell the Guards if it's for the best.'

'I'm just taking it in at the minute, Charlotte.'

'It's odd Stella doesn't suspect it was me,' Charlotte said with plain curiosity.

'Yes, well . . . ' Magnus was waiting for his brain to function. There was traction, but temporarily, no engagement.

'*I'd* suspect me.'

'You would, wouldn't you?'

'She said nothing to you?'

'I'm still taking it in, Charlotte.' The voice was darker now. His breathing was shallow, his eyes wide, his gaze steady.

'Of course. But don't take all day, dear.'

'No. She said nothing along the lines that you might try to kill her.'

'I could never tell her how much your father means to me.'

Behind their calm words, both were expecting a boundless charge of emotion, each from the other. Each utterance was a kind of baiting, but it wasn't working, except that now, Charlotte was flushed. She swayed on her feet and suddenly appeared very weak.

'It's a terrible thing you've done,' Magnus declared in a perfectly reasonable pitch. At last, he was trying to implement the programme he had in his head for his father. He realised, however, that the programme was almost entirely a strategy for remaining calm, overlaid with a jumble of blindingly obvious statements of varying lengths.

'Yes,' she admitted. It was a terrible thing. Now what? Did anything need to be done?

'A terrible thing,' he repeated, sounding ever more reasonable than before.

Yes. But did anything need to be done?

To ask if she might, under any circumstances, make another attempt seemed ridiculous. So, what indeed needed to be done?

Aunt Charlotte pressed her hand to her breast and smiled at her darling Magnus. 'There's a lot of things that shouldn't happen to a person,' she said. It was meant as a humane and all-embracing statement, but she felt she hadn't spoken it out with conviction. She had blabbed, not confided, but there it was, and she was glad to be in her beloved garden, the garden Edwin so admired. Glad she could feel the faint evening sun on her face.

CHAPTER 36

We Do Not Speak Out

Magnus found his father in the garage, under the bonnet of his car. His back brace was draped over the hood of one headlight. There was a pair of long-nosed pliers, a Phillip's screwdriver, some screws and nuts laid out on it. Edwin was deep in the maw of the vehicle, which was a fascinating hell for him. This architect who loved his cars and driving, wasn't much of a mechanic, so there was endless tentative fiddling.

When he heard Magnus, he surfaced with difficulty. His back punished him severely. 'Magnus,' he said lightly because of the pain, 'it won't start.'

'Won't it?'

'Look,' his father said, generating a few sparks, 'it's not the battery.' He invited Magnus to get in under the bonnet with him. He knew his son was no better at mechanics than he, but now there were two of them to fiddle and worry.

Magnus went under from the opposite side, but only so he could engage his father face-on. 'I've been to Aunt Charlotte.'

'Oh, aye?' Edwin didn't look up. He kept tinkering. When he did try to rise again, his back gave out. Magnus quickly came around to his side, but his father wouldn't accept any help. When Edwin was finally straightened, and the pain had subsided, he said: 'She told you Stella invented all this?'

'No,' Magnus replied weightily.

'Ah, I see . . . .'

There was a new authentic silence that signalled more than the sharing of a burden, father with son.

The questioning had ceased. The will to eclipse Charlotte's malicious act came to Magnus as effortlessly as it had to his father, the secret and imperfect ways of love reason enough. For these Sparlings, love required being properly damned in a manageable, domestic way that did not deny feelings or punish failure.

'We need this car to go,' Edwin declared.

Magnus couldn't speak, but nodded stiffly. 'Are you all right?'

'What?'

'Your back.'

'Yes, yes.'

Edwin called the AA. They came and got the car started. He was embarrassed that it was in his garage with tools and such, but he was right about the fault not being the battery.

Edwin stood beside his son looking out from the mouth of the garage. He hadn't let go of the Phillip's screwdriver. 'I used to do all the digging for your aunt Charlotte in that bloody great garden of hers.' He made a broad pointing gesture with the screwdriver. 'Not to mention all that out there, front and back. Now, I get tired grating a piece of cheese.'

'I should do a bit of gardening,' Magnus said without enthusiasm.

'Charlotte wants to come round here and tackle it,' his father continued, ignoring his son's lame offer. 'She's on at me regularly about it. I've been fending her off. For her own sake, you understand. You think I should get somebody in?'

CHAPTER 37

Edwin Vacates

Stella was coming home – moving back in, was a better way to put it. The neighbour's dog wouldn't be visiting Stella. Not of its own accord. Jack, the neigbour, would be encouraging it, of course, but the dog had never taken to Stella. Nor would it go the short distance to his new abode, Edwin was convinced. *C'est la vie.* He'd toss the ball-throwing thing over the wall, and that would be an end to it.

It was very early when Edwin took up his position in the hall. The lobsters he liked to eat weren't awake in Sawers' tank in Chatham Street. He hadn't been to the fishmongers since this crisis began. There had been no lobster, no tripe, no kidneys. None of the food he saw as a special treat for a solitary man accepting of his lot. Noel wasn't keen on shellfish, but he liked his offal. Edwin would get liver and kidneys and get him round to the new place to warm it up. End the hiatus.

Sleeping lobster, eh? How did it get to be 9 AM? He'd been up sorting for a little over three hours, and now he was standing there listening to *Desert Island Discs* coming from the wireless in the kitchen. He stood between the two bags he had packed. These bags had got bigger, or he had shrunk. He didn't know which. The latter, he decided.

It was a quiet end to the disembodied life with Stella. Together, they had made this plan to separate – which was a remarkable act in light of all that had occurred. Standing as he did, it looked as though he was waiting to be airlifted out.

His wandering eyes came to rest for a moment on the series of neat horizontal lines on the architrave of the kitchen door, each identified with a date that marked his son's growing. Edwin had inked these incisions so as to be a permanent record. They stopped, aged fourteen, when they had returned from their momentous visit to America. There he had stood, Magnus, that serious boy, daring to lift his heels off the floor, then finally refusing to be measured.

Edwin waited for the impulse to leave. In the meantime, he contemplated his Radio 4 desert island existence. He had done this many times before. It was a comfort. As a retired architect he would, of course, be seeing to some sort of viable tree-house or semi-fortified cave-dwelling. When speaking about his survival, he would refer to Stella's enduring respect, and not joke about her being responsible for his being cast away. He would give his potted history and his musical choices in a modest but assured voice, providing Noel with no cause to mock.

He was vacating the house for what was called a modest bedsit just a few minutes' walk away in the same neighbourhood. It was the kind of dump many disaffected men chose for their exile from the family. The most equitable cleaving often meant that these bolt-holes were not more than a few streets away from the family home. These men could still be responsible in their decline. Literally, they could be called upon at short notice.

He decided to leave the radio on. The impulse to move came before *Desert Island Discs* was over. He would listen to the repeat on Sunday morning in the other place. He would then go to the corner shop he usually went to for the Sunday papers. Normally, he didn't meet Noel on a Sunday, but this Sunday they were meeting to make plans for a week in Sóller. It would be very hot in Majorca this time of year, but what the hell. He hadn't yet told Noel about the move to the flat. He felt it was important that he make the decision and take action entirely by himself. He didn't want Noel dogging him to come and stay in his house. On Sunday he'd tell Noel about the move, they'd make their travel plans, have a drink, and later he would listen to *Sailing By* and the shipping forecast. Then, he would go to sleep in the new bed. Magnus had observed some of his actions about the house, his sorting, his rearranging, but hadn't been around for his clearing out of the wardrobe, his oiling of the stiff locks, ordering in fuel for the central heating tank, putting a fresh battery in the kitchen clock, and the packing of bags.

Vacating – yes, that was the word that best described what he was doing, Edwin decided. It gave him the cleanest entry into the new phase.

He was *vacating* his house. It was a mysterious business, really. His head told him to blaze his way out through the hall door, but he did not. Instead, he drifted out with nothing more than the pull of a kite.

For his part, he was glad Magnus wasn't present for this episode, fussing about sternly, questioning the action. Edwin didn't want his son watching him try to be kind to himself.

He had come to treat his wife as dead. It was a pragmatic approach, and he was able to appreciate the irony. It was a means of achieving an intimacy that otherwise was unachievable. It was the kind of intimacy he had failed to find visiting his natural parents all those years ago in Bakersfield. Driving across the desert with Magnus, he had fixed in his mind a picture of himself as a boy in his field, making a giant armchair in a haystack from which to look out over the broad countryside and take in what was his domain. What his blood-parents had abandoned. The distance could now be properly set with Stella, the woman with whom he was insolubly bound.

Magnus liked the house, Edwin knew. He had been happy there. It was a beautifully proportioned and well-appointed house that, admittedly, needed to be better maintained. However, Edwin's secret life of wandering the place in the dark while Stella slept upstairs, or somewhere else entirely: those days were over. These nocturnal wanderings produced a map that could not be passed from father to son. He would not be able to convey all that he felt about the house. Nevertheless, that stuff would come with him. Memory, Edwin had learnt, was in the body as well as the brain, and wouldn't be let go of easily. No doubt he would be up at night, in the dark of the new place, bumping into cheap furniture.

Solitude, too, was mysterious.

CHAPTER 38

Another Trip to Hearten Two Old Men

Sitting in the departures lounge at Dublin Airport, Noel observed Edwin flexing his fingers, then letting his arms hang straight down on either side of the single bench chair.

'What's that you're doing?'

'It's for circulation.' Edwin told Noel that in the bed at night, he avoided crooking his arms at sharp angles. He imagined that the chemistry of his blood was now such that it had thickened and could be impeded by acute bends in the veins, causing severe pins and needles, or numbness.

'You're on the Warfarin?' Noel asked.

'I am.'

'That should keep you flowing. And the back?'

'I'm wearing a brace.'

'I know about the brace. Are you wearing it now?'

'I left it behind.'

'Practising without it?'

'I forgot the shagger.'

In the baggage hall at Las Palmas Airport, Noel's glasses slipped off his face onto the carousel. He was having trouble with his glasses, or his head, he told his old pal. Either the glasses were getting ridiculously loose, or his head had diminished. In any case, the glasses had slid off his ears and into the toilet bowl when he was having a pee. They clattered into the bowl with a pleasing skitter.

'All this shrinking,' mumbled Edwin.

Noel just continued with his account. Told Edwin he didn't hesitate to roll up his sleeve and reach into the water-trap, but now, he said, his back trouble was back.

'Back trouble back?' Edwin muttered, but how good it was to be here again. They had landed early enough to allow them to catch the train to Sóller. They'd rattle through damp mountain tunnels on the narrow-gauge to the town, then on to the port to dump their bags in the seafront hotel. They'd be eating in the open air with time to spare. There might even be time to take in again the Miró and Picasso exhibition in the tiny gallery in the station building before getting on the tram to Port Sóller.

It was eight o'clock in the evening when they came out of the hotel with only their straw hats as baggage. The paintings had lightened their mood. They intended to walk the full length of the seafront, around the placid bay. With the sun sinking fast, the pale green water was changing to dark blue. It was quivering with floating sticks of reflected light. At this end of the promenade there were large parties of German pensioners dining in the open air, taking the early sittings. Edwin and Noel set off at an ambitious pace. It was good to force the pace a little. Good to get out from among the pensioners quickly – though Edwin and Noel were pensioners, too. They could always drop down a gear if the balmy breeze they had in their faces fell away.

'The madness is done with?' Noel asked.

'I think I'm saved, Noel.'

'You'll not be doing that again.' Noel was swallowing great gulps of air, which he needed, to say what he was saying.

'I didn't do it.'

'Finally, he tells me. So, Stella really has it in for you. God almighty, what drama.'

'There was a cup with paraquat in it. I'm going to tell you a secret.' This sort of conversation between two men was best conducted walking side by side. He told Noel Charlotte was responsible. That she did it for him.

'What was she thinking?'

'That she and I might be together.'

'Be together,' Noel bellowed in disbelief, then immediately lowered his voice and repeated the phrase.

'You tell no one this,' Edwin said. He said it as though he was referring to a personal tragedy – which, in a sense, he was.

'No one,' Noel repeated. Edwin knew that he would be as good as his word, so he told him what he knew, said he'd be carrying on as before, that it was up to others to adjust.

'Stella knows the truth?'

'No.'

'God almighty.'

'She'll not hear it from me – or from you.'

'Or from me.' Noel put his hand on his heart. 'Let's stop in here. I need a drink.'

They made an unscheduled stop. The alcohol was hugely satisfying, sliding down Noel's throat. It was so good, he had another. Edwin was remarkably relaxed, he thought, and said as much.

Edwin threw down his Pimm's and declared: 'I'm hungry. Aren't you? I could eat a horse.'

They paid up and went on their way, strangely elated. They walked the full curve of the bay to the navy buildings in the lea of the lighthouse, then they marched all the way back to their favourite restaurant. Edwin held up well without his brace. Noel Ffrench, with two 'f's, was lost in admiration for his friend. He'd be paying for this dinner without a doubt. They ordered the combination platter and the best wine on the list.

'And Magnus . . . ?' Noel enquired.

'Magnus . . . he knows, but you won't get it out of him.'

'Good boy.'

They both let go. They got drunk. They were giddy with relief: astonished, too, in an exhausted way, at what life had delivered to them both. Their work as architects was their salvation. They would go and sit with the other old fellows at the fountain tomorrow morning, try their faltering Spanish on them again and ask if they, too, had had the cosmic wind knocked out of them by their living their lives.

It was after midnight when they cut a wavering path along the promenade back to their hotel, keeping themselves upright by pressing shoulder to shoulder. Somewhere in the wash of tame music from a synthesizer, Edwin collapsed. He went down hard. It was a major seizure.

An air ambulance was not required. Noel was able to take him home on a scheduled flight, but both men knew it was serious heart trouble. No doubt about it.

An operation was needed. Edwin wouldn't stay in the hospital. The consultant was used to patients resisting. She understood. Hospitalisation prior to surgery, if it could be avoided, should be avoided – if it was feasible. Her judgement was that in Edwin Sparling's case, the condition was such that immediate hospitalisation was not essential. However, she strongly urged that he be admitted to a convalescent home for the intervening period, given his solitary domestic situation.

Edwin said he would think about it. Think about it from his new home.

CHAPTER 39

Gathering around Edwin

Magnus was on his way to the 200 Task meeting that was looking into the overspend. He delayed in the corridor because he needed to catch Freddie, who was attending the steering-committee meeting. Magnus got his timing right. Freddie came out flirting with his colleague Muriel Geoffers, spouting effusively about getting seduced politically: it was the democratic way. There was something about absolving rebels, combining renewal with tradition. Freddie's most fluid line in flirtation invariably relied on gossip, which was plummily inflated for self-protection. He saw that Magnus wanted his attention. He made a point of concluding with M. Geoffers in front of Magnus, before greeting him. 'In England one will be rehabilitated if one lives long enough, wouldn't you agree, Muriel? If the disgrace can be lived with, it becomes part of history.' Freddie didn't seem to care that Muriel was unmoved by his observations. 'Ah, Magnus . . . you look pale.'

'No, he doesn't,' Muriel Geoffers declared, and smartly moved on.

'I need to ask for more time.' Magnus blurted. 'Forty-eight hours.'

'Poor Magnus, in the breach.' He lowered his chin, put a hand on the younger man's shoulder. The sympathy was genuine, in spite of the tone. 'Look, you go right ahead. I'll clear it with the Permanent Secretary.'

'I'll clear it with him myself, Freddie. You'll be carrying my load. For a short time, I assure you.'

'We shan't manage,' Freddie said kindly.

The Permanent Secretary had just come out of the Wednesday-morning meeting. He didn't look like he was about to let out one of his belly-laughs. He was preoccupied with overspend. For Magnus to be seeking more leave on compassionate grounds was excruciating under any circumstances, and this was bad timing.

'Permanent Secretary . . . '

'Yes, Magnus?'

'I'm dreadfully sorry to ask . . . '

'You're off again?'

'I know the timing is appalling. It will be a short visit.'

Picking up on Magnus' reluctance to elaborate, he came out with: 'Your mother is in hospital again?'

'My father – he's had a heart attack. He's all right now, but . . . '

'Dear God.' A jaw-slide was checked in a show of solidarity. 'And how is Florence in all of this?'

'She's doing well.'

The Permanent Secretary gave him a single nod of encouragement. It was a nod that also acknowledged loss. 'You take the time you need.'

When Magnus arrived, his father was not resting in bed. He was sitting in the park with Jack's dog lying at his feet.

He saw him first through the park-railings; back view, hunched on a bench. His frame was more delicate than he recalled from his recent visit. The hunching suggested the old man had lost his stuffing and was relying on wigwamming his bones to maintain any kind of upright position. He appeared to be impossibly deep in a book, or dead.

Magnus called through the railings. His father couldn't turn around, but he responded by calling Magnus' name. Magnus hurried into the park.

'Well now, you should be resting.'

'Bloody hell. I *am* resting. What has you back, anyway?'

Magnus bent down awkwardly and kissed Edwin on the cheek. The dog had to get out of the way.

'I've had a full report. Don't think I don't know about your bad turn in Sóller.'

'That Noel fella has been blabbing. He exaggerates.'

Magnus sat down beside him. 'Maybe . . . '

'You're not to worry about me, Magnus. How many times is this you've been over recently? Have you been fired?'

'It's getting difficult, I admit.'

'Look after your job.'

'I'll talk to the doctor and see where we are.'

'I talked to that detective.'

'He called you again?'

'I called him. I wanted to finish him off. "Are we done?" I asked. "Are we through with this whole bloody business?" '

' "It rests",' he tells me. What a bloody phrase.'

'That's all behind you now.'

'And here I am – resting.'

'Things are looking up, dad.'

Edwin was struck by his son's lightness of tone. It went beyond the bone-relief they both felt over recent events. 'Florence,' he said, his face clearing, 'is she better in herself?'

'She is. She's with me. She's waiting in the house.'

'Is your mother there?'

'No, she's out.'

Edwin rose from the bench and turned to look through the railings at his house across the street. 'In the house,' he repeated to himself. He had never expressed the extent of his worry over Florence, and now she was here and she was fit and well. He steadied himself with a hand on Magnus' arm. 'Come on, then.'

He gave the dog a dithery kick to get it out of the way.

Though it was early in the day, Edwin took down the bottle of Champagne he and Stella had ready for the birth of their grandchild, the bottle that now had such tremendous weight, and a ghostly power. He popped the cork without ceremony. He did not reveal the significance of the act to Magnus and Florence. He got cheese and crackers from the kitchen. He insisted that Florence have butter on her crackers with the cheese. It was a rich excess that was fitting – one that his daughter-in-law deserved on any day of any week in any year.

'Go on.'

'No thanks, Edwin.'

'Ah go on. You'll have the butter.'

'She doesn't want it, dad. She prefers to have just the cheese on it.'

'Have the butter, Florence.'

Florence relented and spread butter thinly on her cracker before laying on the cheese.

It was only because of Florence's reemergence, her coming to see him, that Edwin agreed to spend time in the convalescent home.

'You can't bring those,' Magnus said in a sweet, quavering voice. He was referring to the pyjamas his father had packed. Magnus had taken the liberty of inspecting Edwin's grip-bag of clothes for his stay in the convalescent home.

'No?' his father replied. His sheepishness belied his bravery.

'We'll get you a new pair.'

'I'm only going in for two weeks.'

'Nevertheless. We can't have you looking like a tramp.'

'No.'

So, Magnus took him to Brown Thomas to pick out the most expensive pyjamas he could find. The old man needed the reassurance that would go with a trip to a department store on his own steam. This was the department store that was once Switzers, where they had come to buy clothes for their trip to America. They moved slowly through the aisles of men's tailoring, Edwin as though he was naked. Both men knew that the two weeks might turn into forever. They had to be strong for this pyjama-buying.

'What do you think?' Magnus said, turning over the neat cellophane package.

'They're far too expensive,' Edwin replied. It was a predictable answer from a modest man.

'You're right. But do you like them? I'm getting them for you.'

'No, you're not.'

Edwin slumped discreetly against a pillar.

'Are you all right?'

'I'm all right.'

'I shouldn't have made you come here.' Magnus hadn't made his father come to the department store. It was an agreed trip.

Edwin waved his son's concern away with a weak turn of the wrist. 'How much are they again?' He reached awkwardly into his inside jacket pocket for his chequebook.

Magnus stayed his father's hand. 'I said, I'm getting these. You'll love them. They're silk.'

'Your mother likes silk,' Edwin said, beginning to panic. His shoulders were hunched. Both hands were limp in the air. It might have looked like he was being arrested.

'She'd approve,' Magnus said, patting down one shoulder.

'Oh, everything loved for its quality, that's your mother.' The stab of panic passed quickly. 'She likes that fucking awful paisley pattern,' he said, pointing to another pair of pyjamas.

'Fucking awful,' Magnus echoed, taking heart. 'We're not putting you in that.'

'So, you're buying me my pyjamas?'

'I am.'

Edwin's eyes skidded uncomprehendingly over the cellophane under which the maroon silk pyjamas were neatly folded. He wanted to stay muddled on the subject of being abandoned in a convalescent home till the end of his days. He pushed himself off the pillar. 'Remind me: I need petrol.'

Stella had stayed overnight with Charlotte. Edwin dressed and ready by five-thirty in the morning. He went out into the back garden, planted his feet firmly in the clover, and stood listening to the birds.

Secretly, Magnus was up, too. He left Florence to sleep in the bed and observed his father from the bedroom window. Magnus had been getting up progressively earlier himself. Where was it leading, he wondered, this alertness in the quiet, this getting out of the house into the spacious mornings and tramping the streets? He liked to see the early buses with their interiors lit, to hear the dawn chorus. It didn't matter if it was raining. He put on his coat and took an umbrella. One his father had given him from under the stairs. It had a reinforced frame.

Magnus had sought to live a life of regularity, of anticipation. The acquisition of relevant in-depth knowledge was central to his work, and could be relied upon when a dilemma presented itself for those in authority. What had happened at work had its logic. His loyalty had been tested and Magnus had not been found wanting. However, he had come to recognise that it was the unpredictable and random acts of fate that had given meaning to and had governed the conduct of his life and made duty sacred.

Edwin went inside but kept the back door open, in spite of a strong breeze. In spite of his ailment, he spent the remaining time waiting to leave for the convalescent home, standing, flattening his feet, willing himself not to be afraid. He made small movements, like an animal in the zoo with the cage-gate open. Though he would not be going to the convalescent home that day – there was no bed for him yet – he seemed to be saying, *Here I am. Come and get me.*

He wanted no pity. If he wanted pity, he wouldn't be standing.

'You want that door closed?' Magnus asked.

'No.'

'You should sit down, dad.'

'I'm all right.'

'You sure you want the door open? There's a hell of a draught.'

'Yes. I'm sure. For the air.'

'Do you want to go out?'

'Out . . . ?'

'For a walk in the park.'

'No. Maybe. Later.'

'All right, then. We can go somewhere nice for dinner.'

'There's food here.'

'I know there is. Just for a change.'

'A change? Things have changed enough, son.'

'We could go for a drive.'

'And talk, yes.'

'Yes.'

'And we could have the dinner.'

'Yes, we could.'

'Bring Noel, if you like.'

'Yes.'

Edwin gave out with a polite, if formal, clearing of the throat that went into the corners of the room. It was a little sound he had made all his adult life; a skilful sound that harboured no expectation or despair.

'Thanks for this,' Edwin said, 'for coming home again, and with Florence. You know how happy I am that she's with you here.'

'I know.'

'Things are looking up.'

'They are. We'll get you sorted. Don't worry.'

'I'm not worried, son.'

It was Magnus' desire to connect, bone to bone, to give and get help in a grown-up manner. He stood beside his father and gazed out into the garden.

'You never went back to see the bloods, did you?' he asked, knowing his father had not returned.

'Never . . .' Edwin replied. He had not heard his parents referred to in this phrase in all the years since his extraordinary visit. He smiled.

'I've thought about them,' Magnus said, but Edwin did not rise to this. Did not say whether or not he had entirely banished them from his thinking. 'I've been going over our visit there . . .' Magnus continued.

Edwin was silent.

'I've been remembering,' Magnus said, as if to affirm a good deed.

'You think I should have gone back?' Edwin asked.

'I don't know. Yes, perhaps it would have been better a second time.' Even as these hollow words came out of his mouth, Magnus rebuked himself for being as quick to judge as an ex-lover, and for judging with the same arrested concern.

'I don't want to go back,' his father said with conviction. 'But you . . . ?'

'I've thought about it, but no.'

'Visiting was a mistake, you think?'

The word 'visiting' was so purposefully inadequate. 'I was going to ask *you* that.'

There was another silence, then Edwin spoke again. 'I'm glad we did it, you and me.'

'Well, so am I.'

His father was going to say more, but instead scoffed and shook his head in a kind of thwarted admiration. 'Your mother never forgave me. For my sake, as far as I can gather. Funny, that.'

This time, it was Magnus who created the silence. 'What I really want to say is it was a good thing you did. A brave thing.'

'Going back again: that might have been brave.'

It was awkward now – more so than before – but it was also easier to speak. After they had returned from America, the distance that had opened between father and son, neither could explain. It was important now to acknowledge the bond they had that could not be extinguished by will or circumstance. 'I'm glad I got to go with you,' Magnus said.

'It amazes me,' his father replied timidly.

'You must think about them a lot,' Magnus ventured.

'It's all a wonder,' Edwin declared, his words even lighter, and a little more confused than his previous utterance. When Florence appeared in the doorway, Magnus took it as a gift from the gods, a sign of good fortune.

'I couldn't sleep,' she said.

'Come in,' Magnus said, stretching out his hand. 'Sit with us, my love. We're talking.'

The expectation that father and son might continue to speak about their journey to the bloods in America all those years before was astonishing to both men.

CHAPTER 40

Stella Adrift

Stella had begun to appear in strange clothes. Over garments and accessories, that is. Coats and scarves and the like that were cast-offs, not secondhand vintage. But who had cast them off? Who had said, 'There now, Stella, that's for you. You'll look great in it. That'll keep you warm. Suits you down to the ground. Take it, take it. I insist.' These were men's cast-offs, so far as Magnus could judge.

When she appeared in a leather bomber jacket, Magnus declared: 'That's disgusting.'

'What's disgusting?' his mother demanded.

'That jacket. That thing you're wearing. Where did you get it?'

'Never you mind. There's nothing wrong with this jacket.'

'That's a man's jacket, and it's grubby.'

'I wouldn't want to be relying on you.'

'What?'

'When was the last time you bought your mother an item?'

Magnus looked about theatrically for this third person. 'An *item?*' he repeated, incredulous at the archaic term used. 'You think I should buy you clothes?'

'It would be a nice gesture occasionally.'

He couldn't believe his ears, except he knew that this was her looking for a reaction, whatever the price. 'You're not short of money, are you? You have a wardrobe full of fine clothes. Quality clothes. Classic clothes.'

'That's where I got this jacket.'

'Look – wear what you want. I really don't care.' But he did care, and he was shocked to see her in anything dowdy, anything inappropriate, any tat. 'It's just that – *item,*' he added belatedly. 'It looks appalling.'

She seemed to derive satisfaction from his being put out. She wasn't going to give on the leather bomber jacket. This brought out a morbid fascination in Magnus. He'd be watching to see if she would appear in trainers and tracksuit bottoms. He'd get Charlotte to keep watch and tell him if she sank any lower.

While Stella was upstairs in the bedroom, looking at herself in the tall mirror, Florence was downstairs with Magnus and Edwin. She was smiling at her father-in-law, offering modest reassurance with every other phrase effortlessly blown to the extremities of audibility by a little jet of air. Edwin grasped that she saw beyond the fizzle and vinegar of an old man's complaints.

Edwin got marmalade on the cuff of his shirt when Florence finally got him to sit down at the kitchen table to a breakfast he didn't want.

'Don't worry,' he said, 'it's not an important shirt.'

'You have important shirts?' Magnus asked, as he wiped his father's sleeve with a damp cloth.

'I do,' his father replied, grinning at Florence. 'I'm not wearing one today.'

'This is only for a short time,' Magnus said guiltily.

'I know.'

'It's convalescence.'

'I know what it is.'

'Get you rested.'

'Oh aye.'

'It will prolong your life, for Christ's sake.' Magnus went to the bottom of the stairs and called his mother, shouting that it was time for Edwin to go.

Stella came down.

Edwin slipped out quietly, linking arms with his daughter-in-law, and exhibiting the humdrum bravery of being ordinarily old. Magnus led the way with the car keys in hand. Stella followed the short distance to the open garage doors, where she let them in.

For an instant, Magnus is a feverish child again, throwing up in the bathroom.

'That's it, that's good,' Stella tells him, 'get it all up.' There's no need for the doctor. They can take him to the doctor in the morning if – if what? His parents have neglected to tell him that he will not die from his vomiting. He rides the waves of nausea. He knows there is a rhythm and he tries to go with it. Not to go with it means certain death. He doesn't dare close his eyes.

CHAPTER 41

Edwin Anchored

For all his work on hospital and asylum buildings, Edwin seemed not to know about such places when he set foot in the convalescent home. Perhaps he judged that this was the best way to make his entrance. To play it familiar might send the wrong message. A short period of convalescence demanded that a man keep his eyes fixed on the hard horizon.

'Happy cake-day,' one old man called out. The word 'birthday' would not come quickly enough.

'Sit down, Johnny,' the sparrow woman with the collapsed jaw shouted. Johnny, the self-appointed toastmaster, would not sit down. 'Sit down, or you'll fall down.'

Johnny was too excited to sit. He was looking this way and that, shuffling in and out of the doorway. There was a young girl from the college of music coming to play the violin. Where was she? She probably didn't know they were assembled in the sitting room.

'All the good people,' Johnny said, getting more agitated. Who were the good people? Not this assembly. It was another group he was referring to. He must have been talking to Edwin.

'All the good people,' he repeated, but this time in a softer, more wistful tone. He could see the girl with her violin case. Magnus was behind her. Edwin was at the end of the hall and beckoned his son away from the gathering.

'A birthday,' Edwin said. This was something grizzly to be avoided. He led Magnus back down the hall to the lift. Though it was a convalescent home and not an old people's home, Johnny, he explained, was sure he'd been dumped. He spent much of his time shrouded in rugs in what passed for a garden, shell-shocked and dumb. This birthday celebration had brought him out of his shell. Apparently, he went missing regularly, but wasn't a true escapee, because they could always find him in the same pub: he didn't know where else to go. He had no interest in turning up on the doorstep of either of his daughters and their families.

'Goes out through the kitchen, apparently.'

There was a nurse with a ninety-five-year-old woman in a wheelchair waiting by the lift. 'My father and mother are dead, of course,' they heard the elderly woman tell her nurse. The utterance hurt Edwin's ears. 'Come on,' he said, though he was hardly able, 'we'll take the stairs.'

Because of the micro-dirt and the bitterness that had seeped into the leatherette of these high-backed hospital chairs over the years, Edwin chose to sit on hard chairs. Wood was a better processor of human fallout. Once in his room, he put Magnus on a hard chair. He went and stood by the window and looked at the leaves lifting in the breeze, showing their lighter undersides. He didn't last long there. He tipped his bones onto his bed and lay scattered in all directions.

'How do you feel, dad?'

Edwin said he was watching for any sudden change of mood, any bout of euphoria that traded on the fact that he was still alive. It could herald malign chemical changes in the brain, or a blockage. It wasn't his heart he was worried about. The steady little pant generated by something no bigger than a pair of spider's lungs might cease somewhere in the system, and transform him into an imbecile. Places like this seemed to bring it on. Particularly in men. You could only be brave.

Magnus studied Edwin's frail, crooked frame. The raindance for which he had not forgiven his father, came back to him now. The strange, loose shuffling in that bare motel room, Edwin's crumpled face with its squinting eyes and tight lips, now filled him with compassion. Magnus finally grasped that this was no humiliating or shameful act, but rather a performance from a modest man not given to expressing his emotions; expressing, nevertheless, his profound sadness and his relief; a solitary orphan-man trying to love himself as he loved his son.

Magnus told Edwin that he had contacted Irene at the time of his wedding to invite her to the civil ceremony in London. It was, he explained, for selfish reasons that he had rung. He didn't want any pangs of guilt. She was family, after all. Besides, he wanted to pry a little more. In any event, she had declined, so he had not mentioned the matter to Edwin. He was telling him now, because it was unfinished business. He wanted to ensure that his father had no such pangs of guilt.

He had asked her why she had returned to the Sparling house in Wicklow. 'Remember', he said to Edwin, 'she hadn't come back to visit you. Remember, she denied having talked to the Dooley girls. Well, she had a change heart. "I visited," she said, "because Edwin might think I was dead." 'She had heard stories of children who had been told all their lives that their birth-mothers were dead, who nevertheless sought them out, only to find they had died just a few months before. "This dying again is a terrible and unnecessary hurt," she had told Magnus. She didn't know what his adoptive parents had told him. She knew only that they were good and honourable people, and not likely to allow such cruelty.

'I asked her why she had not formally presented you for adoption. She was terrified of signing papers that would bar her from all contact forever. She knew girls who had been forced to sign such documents. It was standard practice for a minor at the time of your birth,' Magnus added. His father was staring impassively, not weighing the words, but recognising their sounds. Magnus continued. 'Had she signed such papers, they would not have held in law,' I told her. "I was a girl," she said. "Was there any girl giving up her baby who didn't sign? My mother and father wouldn't have known any better."

'She was right, of course. "You wanted the possibility: the hope of contact, however remote," I said. I was putting words in her mouth, I'm ashamed to say. "Yes," she cried out. I think she might have put her hand up in the air to stop me, though we were talking on the telephone. Then she said Ned was coming home. "I hear him pulling into the drive," she said. "I'll go now." She asked for my number. She and Ned wouldn't be coming to the wedding. She thanked me for the invitation and wished me a happy life.

'"What is your fiancée's name?" she asked.'

'"Florence," I told her.'

'"Florence," she repeated, as though she knew who she was, and very much approved.'

Magnus wanted his father to take this in, to know that his son was still working for the family. Nothing bad had come of the visit to Bakersfield, he wanted to say, and it should be looked upon even now as a kind of liberation he felt. But Edwin only stared, with tears coming out of him. He made strange shapes with his mouth, because he had bitten the inside of his cheek.

And so it was that Magnus was a boy again, splay-legged on the beach beside the body of a stranger, much like he was with his father in this moment.

'There now,' he said.

'There now,' his father repeated, without comprehending.

When Magnus told him that he was thinking about finding the dead man on the beach, Edwin asked his son to tell him the story again. He insisted he tell it.

Magnus told him the story. It was as if he was telling it for the first time. He felt again the weight of the body fill his arms. Edwin listened attentively, and appeared to be gloriously winded when Magnus was finished. He nodded and thanked him. He was full of blind pride. 'Your mother's coming here,' he said, 'you know that?'

'Yes. She told me.'

'You talked to her already? Good.'

'She's late.'

'She is. She's late.'

'It's good she coming.'

'She's in a state of high anticipation,' Edwin explained. 'The idea of me being properly dead and her fully alive has only just formed up in your mother's head, and she can't get over herself.'

'Will you stop with that carry-on.'

'The distance between me and her makes sense to her now. It has its purpose. But it's all very . . . ' Edwin winced and rocked a claw-hand in the air, 'it's all very polite. I get wiped out even before I croak,' he explained. 'It's part of her preparation, her purifying herself. That's all right. Tell your mother not to keep faith with me.'

Magnus baulked. 'Not to keep faith? You think she's been keeping faith with you all these years?'

'We don't want her starting now, do we?'

They both laughed. Edwin was the first to stop. 'She'll be afraid to be without me.'

'And you?'

'I'll be a dead atheist, son.'

'I mean – now . . . .'

'Keep well clear of her for a time when I'm gone: that's my advice. Talk to her on the phone. Visit her. But keep your distance. It's all bearable.'

'Come on,' Magnus said, bending his knees and putting his hands under his father's oxters and raising him out of the chair, 'the doctor says you need to walk.'

'Yes,' his father replied, in a voice that trembled, because of the physical exertion required to stand, even with assistance. 'And we can talk.'

'And what the hell have we been doing?'

'Passing the time, son.' There was a brief pause, then he spoke again. 'If something happens to me, I don't want a . . . what do you call it . . . ?'

'A wake.'

'Your mother, however, will make an event of it.'

'She'll want the attention. She'll have them all in the house.' He didn't specify who *all* referred to.

Magnus shrugged. 'You want no drama. I understand. We don't need to talk about this.'

'There'll be a handful of genuine mourners. Noel. If he's still above ground. Your aunts. The boys.'

'Don't waste you time thinking about this stuff. You'll be dead. You'll be in another place.'

'There'll be others paying their respects. Neighbours and the like. Jack, for fuck's sake. Be warned. There'll be a third category. Another gang.'

'Who could they be, dad?'

'A few gougers come for a gawk. Come for a poke around. Come to show off.'

'Show off?'

'Present themselves.'

'What are you talking about?'

'They'll be wanting to have a crow.'

'It's all in your head.'

'Enemies,' Edwin declared hotly, after a brief glottal-stop. He wouldn't elaborate.

Stella's lovers, it had to be. They were ancient crocks, but that seemed not to enter into it.

'Charlotte will spot them for me,' Magnus said.

'She will not,' his father replied indignantly.

'What do you want? What arrangements am I to make?'

'I heard of a woman, a singer and dancer, who put her husband's ashes in her pair of maracas.'

'As punishment?' Magnus was fully in the madness now. He was quite enjoying it.

Edwin shook his head with easy conviction. 'She was happy shaking her maracas.'

'It was agreed in advance: he would go in the maracas?'

'I wasn't told. She was happy making music with him. That's the sum of it.'

Magnus nodded. 'They can do egg-timers, no doubt.'

'I like the maracas,' his father said wistfully.

'They can compress the ashes and produce a diamond. I know that.' He realised he was annoying his father by spoiling his sense of wonder. 'You want to be put in a pair of maracas?'

Edwin looked away for a long time, then returned with a brave smile – to which Magnus responded with a short, barking laugh.

Edwin led on by declaring that he was a resistant atheist.

'A Protestant atheist?' Magnus asked, seeking clarification.

'An atheist in spite of myself.'

'You're contrary,' Magnus observed, trying to be helpful.

'I have contradictory views,' his father said. 'The usual stuff. It seems entirely natural to me but, of course, its an impossible situation.'

There was a lovely vagueness in the old man's assertion. Magnus wanted to respond. 'You might just as well be . . . for instance, an underwater druid.'

'No.'

'Ah . . . '

We'll leave it at "Protestant atheist".'

'I'm with you.'

There was a brief pause. Some tentative nodding. 'Your mother still believes.'

'She does?'

'Oh yes.'

'Good for her.' Magnus was in a positive mood today and was determined to hold on to it.

'I've told her. "Good for you," I've said. She thinks I say it out of weakness.'

'And what do you say to that?'

'I blast her, then I weaken. I tell her she may have it right.'

'A sensible approach.'

'You think?'

'I don't really know.'

It is a daydream Magnus has. He is walking up the hill to the shady churchyard with the monkey-puzzle trees. His father's ghost comes down the pavement, but strangely, he is unghost-like. He is real and vital, made so by a life that has worn him out. It is a hot summer's day and he is wearing Aunt Charlotte's gardening hat. She doesn't want him getting skin cancer. Magnus wants to shoo Edwin back up the hill and into the grave, where he will sit at those precise coordinates, eat an apple, hope for a soft breeze in that heat. But Edwin ignores him as he draws ever closer, then passes. The face is remarkably well-defined, given that it is made of spectral mist. Magnus, it appears, doesn't register with him at all. Edwin is out looking for the neighbour's dog. Magnus knows this by the craning of the neck, the patrolling eyes, the way they search the spaces between pedestrians and cars. His father passes through him. If it were a sleeping dream, this would be the moment of waking. It is not unsettling. Rather, it is to be treated as normal. His father needs to be more attentive, that's all.

CHAPTER 42

Keep Pedalling

Jack, the neighbour, came to visit. He brought the dog, or it may well have been that the dog had brought Jack, Jack being, in Edwin's eyes, a biddable tower of jelly. Still, it was good of them both to come.

There were flakes of white paint lifting from the surface of the one park bench in the grounds, where Jack sat down with the dog. 'You have a visitor,' they told Edwin. The phrase didn't sound right at all. The nurse pointed to the garden, such as it was. It was really a car park with grass margins. The flaky bench made Edwin think of decrepit old people on bowling greens, and damn him, Jack didn't look at all clapped out.

'Ah, would you look,' Edwin called as he advanced unsteadily. The dog was more stiff than ever, and Jack ever younger.

Edwin's hands were surprisingly strong when he wrestled the dog's head and pulled at its ears. This dog's tail beat against its master's legs, beat the bench, beat the ground. It panted its fish-breath up into Edwin's mouth. Edwin spoke to Jack through the dog.

'Hello, Jack. Thanks for coming. You shouldn't have bothered.'

'You're looking well,' Jack lied. 'They must be minding you well in here. Marie is asking for you . . . .'

Edwin appeared to be looking at the dog as though Jack was working it like a ventriloquist's dummy. 'Is she? That's kind of her, isn't it?' He held the animal's muzzle to make direct eye-contact. The dog knew to freeze, but its eyes rolled to its rightful master.

'She'll be up to see you.'

Edwin now made the same eye-contact with wobbly Jack. 'Until Magnus is back, I'm stranded. I can't get out to walk. Maybe with the dog . . .'

208

'Or with Stella . . . '

'Or when Stella visits,' Edwin said, his eyes hooded – which seemed to make old Jack wobble even more. 'I meant to ask you, can you see to our bin, Jack. It's not that Stella can't, it's just she won't remember.'

'I can, Edwin. Of course I can.'

'Good man.'

In Magnus' eyes, Aunt Charlotte was obvious in her affections. This was in marked contrast to his mother. Stella's show of affection was occasional. Though genuine, it always came as a surprise and, he thought, demanded some indeterminable reward. These rare moments, he believed, had something to do with loneliness, and were to be dodged if possible, as they meant that he received too much attention, instead of being left entirely to his own devices. Aunt Maureen was somewhere in between with her loving-up. She would lavish affection in shorts bursts, then run away with flushed cheeks.

Rarer still were moments where affection was combined. One such moment related to Magnus' tortoise. Edwin had told his son that his tortoise would probably live to be one hundred years old, or more. When the tortoise died, Edwin was away on site in the north-west. Stella said: 'We'll bring Knute over to your Aunt Charlotte. She'll handle it.'

What did 'handle it' mean, little Magnus wanted know.

'She'll know what to do.'

And so, the tortoise was put in a Cornflakes box and Stella cycled to her sister's house with Magnus on the cushioned back-carrier clutching the flimsy cardboard. Every boy knew the cruelty of turning a tortoise on its back. Little Magnus was morbidly amazed that he could now tip it any which way, make it slide upside-down from one end of the box to the other, and it didn't matter. It was only when Aunt Charlotte received the package that Magnus cried.

'There now,' Stella said, petting his head, 'Aunt Charlotte doesn't want to see tears.'

'Let's have a look,' Charlotte said, opening the box and peering in respectfully. 'Oh, there he is.' She gave Stella a significant frown that clearly carried an instruction to stay put with Magnus. 'I need a little more light,' she ad-libbed, and went into the kitchen momentarily to make sure the tortoise was indeed dead. She turned it over. Lifted its lolling head with the side of an index finger, She was back in a jiffy. She let Magnus have another look in the box. 'He looks content. What do you think, Magnus?'

'*I* don't know,' Magnus declared with a sob.

'Well, I think he's content. You think he's content, Stella, don't you?'

'I do,' her sister replied. Stella made the mistake of not looking into the box. She was glad to have it off her hands. Charlotte was always the one for the animals. Even better than Maureen, she thought.

Charlotte moved the situation along quickly. 'You did the right thing bringing him to me. I have just the spot for him.'

She wrapped the dead tortoise in a tea towel, and gave it to Magnus to hold while she dug a hole in the soft terrain at the bottom of her garden. When they had buried Knute, she rang an ornamental bell she kept on the mantelpiece, and stuffed a five-pound note in Magnus' breast pocket.

That evening, Magnus talked to his father on the phone, Stella holding the receiver to his ear.

'Knute is dead.'

'Your mother told me. I'm sorry to hear that, son.'

'Aunt Charlotte buried him in the mud in her garden. She wrapped him in a cloth. I'll show you the place.'

'I'd like that.'

'She rang a bell.'

'Did she? That's a nice thing to do.'

'Mam was useless.'

'Was she? Oh dear.'

'You should have taken me with you.'

Aunt Charlotte was good with money. That is, she was good at parting with it, and was attentive to a boy's fiscal needs, thereby earning her right to be fully and mischievously involved in his life. There was no question of getting a few bob for cutting the grass at Charlotte's. She cut her own grass, front and back, with a push-mower in a great military whirl. The few bob usually came without any task to be performed. The money was handed over without ceremony, stuffed into a pocket or folded into a hand, which was then pushed away.

Charlotte used to play hockey and tennis. Would give young Magnus a chase in the park or a race around the garden. Would play football with him, and would readily give a push to knock him off stride. Magnus liked to play boy football with her. Liked to push her back.

Magnus' father had him write his name and telephone number on the good leather football he had at home. 'You don't want to lose anything that's yours, now, do you?' Edwin had said patiently. Magnus had the best of clothes and shoes, the best of footballs. That was something on which his parents were both adamant. Don't buy cheap, was the policy. If you can't afford it, do without. And hold on to what you've got.

'You want me to write my name and telephone number on this ball?' Magnus asked his aunt when her football was first produced. It was an inferior thing, but that didn't take from the excitement.

'God, no,' Aunt Charlotte retorted. 'Write your name on the ball? We don't want anyone knowing where it's come from if we put it through a window, do we?'

'No.'

'If you knock some poor child senseless with it and have to leave it and run . . . .'

'You're right.'

And they were off, Aunt Charlotte taking advantage of her nephew's distracted thought, kicking the ball up the wing and scoring between the two central fence-posts at the bottom of the garden. This was when she kept a more ordered bank of shrubs and plants and you could still see most of the back fence. She walloped the ball against the fence-boards. 'One-nil,' she shouted.

Magnus loved it. Loved the quick turns she made, the barging. When one or other of them sent the ball over the fence, she didn't ask him to retrieve it, but went herself into the neighbour's garden. That was in her rented house in Dublin. That was before the Dooley sisters' parents died. Before Maureen moved away and she returned to the house near Laragh, where a hand-mower was of little use, where no freshly dug hole would be right for Knute, and where a boy could kick a ball any which way and the world would remain indifferent.

Edwin had been transferred to hospital. Magnus imagined that at the point of passing, his father's head would become progressively heavier. That it would loll and knock against the bedstead, as his blood-brother's head did on the banisters.

'What are you at?' Edwin asked, meaning: what was he thinking? The words were short and gravelly because he hadn't spoken for some time and his throat was dry.

'Are you worried about me?' Magnus asked.

'Your work. You're in for a lemoner if you take any more liberties.'

'Stop your worrying.' His father's antiquated words made Magnus want to throw his arms above his head and dive backwards over one shoulder. He found that he was covering his heart with the palm of his hand.

'It's not you I'm worried about,' Edwin continued. It's Florence. Go and mind her.'

'I'm minding her.'

'Well . . . are you going?'

'I am,' Magnus replied.

'Good man.'

Magnus made ready to go, but shilly-shallied. 'When you're out of here, we can go fossil-hunting if you like.'

'We started out as sponges, son. Then came out of the sea as armoured creatures. Now we have brains that fill our skulls as surely as our feet fill our shoes. You wouldn't think it, looking around you here.' He grinned. 'Still . . . .'

Magnus left the hospital, convinced that he had no proper feeling of privilege or honour. He did not want to be present when his father finally turned in the world. He slept with Florence in his parents' house, sure that the call from the hospital would come in the night, but the phone did not ring. Stella was considerate, even kind towards them, but she was a widow in waiting. A biblical justice was soon to be meted out. Early in the morning, Magnus returned to Edwin's bedside to wait and to ponder.

When he found that Edwin's eyes were open and fixed on him, he felt he should speak. 'A bike has a will of its own. Remember you told me that when I was a kid?'

'Keep pedalling,' his father said, parodying himself in a weak voice.

' "It wants to fall down," you said. 'Or it wants to lean against a wall," I said. "That's a wall being in the way," you told me.'

In this moment Magnus let go of his body on the beach. Let it go forever. He closed his eyes for an instant. He is a boy again, shaky on his first two-wheeler. He sees the road surface pulled under the tyres by his father standing behind him.

'Head up,' he hears the old man shout. 'Keep pedalling. Don't be afraid.'

He does not look back. Instead, Magnus imagines the light in his father's eyes. He replays his shout with the soft volume in his head up full. He keeps pedalling.

Edwin mumbled something from his pillow. 'Oh dear.' These were the last words spoken by this oddly blessed man.

'What's that?' said Magnus. He didn't quite hear. 'I'm not leaving yet. I'm in no hurry.' I'm not taking that bike in the garage, by the way. That's your bike. I'd get killed on a bike in London.'

You lie still, my daddy, or don't, Magnus wanted to say. Take my wrist, see that I have taken yours in my hand. It is the sailor's grip you taught me, the grip I made with my baby.

CHAPTER 43

All Things Bright and Beautiful

The Permanent Secretary found Magnus standing in one corner of his office clutching tightly a sheaf of papers and staring at a patch of pale sunlight on the floor.

'Permanent Secretary,' Magnus declared with a sudden brightness. He lurched out of the corner and slid the papers onto his desk. He canted his head to signal presence of mind.

'Magnus, I'm so very sorry.'

'Thank you.'

'You shouldn't be in here. Take the time.'

'I will. But first, the brief.'

'You've heard, of course, there's a Members'-expenses scandal brewing.'

Magnus put his palm on the bundle of papers he had laid on his desk, to indicate that he was already on the case.

'Get Freddie in. We'll talk. Then, you go.'

Magnus got Freddie in.

'You're telling us there's been a collapse of integrity, Permanent Secretary?' Freddie said, sucking in his cheeks in mock surprise. The 'rowdies', as he called them, would not be caught out. You wouldn't get a single one of them on any class of excess liberty.

'When the new expenses regime is created, the same amount will be coming out of the public purse, is that what you're saying, Freddie?' Magnus asked.

'Do you know, that's a bloody shrewd question.' Freddie had offered his condolences and very much approved of his colleague presenting himself for work, albeit for just a few hours.

'Standards and Privileges Committee . . . ' the Permanent Secretary muttered, knitting his brow and beginning to pace the pale rectangle on the floor.

213

'Committee on Standards in Public Life,' Freddie added, trying to match the brow-knitting of his boss, and failing.

'What I want from you, Freddie, is to ensure that we are fully prepared when this breaks.' What the Secretary wanted from them both was to know what could be ascertained regarding false claims; he wanted names, and a full account of sums drawn down. He wanted to know about any foolishness, any blindness. He wanted the mechanics of facilitation in minutiae. Every civil servant knew it was their task to provide reliable information when a scandal broke, but Freddie was too choked at the prospect of such an enormous dig; he hadn't done more that nod when Magnus said calmly, 'Yes, of course. We understand.'

Hours later, Freddie was fully engaged at their digging. Magnus was turning the key in the lock to his father's newly rented flat in Dublin. He paused for a brief moment to wonder at the relief he felt with this new pressure he was under at work. The rain drummed on the cheap black umbrella he held aloft. Yes, he thought, I have my father's ability to make normal. For better and for worse, to take the hurt.

Magnus turned the key deftly, stepped into the dingy basement flat where his father had spent just a few solitary nights. He let down the umbrella, which folded like a headless bat. He rolled it tightly and fastened the restraining tab, in spite of it being wet. He went looking for the back brace, and some of Edwin's clothes.

Florence flew from London on the first available flight. She drove Magnus to the church in Wicklow. She insisted she was comfortable driving Edwin's car. Magnus, she could see, was in shock. She got him to give her road directions. At the church, she wanted to show support from a discreet distance. She hadn't grown up in a house with religion. She had no religious affiliations. Magnus introduced her to the Reverend Meldrum, successor to the late Reverend Tuttle. The reverend would have received them in the rectory, but he had business in the church with an electrician who was late. He apologised for the lack of artificial light, and offered tea and biscuits just as soon as the electrician was fully briefed.

Florence then wandered to the back of the church, and the reverend asked after Stella.

'She's holding up,' Magnus said.

'Ah,' Meldrum said, 'good. I'll visit her. And Charlotte and Maureen? I often see Charlotte, of course, out in her garden in all weathers.'

'They're with Stella.'

'I hope to see them all, then.'

They set to discussing the arrangements for Edwin. Magnus could remember the titles of Christmas carols, yes, but hymns . . .

Then, something came to him without effort. *All Things Bright and Beautiful.*

The manner in which the reverend repeated this title gently suggested that Magnus should try again.

Magnus could remember some of the tunes – ones that he liked, that had good childhood associations – but he couldn't hum them. He did try with one. The reverend knit his brow. He very much wanted to recognise it, wanted to connect, but failed.

There was no rebuke, no trace of criticism in his words. Nor was he humiliated by the pathetic effort of a stray member of the flock. Any gesture, any attempt to worship or merely acknowledge was to be encouraged these days. The reverend was as patient and attentive as the brass eagle supporting the Bible on its outspread wings by which they stood.

Magnus looked to the font, where his father had been baptised. *All Things Bright and Beautiful.* He turned slowly on his heels, as if to suggest a memory technique, but really, there were no hymns forthcoming. He looked to the rose window above the entrance, to the nearby stained-glass window, where he observed a big spider in the spangled light. He had a strong urge to call on Florence. She was leafing through a hymnbook she had lifted from a pile by the door. Should he call her up? He could whisper her name. It was a small country church. The distance wasn't great.

'We can keep the service short,' the reverend said, feeling Magnus' rising panic.

'No, we don't need to do that,' Magnus blurted out.

'Something rousing, wouldn't you say?' the Reverend Meldrum said mildly, to smoothe over his miscalculation.

'Yes,' Magnus replied very quickly.

The reverend nodded. He looked away, seemingly with an air of indifference, but came back with the opening of *Shall We Gather at the River?,* which he sang with complete conviction at half-volume, to signal that this remained a personal interaction, not something for the wider spiritual world, for any imagined congregation.

Magnus was deeply moved by this man singing to him. Making a lullaby for the dead. Florence must have thought he had asked the reverend to sing.

Yes. Magnus wanted this hymn. He didn't want to interrupt, so he gave an emphatic nod.

The reverend stopped and said modestly, 'We'll have that one, then.' He maintained direct eye-contact, to make clear that this help would extend to at least two other selections that would be needed. There was no sign of any electrician.

Magnus was relieved to see Florence making her way towards them, carrying the hymnbook. She wanted to be party to this, after all. A spiritual, she was thinking. Another one with a river theme. *I Went Down to the River to Pray . . .*

Stella was wearing the leather jacket Noel had given her when she went to meet him.

He had been given it by his late wife. He had always thought it was too young for him, too feminine, with its elasticated bottom and pocket stitching, so he had given it to Stella.

He was glad to see her wearing it, but on her it looked too masculine.

Noel made a conscious effort not to mumble through his moustache. He would let her work her charm, though he had a fear of toppling. Secretly, he revelled in her dark passion and wanted to get close to it, kiss it, even, but withdraw quickly. What now that his dear friend was gone, and he was suddenly old and pathetic?

He knew Stella liked his easy manner. His noble chin. She admired him as her husband's colleague and companion. But what now?

'Hello, Noel.'

'Stella, I am so sorry.'

'You are, I know. And I'm sorry you lost your friend.'

These were uncommonly empathetic words for Stella. 'You look great, so you do,' said Noel.

'Thank you, darling.'

'May I sit beside you – there, I mean?'

Stella reached out her hand to draw him to the seat beside her.

Noel discreetly inhaled her perfume as he settled. He had a sudden urge to weep. Life was extraordinary. There was Bart and Phil in the snug. And there was Shea, the barman. Bart and Phil knew life was extraordinary. 'I'll get the drinks,' Noel said lightly to Stella.

'No no,' replied Stella. 'I'll get this.' Which implied there would be more, and perhaps a real risk of Noel toppling. She smiled at Shea, and Shea was there in an instant. 'You know about all this killing business?' she said, after the drinks had arrived.

'I do, Stella, except nobody was killed.'

'No thanks to your friend. You must see him in a new light?'

'He's gone, Stella.' This came out as a mumble. She patted the back of his hand. He reset the glasses on his nose with a riding-up of his moustache. 'We'll never know what was going through his mind to attempt such a thing, will we?'

Stella considered this carefully while she rooted money out of her purse. She liked to put money on the table in pubs. When she looked at him again, it was clear she wasn't happy with Noel's lame attempt to mollify her.

'I went to see him in the convalescent home,' she said.

'Did you?' Noel spluttered with surprise.

'Just the once. I wanted to see the setup. 'After all, how many years' service did he give to the Department?'

'Absolute loyalty,' Noel mumbled, but immediately wished he hadn't used these words.

'I went to show I'm still useful.'

'There was never any doubt, Stella.' She could still cut a path through the atomic particles of old age.

'I couldn't see him as a patient, you understand. And I had to pretend he didn't try to poison me.'

'I can imagine how difficult that must have been,' Noel said, utterly disgusted with himself for caving so readily.

'No, you can't. Anyway, I was a Red Cross envoy. "They're looking after you?" says I.'

' "They are," says he.'

' "That's good." '

' "Yes." '

' "Do you want anything?" '

' "No. Thank you. I'll be out shortly. Is there any post?" '

' "No post," says I. "Were you expecting something?" '

' "No." '

' "If anything comes, I'll see you get it." '

' "I'll be out anyway." '

' "You will." Of course, I knew just by looking at him . . . My husband, this man who tried to poison me . . . .'

Noel couldn't bear the sorry state of affairs, but he had to, for Edwin. 'That was the last time you spoke to him?'

'It was. Not a peep out of the old bugger about me.'

'Ah well.'

'Ah well?'

Noel gently broke open his regret with two rigid hands. He had sworn not to tell her what he knew. It was all he could do to repeat with resilience his 'Ah well'. He made it sound softer, but very much bigger.

The morning after the funeral, Magnus put coins in a slot and had ten minutes in the vibrating massage chair at the shopping centre. Florence stood and watched. Then, while he was still vibrating, she took his hand.

CHAPTER 44

Three Sisters on the Pier

Had any observant stranger seen three elderly sisters get out of a car? Active women for their age, used to walking the pier in all weather.

Had they heard one say: 'Stop it, just stop it.'

And the reply come: 'Stop what?'

And the rejoinder: 'That face.'

They would have seen two set off before the third was quite ready. Seen the two talk to each other with exactitude and a properness that was at the expense of their disgraced sister. Would have seen them take to the pier at a pace, leaving the third to follow.

Would have seen the two steam ahead into the light morning mist, greet an acquaintance with a forced heartiness, a person who on any other occasion would have received the slightest nod; a heartiness they knew would not be matched by their sister, trailing behind.

Yes, it was indeed a beautiful morning, but there was something more required than the simple application of a set of rules, their punishing pace suggested. That bracing fresh air fuelling their progress was thickening in the lungs of their sister. Perseverance proved nothing. Didn't they all persevere? Hobble all you like. We're not looking. Shame retarded the guilty.

The observant stranger would have seen those two elderly women reach the end of the pier, turn around without stopping to gaze across the bay, and begin the return journey at the same impressive pace.

They would have seen them pass their sister without acknowledgement, and her still on her way to the end. Would have seen the disgraced sister belatedly reach the end of the pier and turn on her heels as the others had done, her goal to maintain a constant distance.

That distance would close. It was a temporary rift, a spat between sisters. One had said something to another about neglectful behaviour towards her recently deceased husband.

Stella had won Edwin from Charlotte all those years ago. She had had him for such a long time, and had made such a bad job of it. Ask their sister, Maureen, about the matter, and she would tell you Charlotte had been scorched by Stella. Ask Charlotte, and she would pass it off as girlish stuff. She would pretend to be dreamy – which was difficult for a woman of her age. Ask Stella, and she would deny any competition, and be inexplicably cutting about most of her married life with Edwin. She would lend these remarks an air of tragedy by suggesting that the courtship was truly spontaneous and romantic – which, she would claim, is a feat for any architect. It was this that had given rise to the spat prior to the walk on the pier.

What would that stranger think, had they known that the elderly woman trailing behind had, in one mad, despairing moment, tried to poison her sibling out of love for her brother-in-law?

Magnus didn't tell his mother, because he wanted to protect Charlotte. That was what Edwin wanted. In this regard, Magnus was carrying out his father's wishes. The doubting had been stripped out. Stella had it wrong. In this knowledge, Magnus could indulge her or rebuke her for her unreasonable behaviour, while letting her believe what she believed.

How easily this secret privilege was obliterated by a newfound clarity. Stella told Magnus that Charlotte had confessed to her and Maureen shortly after she had told him what she had done.

'You were going to keep it to yourself, Magnus?'

'It's what Edwin wanted, isn't it, Stella?'

'Yes,' she said. 'I see that.'

'We all see that. Now you say nothing about Charlotte?'

Stella gave a sentimental smile, let her eyes water, offered no reply. The facts had been accommodated. The deed was being assimilated. Collectively, the three sisters were making a drama of it. They pointed to the impossibility of any such extraordinary event being repeated. Acknowledgement was key, not forgiveness. Forgiveness was forever located between too early and too late. That was good enough.

In future, Aunt Charlotte will keep in touch with her nephew as never before. If he and Florence are ever to have another child, and she is still alive, she will tell the child her story of two good men. One, who couldn't type without stamping his feet. The other, who kept his love secret.

CHAPTER 45

Small Miracle of Judgement

Stella returned to the house mid-morning. The neighbour's dog gave out with a coarse, unconvincing bark. The sun streamed through the windows and showed up the worn patches of the soft furnishings in the living room. It was Stella's house now, and it surprised Magnus to see that she felt entirely at home. Maureen had not yet returned to Edinburgh. She was patient and attentive, and shadowed her sister's every move in what Magnus saw as a religious way. Charlotte stayed in the Dooley house in Wicklow, preparing a big dinner.

There was no food for lunch. The cupboard was bare. Magnus went to the supermarket to buy groceries. He was in no hurry. He sat in the massage chair for a time without putting money in the slot, then he put a euro in the red plastic slot of a trolley and set about buying his mother her groceries.

Maureen was not there when he returned. Had they rowed, Magnus wondered?

'Would you like a drink, Magnus?' his mother asked. She was unusually meek.

'No, thanks. Maureen's gone for a walk?' he asked casually.

'She's gone ahead to Charlotte,' Stella answered. There was something like a sigh of admiration. Magnus didn't want to spoil anything by asking why his aunt had left early. 'Tell me about Florence.' This was a robust instruction from Stella. She didn't want to talk about the Dooleys.

Magnus was glad to speak on the subject. 'She's doing well. The time in the open clinic has helped enormously.'

'Florence is a lot like me,' she said. The statement was mystifying, but its meaning was clear. Stella was contrite, desiring to reconnect, then to carry on regardless. 'I want to come to London soon to visit her. You and Florence,' she corrected herself.

'Of course.'

'I'll not impose.'

'It won't be an imposition.'

'I can spend time with her.'

Magnus could see his mother getting more alarmed at her own words. 'She'd like that.'

'Go to the theatre together, and such.'

'I'd like it, too. We'll set a date.'

'Are you sure you don't want a drink?' Stella asked.

'Yes, I'm sure.'

'I'm having a drink.'

'You do that.'

'I don't know what I'll do with all this stuff,' she said, without looking around.

Magnus turned his head very slowly to the left, then to the right. He tilted his head slowly up, then down. There was no gravelly squelch. Though satisfying, this exercise told him nothing other than that, for now, there was no neck-grinding. There'd be more of this, he was thinking. Probably in the family bones: the Dooleys or the bloods. In future, he'd move his head with more caution. 'You'll think of something,' he said presently.

'You have his watch, I see.'

'Yes.'

'There's money, you know. He left you something worthwhile.'

'Yes. I know.'

'I don't need to tell you he was tight with money. Every penny a prisoner. Perhaps this is the pay-off.'

'That's generous of you, Stella. You're getting soft in your old age.'

'I was thinking I'd take a pebble from his grave, put it in my shoe. He tortured me when he was alive. I shouldn't rob him of the pleasure now. What do you say?'

'Romantic . . . you?'

She cackled with satisfaction. 'Oh, all right.'

Magnus wanted to mark his parents getting together. It seemed proper under the circumstances, so he asked about it. Though she didn't come out with it here, of her own volition Stella determined that love was beyond her. There had to be another arrangement: he would love her, and she would always be there, toughing it out until who knows what happened. Something good, perhaps. In this arrangement, Edwin would never be bitter. She'd see to that. They could

221

relax and enjoy themselves. They would be safe and secure. They could have a life together, and who knows, who knows.

'We were wildly attracted,' Stella said. This came out of the blue. No, it came out of the fog of bereavement.

'Were you? Really . . . ?' She had not said as much before. Magnus wanted more.

'But we began to fight, and we didn't know why.'

'On, come *on* . . . .'

She was launched now. It didn't matter what her son said. She would finish. 'We used to have sex to make up.'

This wasn't shocking, but did he want to hear about it? Stella was perfectly relaxed, and more thoughtful than Magnus could have expected. 'Then,' she said, 'we had you.'

'Ah.'

'You came along, and it was different.'

'You should have split.'

'It was better between us, and we didn't know how or why.'

'It must have been me.' Here was more of that heavy irony, wasted.

'Your father was going to call you Richard. I wouldn't have it.'

'Hector. You were going to call me Hector.'

'We were not. Bloody awful name, Hector. Who told you that?' She wasn't looking for an answer.

'You could have changed your lives, either of you. Both of you.'

'He tried that,' she said, tapping the rim of her glass with the back of an immaculately varnished nail.

'You don't learn, do you, Stella?' Magnus said.

'I've given that up,' his mother replied moderately, and took a loving sip from her glass, draining it. She rose to her feet with her chin in the air. 'Edwin taught me to swim,' she said.

Her wistful smile took Magnus by surprise. 'You never learnt when you were a child?' She didn't seem to hear his question or, at any rate, chose to ignore it.

'In the sea,' she added. 'He insisted it be in the sea.'

Magnus had never swum with his mother. He'd seen her in a bathing suit, but never seen her swim. 'You've given up the swimming, I take it?'

'When I got pregnant with you, it helped.' She let that hang in the air a while, as did he. 'I'd be down to the baths to do my twenty lengths. It helped with the birth.'

What was Magnus to say? He wasn't comfortable with talk about his birth. 'Yes, well . . . it would.'

'It was good of him to teach me to swim.'

'And me.'

'You never liked swimming, Magnus.'

'No. That's true.'

'It's important to know how to swim.'

'Yes. Very.' He let her drift from here. She wasn't really engaging with him. The heart, temple of love and goodwill, centre of purpose, seat of courage, relied on liquid engineering. Stella went to the sideboard. She moved as though she was stepping across the sky on a set of railway sleepers. She was planning on having another Jameson, and went in search of what she called her 'dilute'.

'You were a difficult birth,' she said distractedly.

'But thank God for the exercising,' Magnus put in on her behalf.

'Still . . . ' his mother gave out with the same wistful smile, 'you came out.'

'I don't want another drink,' Magnus said, continuing to be helpful. His mind, too, was drifting. A scene presented from early childhood: the family is on the way to Brittas Bay. He is in the back seat of the car; his father is driving; Stella is in the front passenger seat smoking her Piccadilly. It's taking an eternity. That's what happens in those rare moments when his parents appear to be content in each other's company. Little Magnus has his sandals off, and the white socks he hates. He presses his bare feet into the back of the seat. 'Are we there yet?' he asks.

'Not yet,' Edwin says, in that soft, vague manner he uses with all children and dogs.

'Soon,' his mother adds.

'Daddy, what will I do now?' little Magnus asks. It's a big question to ask, he knows.

'Do nothing,' his father advises easily. 'Just daydream.'

Stella smiles at Edwin. It's that same wistful smile.

'OK,' little Magnus replies. And he does. He commences to daydream.

'How's that job of yours?' Stella asked so suddenly out of her glass, it seemed like an ambush.

'Difficult.'

'Get people round a piano, that's my advice.'

'Thank you, Stella. Now . . . Charlotte . . . '

'Yes?'

'Are you speaking?'

'We talk on scraps of paper.'

'You must forgive her.' Stella did not respond – and what could Magnus expect of her? 'You can't speak about this business. We acknowledge what has happened, and we put it behind us.'

His mother agreed it was best not to speak of it. Her resolve impressed him. 'We've buried the hatchet,' she said. Said it in a way that signalled that she knew precisely where the hatchet had been buried. This small miracle of judgement stopped Magnus dead with his prepared lecture.

'Good,' he said patiently.

'I see what has happened,' Stella said.

Magnus was compelled to kiss her on the cheek. It was a kiss she graciously accepted. 'It's taken us a while, hasn't it?' he said.

'Huh.'

Magnus smiled easily.

Stella rotated a hand in the air above her head. 'You should take most of this stuff,' she said.

'I can't.'

'Don't you want it?'

'I can't.'

'*I* don't want it.' There was a brief pause. Then, 'You should take some of it. It would be wrong not to. Do you want to make a list?'

'No.' What he would take was a private matter. He would inform her after he had taken what he wanted.

'You're right. Not today.' There was another brief pause. 'Such a clutter,' she said, finally looking around. 'I could talk to Noel. He might help you. Except, Noel's a bit dead and alive.'

'He might not want to get involved.'

'He asked me if I wanted any of his wife's clothes: the good pieces, of course.' I'm sorry about her passing. I never did speak to him about that.'

'He knows you're sorry, I'm sure.'

'I'd see her about. She made these faces: there were sudden hoots of laughter, exaggerated frowns . . . .'

'Yes, well, she was a good-natured woman.'

'It made me feel like I was in a pantomime.'

'Now, Stella . . . .'

'She had eczema.'

'Please . . . .'

'She might have used the cream, but I think she liked scratching. And now, she's gone.'

'Listen to yourself.'

'I'm only saying . . . .'

'Yes. Well, don't.' She was goading him, Magnus knew. She needed to do this sort of thing to signal that she really cared. The acute angles at which she dived at the world were as infuriating as ever.

Then, she said, 'I was thinking about you and your father in America. He told me about it – eventually.'

'It took him a while, did it?' Edwin didn't tell her much, if he told her anything at all, Magnus was thinking. That was *their* trip – his and his father's. It was utterly personal. Man and boy.

She saw the furrows in his brow, and misread his expression. 'I would have gone with him, but he wouldn't have it. He thought I would interfere.'

'He needed to go by himself.'

'He took you.'

'I didn't interfere.'

'Had I been asked . . . .' She didn't finish.

'He told you about the bloods?'

She didn't know what this meant. 'The bloods?'

'That's what we called them,' Magnus said triumphantly. 'His mother and father.'

'Oh, yes. He told me.'

'He did? I don't think so. It was a disaster, him meeting them. Did he tell you that?' Magnus said this, even though he did not hold it to be true. It was some kind of failure, yes, but that was to be expected.

'He's right. I would have interfered.'

'Never mind.'

'When you went missing . . . I regret I wasn't there for that. For your father finding you gone.' There was a brief pause. She tightened her face. 'He was never right after that.'

'I said never mind, Stella.'

'When he first found his mother, he should have written to her and left it at that. Your father wrote a good letter, as you know.'

'He had to go. How could he resist?'

'He should have talked to me.'

'A letter . . . ?' Magnus was indignant.

'A letter or two, with a few photographs. And a card at Christmas.'

'You're a hard woman.'

'That's his mother you're thinking of, Magnus.'

'You're saying you could have guided him – you?'

'I could have interfered.' Stella went upstairs. Returned a short time later. She produced two items. The first was the pale yellow blanket the baby, who would be called Edwin, had been swaddled in; the only object in the world that was both his and his birth parents'. Unfolding it, Magnus was struck by how small it was. Why did he expect it to be large enough to swaddle an adult?

'Good as new,' Stella observed, but there was no doubting the special power this soft rectangle of fabric held. Magnus' jaw locked momentarily, and he smarted with emotion as he passed the blanket up through his fingers. 'I'll keep that,' Stella said, in the same practical voice. Though she would not declare it here and now, she had kept it in a silk pillowcase for her grandchild. She had it stored along with other baby outfits she planned to give Florence.

The second item was a letter from the local Garda sergeant wishing the abandoned child well for a full and happy life. The opening paragraph presented the sparse facts relating to the newborn being reported as found on the Sparlings' doorstep early one September evening, wrapped in an infant's blanket. Though it was not he, the sergeant, who was fully in charge of the investigation, he had made himself entirely acquainted with the facts, as he had great regard for the Sparling family, long of this parish and much respected.

There was another silence between them. Then, Magnus spoke again. 'I drove out into the desert in that hired car. Isn't that something?'

'You were a little tyke.'

'I told him about the Mojave Indians. Did he tell you about the Mojave?'

'No.'

Magnus told his mother now about his rescue. About Hunter Dobbs, the cop. The gas-station man with broken teeth. The doctor at the police station. Stella was the perfect audience. She listened intently. She was proud of her son. She would have preferred it if his father was still alive, she supposed, in the way Edwin had all his life wished for his mother.

There was another silence, this one longer than the others. Magnus imagined his father in the heat of a Mediterranean afternoon, shuffling in the shade of his four trees; imagined him running cold water from the spout of the drinking fountain over his ancient hands, then leaning against a patch of jigsaw camouflage bark because he doesn't want to sit until the other old men show up. Imagined Noel arriving with two takeaway coffees. Edwin sitting only when Noel sits.

'You'll have to help me here,' his mother said. 'It's too much for me.'

'Not today, Stella.'

She was already at the drinks cabinet. Magnus rose to his feet.

'I'll pour you a whiskey,' she said.

'No. Thank you. I'll be back in a minute.'

'Where are you going?'

'Out to the garage.'

'There's more rubbish there. You'll need a plan.'

Magnus had already left the room. He took his father's car keys from a drawer in the kitchen. In the garage, he sat into the car, looked at himself in the rearview mirror, bared his teeth. This made him think about his father brushing his teeth at his sink in the convalescent home. Brushing them thoroughly and in a precise manner, as he had always done. As he had patiently instructed Magnus to do. For a man of his generation, he had done well keeping all his teeth until the end; done well to keep up with developments in preservation and reconstruction.

Magnus pondered all that good dentistry now gone to waste. Those white fillings that replaced the mercury-laden composites. Those near-perfect crowns. Fossil-hunters weren't interested.

Still. Mustn't complain. That's what his father would say.

Edwin had made arrangements for Magnus to get his car. He had typed a page of notes regarding the general maintenance and unique characteristics of his beloved vehicle. It was a formal note addressed to the common reader, but clearly intended for his son. He had put that sheet in the manual – which Magnus now found on the top of the dashboard.

He read the note, mumbled 'Thank you', and stared through the windscreen at the beaded glass panes in the old doors. The early-evening light made them a wonder. He looked between his legs at the pedals worn down by his father's feet. He inhaled the car smell, adjusted the seat and the rearview mirror, got out and opened the garage doors. The old man had resisted changing these wooden doors for an aluminum up-and-over. He had taken good care of these doors. Magnus was glad to feel the familiar drag on each of them as he swung one, then the other. He dropped the securing bolts into their snug metal rings, sunk in the tar. Edwin had kept these clear of dirt and leaves with a bamboo stick.

Magnus got back in the car and drove. He left the garage doors open – something his father would never have done. He thought he heard his mother call his name, but she didn't appear at a window, or come to the door before he had turned onto the road. Had she poured that drink for him in any case, as she was apt to do for Edwin, though he, too, had often refused? An occasional goodwill practice that had long taken the place of physical intimacy with her nearly murderous dark-horse, recently dead husband.

Maureen was at Charlotte's house. Stella had already declined their invitation to spend the night under the one roof. Magnus had left his mother alone in the house. She was trying to kill off her dead husband. So far as Magnus could judge, she had made a good start. For his part, Edwin had, in his own manageable domestic way, sold his life as dearly as he could.

CHAPTER 46

Listening on the Gate

He was soon on his way to Wicklow. When the engine heated, it purred beautifully as it passed more than its share of petrol through its system.

As before, he took the road that followed the coast, then cut inland. He didn't bother with the roadside memorials that, until now, had demanded his attention. He blasted out on the straight, running his hand lightly across the crown of the steering wheel. On the country lanes, his forearms rested in his lap, his hands steering from the bottom of the wheel. He had all the windows down. There was a cold, blustery wind blowing. He was feeling self-conscious and reckless. In that benign battering, it occurred to him that if there was a coming-together of hostile forces in a life, there might also be some class of redress. A balance struck that was more than the product of one man's efforts.

He thought about Florence, but she didn't want to be thought about. Didn't need it just now, she seemed to be telling him. One day soon, Magnus will come upon the rescue dog on the Kings Road. It will be sitting outside a coffee house tethered to a bar, tongue hanging out. He will see Florence sitting in the window seat of the café with her ex-boyfriend, Rupert. They will be sanguine, talking with a sparkly ease, bathed in a modest wisdom. Magnus will not want to intrude. It will be a relief to see his wife out in the world fending for herself, and for him to feel properly jealous.

Later, Florence will tell him about the encounter. She will describe wandering on the Kings Road, then the dog sniffing her out, Rupert passing her, oblivious, but his dog leading him back. 'Outside Waitrose,' she will say.

'Outside Waitrose,' Magnus will echo. There is no significance to this, but somehow, it lends perspective.

'He's off again this evening,' she will add. 'They're in the air right now,' she will say, looking at her watch.

'I've always liked Rupert,' Magnus will declare.

'He's a good man,' Florence will be glad to confirm.

When Magnus reached the house where his father had grown up, the sun was still above the horizon. The driveway was pitted, and the wheels bounced on lumps of dead wood that must have come down in high winds. He put on a burst of speed as the drive opened out to the front of the house. He braked hard, and the car skidded nicely on the stones.

The house, a fine Georgian farmhouse with large sash windows and a shallow fanlight, had burnt one summer night when there was still light in the sky. Charlotte had seen the flames and the smoke from her bedroom window and had called the fire brigade. For years, what remained of the structure had stood as Magnus found it now. The two chimney-stacks were buttressed with raw wooden beams. All window apertures were braced with box frames and reinforced wooden Xs. The tops of the walls were protected from the weather with opaque plastic sheeting. The garden the Sparlings had carefully tended was growing wild. Charlotte had taken specimens for the Dooley garden. There was nothing more to be done.

Magnus got out of the car. The smell of honeysuckle was constant, even with the breeze. It prompted him to sway. His face was burning from the wind beating on it. He rested his hands on his hips. He let his eyes wander, and he listened. On one side, he heard wood pigeons cooing. On the other side, where branches of trees nearest to the house had been scorched, there were magpies. They didn't like this invasion. Didn't like the ticking of a hot engine. They were too numerous, and too jumpy, for an accurate count, but they were all pristine in their livery.

Magnus peered in through gaps in the boards, but there was nothing much he could see. He tried to imagine his father as a little boy sliding down the banister, throwing open doors, dancing excitedly in front of a Christmas tree, but the vision was forced. A kind of personal hooey.

He imagined a baby being left on the doorstep. He bent down and ran his hand lightly over the granite step. The birds seemed to know what he was doing, and they were indifferent. This was a special place, the point of separation with its own conductivity. It was only when he walked out into the great sloping field behind the house that he felt something. He couldn't say what.

He imagined his father as a boy running down the long slope, gulping cold water from the outdoor tap on the gable end of the house, not crossing the threshold on which he had been left, but going in the back way because he had mud on his shoes.

Magnus walked up to the gate in the far corner, where he would still gain a few minutes' direct sunlight. A breeze tugged at the long grass and made eddies in his path. He passed the hollow. He thought he might be looking to see in his imagination the bloods running away from the house, though he had seen no such thing. When he reached the gate, he called his father's name. He let it out on the sweet, damp air.

What to make of his losses? His losses seemed not to be connected to any gains. They were separate, and not required to be lesser, greater, or equal, but unto themselves. It was this he would remember.

He sat up on the gate. The muscle-tension required to keep him perched on the gate felt good. He listened for the booming of Eureka Dunes across the great distance, but what he heard was wind in the leaves. All that was behind him was behind him. He was not in the pre-sickness state he had thought was permanent. He was no longer afraid.